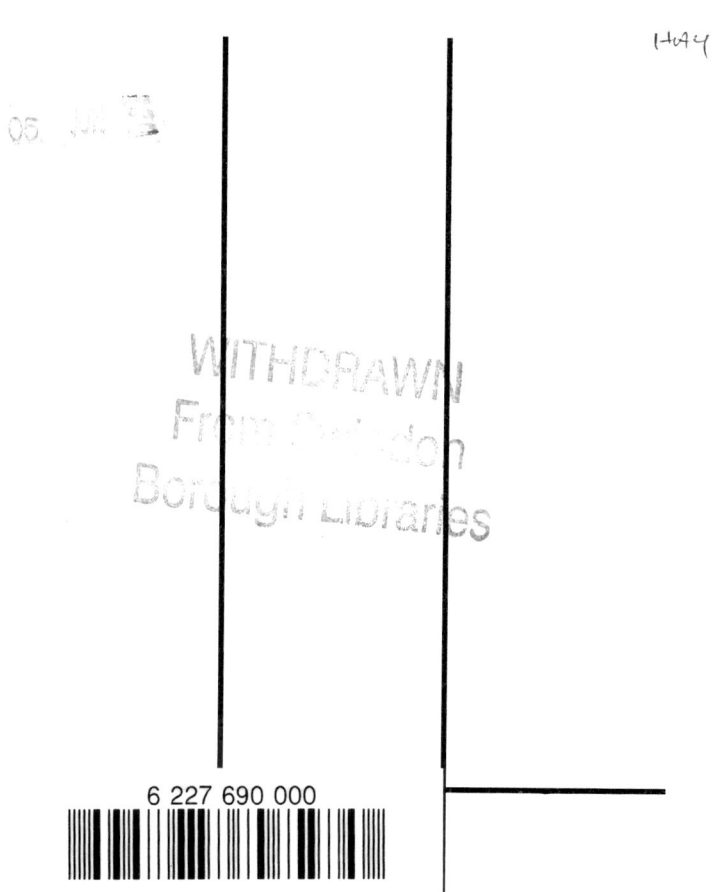

# Into the Shadowy World

Alen Sawaya

The Pentland Press Limited
Edinburgh • Cambridge • Durham • USA

© Alen Sawaya 2001

First published in 2001 by
The Pentland Press Ltd.
1 Hutton Close
South Church
Bishop Auckland
Durham

British Library Cataloguing in Publication Data.
A Catalogue record for this book is available
from the British Library.

ISBN 1 85821 819 5

Typeset by CBS, Martlesham Heath, Ipswich, Suffolk
Printed and bound by Antony Rowe Ltd., Chippenham

# CHAPTER 1

Bakari walked out of the front door and stepped into the street. An old Peugeot, its doors clanging, moved on the opposite side of the road. Bakari stopped to allow it to pass. Sekenke Street was the same he had walked on every day, winding past pools of dirty water. It was not the worse street in Kinondoni as cars and pedestrians had abandoned adjacent Jabu Street altogether.

A boy pushing a cart packed with yellow plastic drums filled with water shouted at the top of his voice, advertising his business. The time was half-past six in the evening, and the sun's rays on that Saturday of July had already deserted the dusty streets of Kinondoni. A few crows crowed above a television mast on top of a nearby house. A school of pigeons flew above the town on their way to roost. A few houses along the neighbourhood had their radios tuned to the popular Radio One, blasting a Congolese Lingala song. The music was subdued partly by a thunderous laugh of a group of women clattering on a pavement, next to a tiny hair salon.

He walked slowly, his head bowed, his eyes on the ground avoiding to step on sewage water or rotting cabbage. Whenever he walked absentmindedly, he would bend his neck so much that it appeared as if it was going to snap. Bakari kicked a coconut shell and it rolled ahead of him: it also spewed a foul smelling liquid on his trousers. He bent down to brush the hem of his aging trevira trousers. As his fingers moved up and down, pieces of loose strings making the trevira material flew out. Unfortunately his greasy notebook also fell from his shirt pocket and landed on the muddy water. That was another trouble for him, and he cursed himself for that.

Bakari brushed the black little book and wiped his fingers on his socks. Then he smelled his hands and poohed. It reminded him of the smell of some stale fish he ate two nights ago at a shabby restaurant in town that provoked a stomach ache and diarrhoea. He had had to spend a day in bed on a blistering summer afternoon, drinking only water and some salty, white powder. His wife had obtained the powder from an informal pharmacy in an

1

obscure section within the Kinondoni market.

There was a folded paper sticking out of the wet notebook. Bakari took the crinkled piece of paper and unfolded it. Inside were some burned specks of tobacco from a cigarette he had extinguished earlier on and tucked in his shirt. In days like these, in the middle of the months when money was a scarce resource, a stick of cigarette had to be conserved to be smoked several times a day; a few puffs on each occasion.

It was not an appropriate time of the day to read a warning letter given to him that afternoon. It was a second warning to Bakari, the first having been given to him for persistently being late to work, disobedience and insubordination. The new deputy logistic manager found satisfaction in intimidating his subordinates with warning letters. The manager himself arrived at work well after eight, a stench of a mixture of alcohol and cigarettes escaping from his mouth. His first activity was to consult with his spies to find out which worker arrived after half-past seven. Just the thought of this menacing man with his set of brown teeth, renowned for going out with barmaids, made Bakari feel sick.

That evening Bakari wanted to rest his mind from the barrage of problems that seemed to be targeting him. He was now heading to Vijana Bar. At a wall leading to the main gate was a partly torn poster of the TMMC Party advertising their candidate for the coming general elections. Bakari pulled a shred of the poster and tore the candidate's eyes. Bakari was satisfied with his unruly behaviour, convinced that the potential member of parliament did not deserve his eyes. If left with his eyes intact, it would be impossible to preclude him from eyeing all the material things he might greedily desire when elected to office.

The chairs were already arranged around the white plastic tables outside the bar. The pedestrians' path, normally busy during the day with people going in different directions, was now clogged with furniture and was thus an extension of the bar. As the night matured, and more clients flocked into the bar, it would encroach further into the muddy road. Pounding Swahili and Congolese music was coming from the speakers hanging on the four pillars of the bar. A fat barmaid wiggled her waist past Bakari as he made his way to the counter. She made no impression on Bakari, and she quickly realised that and continued walking towards the counter.

Bakari did not have any money in his pocket, but came to the bar. It was worse staying at home amidst the incessant clattering of Mwajuma. She would be needing money to pay the vendor at the market for vegetables she borrowed. Then she would be demanding money to pay for the water delivered at the house. Bakari would leave the room before Mwajuma mentioned other needs. Like any other man he wanted to be able to provide for his family their basic necessities. This unkind world would not give him a chance to live such a normal life. Even if fortune came to him once a while in his life, it would quickly slip out of his hands and he would return to destitution.

Bakari found solace at the bar. The loud noise of drunken men, talking as if they were a mile away from each other, made Bakari forget his problems. The usual high pitched noises and shrills of barmaids contesting over a drunk client, sometimes scratching each other's faces, consoled Bakari that he was not the only one facing problems in Dar-es-Salaam. The loud music from all corners of the bars gave him the solace that the world after all was romantic and harmonious.

Bakari's eyes oscillated in different directions to see if he could find one of his friends at a table and join him. His eyes saw a few familiar faces, but they were not inviting him. Those people pretended that they did not see him. Even if he stared at them, their eyes would not be baited to look back. Bakari would be inclined to conclude that his friends were either myopic or that the alcohol they were consuming was rendering their sense of sight incapable.

Bakari wouldn't bother himself; he had drunk from them before and knew they wouldn't invite him today. It was still early in the evening and there was a possibility that more generous people would be walking into the bar. There was a vacant table on one of its corners. Bakari picked a copy of *Majira* newspaper left unattended at the counter and moved to the empty table. The paper was folded many times and was daubed with grease and dust. It was today's paper and still legible. He sat at a chair and spread the newspaper on the table. Bakari searched his pockets and brought out a match box. He drew a match stick, bit it, and started poking his teeth. It was an endemic habit in him, and it had resulted in infections in his gums, but it was a hard habit to kick.

Page two of the newspaper showed a captured tank from government soldiers in the civil war of Congo. Beside the tank were a couple of hungry looking soldiers wearing berets, carrying guns that seemed to be palpitating on their shoulders. At the bottom of the paper was another picture of the rebel leader in southern Sudan. The cap he wore allowed only his fiery eyes and a bush of a beard to be seen. Bakari flipped the paper and went to the back page. The rest of the pages were filled with topics that covered the forthcoming general elections: inundated with pledges that Bakari knew none of the political contenders was able to fulfil.

A shuffle of a chair behind him distracted his attention. A heavy client with a pitch black face collected his car keys from the table and headed for the door. Bakari watched the man belching, making his way around the tables with his big buttocks bumping repeatedly at the plastic chairs. The man shuffled his shoes on the cement floor, implying that they were too heavy for him to lift, or that his tipsy body lost the necessary energy to do so.

Bakari was lucky; the man left his glass half full, and there were nearly two inches of beer in the bottle. In a flash, Bakari took the bottle and glass behind him, and placed them on his table. Being in a season of destitution, Bakari had developed such crafty moves that made him survive from day to day. He continued holding the newspaper close to his face, pretending to be concentrating on an interesting topic. His slightly reddish eyes were nonetheless flickering from side to side to find out if anyone had noticed that swift action. He consoled himself though with the fact that where there is poverty there is no civilisation.

Other clients in the bar were too busy looking at the departing man heading to a shining Mitsubishi Pajero, to have noticed what Bakari had done. In the absence of the paupers who went around scavenging on rubbish bins, no one expected that a person seated in that bar could prey on an unattended drink left by someone else. Bakari lifted the newspaper and spread it wide so as to conceal the bottle and glass from the barmaid who came to check on the table left by the big man. She appeared suspicious, but Bakari's concentration on the paper discouraged her from inquiring from him the whereabouts of the departing client's bottle and glass. She might have thought that another barmaid had been there before her and cleared the table.

Bakari took the glass, peered at it to determine and avoid the area where the other person might have placed his wide lips, and took a light sip. He put the glass back on the table and continued shuffling through the newspaper. A big headline at the back of the paper was about the impending Safari Lager Premier League game between Simba Sport Club and their historical rivals Young Africans Sport Club. Bakari was an avowed supporter of Yanga, as it was popularly known in town. The club's indicative colours were green and yellow. Bakari had several of his belongings chosen following the colours of his club, and would even buy his wife khangas that represented the two colours.

He felt like attending the match, but the two thousand shillings entry fee was a constraint to him. Bakari could not think of a quick business to raise that money for football. If he went to the club's headquarters and hung around

4

there singing words of praise for the club, there might be a chance of a wealthy supporter, driven by self-esteem, to volunteer to buy tickets for the singing fanatics. The chances were however that there might be too many people thinking of doing the same thing, and sympathy from any donor could go to the younger supporters or those who could shove and fight for the few tickets being donated.

Bakari took another sip, moved his tongue in his mouth as if to probe the barley that brewed the beer, then remembered the possible confusion that followed such popular matches. Two years ago, he had a stone aimed at his head just outside the Karume Memorial Stadium which resulted in three stitches on his face. When he reached home, his wife had suspected that he had been beaten somewhere, probably fighting over another woman. Bakari did not understand why Swahili women always thought that if a man encountered a mishap, it happened because of another woman or sexually related activities. It really baffled him.

A short woman was moving in the bar, shoving the plastic tables in her path. She was dressed in an overflowing dress made of African print material, most probably brought from Congo, as the face of the country's former strongman with his characteristic cap made of leopard skin was imprinted on it. To be taken as an up-to-date woman in town, a woman had to dress in material made out of the borders of Tanzania. A khanga from Zambia, kitenge from Zaire or Kenya, was the fashion in town. The body of the lady who entered the bar was shaped like a barrel and had nothing on it to distract a sober man's attention. Bakari was only having his first sips from the beer he had smuggled from a nearby table, and was not yet drunk to be wooed by her bunny teeth and split eyes.

Bakari quickly lifted the paper to cover his face. The move managed to cover his face, but the chequered long-sleeved shirt Bakari always wore in the evening gave him away. It was not the only shirt he owned but the two or three others had one or two areas that needed stitching or patching. His wife had no money to repair them or take them to the tailor working on the veranda opposite their house. Mwajuma already owed him a couple of shillings for fixing the children's clothes.

'Hello Bakari, today you are here quite early?' the plump lady said. She was attempting to execute a captivating body language.

Bakari kept his face buried in the newspaper, trying to give the woman the impression that she had mistaken him for another person.

'Bakari, why are you so quiet while I am talking to you?' She touched him on the back.

5

'Oh, I was so absorbed with this story of the death of TMMC's party chairman,' Bakari said with a frown on his face.

'Tell me the story, Bakari, how did he die?' Her wide chocolate cheeks were raised towards her tiny ears.

'No one knows, but speculations are that he had a painful stomach and was vomiting.' Bakari made a short answer and turned back to the paper.

'I also heard he had began spilling beans, as such endangering the interests of his fellow party members, isn't it Bakari?'

'I don't know,' Bakari answered bluntly.

With the political climate the way it was, powerful parties could be sending out agents to listen to other people's views and maybe victimise them. Bakari was not taking chances.

The lady next to him made a provocative gesture by slapping her big hips with both her hands. If the hips were curved upwards, ending in a thin waist, maybe the gesture could have borne fruit. As she stood with her short hands, she could only be an expert in handling the pestle and pounding maize in a mortar. Her stout, solid body would have earned her praise among other Swahili women as a hard worker in preparing the maize for the popular Makande dish. She then undid the knot of her khanga and re-tightened it around her waist. That move might have exposed a bit of her swollen legs; unfortunately Bakari's eyes were still on the newspaper.

'That is an interesting story, Bakari; may I sit down so you can tell me more about it?' She smiled at him sheepishly.

'No, you see these three seats are reserved for my boss and two other workmates. They are due here any moment now.'

'Aw, Bakari, I can bring another chair then.' She frowned.

'You see, er . . .'

'Sibongile, you mean you have forgotten me?'

'No, Sibongile, I mean, we have very confidential issues to discuss,' Bakari said as he pushed the chair next to the lady further into the table.

'Ai, Bakari, buy me one beer then . . .'

'I gave my cheque to one of the guys coming, to cash for me, so I am waiting for him to bring the money.'

'You mean you have no cash for one beer?'

'I keep my money in cheques or credit cards. Now can I continue reading the paper?' The expression on Bakari's face emphasised his words.

The lady twisted her mouth, turned, pushed Bakari's chair and walked away.

She was disappointed, but Bakari was relieved. The woman was one of those who prey on men's pockets. Even if he had some cash with him, he wouldn't waste it with her. She has been going around with all types of men, and Bakari was convinced that she carried the HIV virus. With two of his friends already having died of the dreaded disease, Bakari was really getting concerned. A week earlier, he had visited a workmate at the Mwananyamala Clinic, and his friend's bony frame on the worn out metal bed had driven a cold chill of fear along Bakari's spine.

Speculation from people saying that the disease was a false alarm by the government to force people to abstain from sex so as to limit population growth was proving to be a farce. He liked women, but this stupid disease, as he called it, was all out to destroy the fun. The idea of using a condom had not gone down very well with him. He felt that using a condom undermined his masculinity: as he put it, 'It feels like eating maize porridge with gloves on your hands.'

Bakari could not think of another alternative to protect himself. He distrusted the loud talking witch-doctors calling themselves professor so and so, or even prophets, who claimed they had enchanted objects that they could offer to a man, and he could go around town conquering every woman without being infected. These bogus doctors would collect many types of roots, shells and other peculiar object, buy megaphones and collect large crowds of people in the market areas. They would begin talking incessantly, dishing out funny and trivial words that were intended to dupe their listeners into passivity. At the same time the agents of these unscrupulous men would be moving within the throngs pick-pocketing their subdued victims.

The time Bakari attended one of the meetings out of inquisitiveness at Tanga, the agents had come to him and demanded that he offered some donations to be used to appease the surging of evil demons in the municipality. Bakari was told that if he did not offer something the demons would visit his house and devour his children. Bakari had no children at that time, and was amazed: how could a shabby dressed fellow with criminal eyes foretell something like that to him? When he dismissed him with a shove, the untidy chap started screaming at the top of his voice, saying Bakari was a surrogate of the demons. The main speaker had jumped in support of his puppet by castigating Bakari and ordering him to be cleansed. Bakari had to turn around and dash for his life as the evil prophet was about to turn the crowd against him by declaring him a witch.

Bakari had left the rest of the throng completely intimidated and none of them dared challenge the lousy doctor's authority any longer. They remained there hypnotised and prepared to do anything the doctor would command them. A time was to come when the doctor's agents walked within the throngs with a straw hat collecting donations from the enthralled crowds. The agents would perform this with fervent ruthlessness. If a person dropped only a shilling, the boys would shake the hat, staring at the giver with bloodshot eyes, thus intimidating him into putting another coin or a note.

There was a good song by Dr. Remi Ongala, blasting from the speakers. Ongala was lamenting in a poetic way about the day to day problems that face the man in the streets of Dar-es-Salaam. Bakari was beating his foot on the floor and shaking his head. The words made meaning to him as he took a light sip. A barmaid came and poured the remaining beer into the glass and took the bottle. Before she left, she asked Bakari if he wanted another bottle. Bakari did not answer; he was buried in the newspaper. A prudent barmaid would not disturb a customer in such a situation. He himself would call for her services when he felt like it.

There was a cock in the neighbourhood crowing at that time of the evening. The sun had gone down completely and there was nothing that made the evening look like daybreak. A cock that crows at that time of the day is asking for trouble. A household that has been starved from chicken meat for a long time will have an excuse to turn the poor cock into a relish. For normal households in Dar-es-Salaam with twenty occupants, a single fowl would not do much to satisfy the craving of all of them, taking into consideration that the two thighs are obviously reserved for the head of the family.

Bakari did not take note of the cock's crow. He was perfecting his skills of economising the little beer in the glass. The beer would eventually get finished. Bakari could not keep on occupying a table for long without consuming anything. Unfortunately for him no one pitched up to offer him a drink, or even shared the table with him. Bakari sighed loudly, but that did not seem to help in any way. No one was going to feel pity and instruct a barmaid to send him a drink. Bakari folded the newspaper, in which he hadn't read even one full story, and placed it under his armpit. It was only quarter past seven in the evening, and still too early to go home.

Bakari left the bar and strode into the streets again. He was not short or tall, but his body was full. His complexion was dark brown, and he had small, round eyes. Bakari's legs were strongly built, the result of long years of playing soccer. Bakari liked to walk with his hands in his pockets, and he had them firmly tucked into his brown trevira trousers as he figured where else to go.

He had been to his friends' homes so many times before, and it was not worthwhile to keep on visiting them. Going home whilst it was still so early was not good either. He had no habit of being at home at that time. He was a man, and it was considered in the Swahili customs that the evenings offered opportunities for women to sit in groups whilst cooking, gossiping about their husband's movements and other things pertaining to their lives. A man who sits at home at this time precludes his wife from speaking freely and becomes a burden to her.

The landlord at the house Bakari rented was the main deterrent that kept him away from home at that time. When Bakari left the compound of house number eighteen that evening, the landlord was not in as yet. Otherwise the burly, middle-aged former fisherman would have held Bakari back. The man who rented six rooms of his compound would have demanded from Bakari the two thousand shillings each lessee was required to donate to meet the costs of mending the single toilet in the compound. The door of the pit latrine that served as a bathroom for the occupants, and those of two nearby houses, had its latches broken. More seriously, the floor was giving in and this could endanger the lives of tenants, especially the children.

Bakari was also required to pay a thousand and five hundred shillings as a contribution to purchase a new LUKU electricity card. The landlord would be waiting for him inside the yard sitting on his usual mat made from woven coconut leaves. He would be sitting there listening to his little radio, with his bald head moving from left to right, following the movements of the women in the compound. With his chapped mouth always half open, his brownish eyes would fix on the backsides of the khanga-clad women, and he would whimper in obsession as their buttocks swayed in different directions. So dishevelled was his character that even his two grown-up and fat daughters were not exempt from his penetrating eyes.

The thought of this landlord, a man from the Mafia Islands, retired from prowling the coast of the Indian Ocean, made Bakari choose the street joining to Morocco Road. The street had also been badly devastated by the rains and cars had made huge ridges and furrows in the middle of it. Bakari was sober; he could easily manoeuvre past the heaps of banana peels, and dirty water. Once in a while he would stumble over a coconut shell, but having consumed only one glass of beer, he would not fall.

There was a Chakacha show at the Biafra grounds and the entrance was free for all. There was a throng of people when Bakari arrived. He slowly and gradually pushed his way to the front. At the back he would not be able to see much, even though he was not very short. His full body made it much more difficult for him to manoeuvre past the throng than if he had maintained the slender body he had had at the time he played soccer.

At the age of forty-three, Bakari had managed to father three children with his wife Mwajuma. He had three other children with other women. He had sired them during his wild years as a Coastal United soccer player in Tanga. As a terrific striker scoring a goal in nearly every major match in the region, all the young girls in Tanga had wished to be identified with this local celebrity. Bakari, in turn, took advantage of them, and exploited their weaknesses. If having numerous affairs could be quantified into wealth, Bakari would have been a very wealthy man. The HIV virus had not been prevalent at that time, so Bakari plundered the female population with impunity. When a girl came to him and reported that she had conceived, insinuating he was the father, Bakari would quickly end the affair and look for a fresh partner.

Bakari had a different agenda for the more mature women he popularly branded as sugar-mummies. He had room in his life for the forty something ladies who fancied him, but for a different purpose. Bakari relied on these financially able women to supply him with extra funds, and use their influence with the authorities to bail him out of trouble. He went out with a lady occupying a high position in the municipality. She had once strode into the office of the regional police commander and intimidated the man in uniform into dropping charges levelled against Bakari for abducting a schoolgirl from Katani Secondary School and keeping her in his house for two weeks. The girl had ended up becoming pregnant, but the same middle-aged lady had come to Bakari's assistance and taken the girl to a doctor, thus ending the possibility of the schoolgirl becoming a mother.

When Bakari's soccer career waned because of women and beer, so did his job prospects with the Amboni Group of Companies. He had packed his bags and returned to Mwaneromango in Dar-es-Salaam, where his parents lived. Bakari's parents had taken him to Kisarawe, then Bagamoyo for a year, for him to get treatment for his foot that had got hurt playing soccer and remained painful ever since. The trip to Bagamoyo, where he got cleansed at the graves of Kaole, was also to help Bakari find a new job, and rebuild his life. He had slept next to the graves for two days, with the rain pouring on him, and had powerful religious leaders reciting famous verses from holy books to restore him with luck.

The oracles of Bagamoyo managed to get him a job at the Port, beginning as a clerk in the Cargo Terminal, before being promoted to the Large Room Section that dealt with clearing imported cargo. The wages in both sections were not enough to pay for rent, bus fares, and the beer he so much worshipped. The transfer to the Large Room was nonetheless a blessing. There were fallouts from the numerous kickbacks and baksheesh clients offered for services rendered to them. The lion's share of the tips would go to Bakari's bosses, after they exempted one or two foreign businessmen from paying import duties. The crumbs that fell from the high table would go a long way into alleviating some of the expenses of the likes of Bakari.

The tips did not allow Bakari to buy a four-wheeled vehicle or put up a one storey building at the Mbezi suburb, but it allowed him to move from the mud house he shared with his parents at Mwaneromango, to rent two rooms in Kinondoni. One room was used by Bakari, his wife and the two young children. The other was shared by Mwajuma's younger sister and the grown-up child. This room also served as a store for utensils, the family's charcoal stove, plastic buckets for preserving water, a big bag of maize meal, a drum always full of white rice from Mbeya, and an array of other property belonging to the family.

At eleven in the morning and five in the evening Mwajuma always moved her charcoal stove into the corridor of the house, and prepared the meals for the family. A pleasant aroma from her cooking would diffuse through the whole compound and fill the other occupants with envy. 'Mwajuma is cooking chicken today; yesterday she cooked meat, on Sunday she prepared pilau,' other women would be heard lamenting. The wife of a neighbour had even stopped talking to Mwajuma, alleging that Mwajuma was proud and did not want to share her good life with her peers.

That was the situation when Bakari still worked at the Port's Large Room. But ever since the big corruption scandal rocked the Large Room, disarraying everyone from managers to messengers, life had not been the same for Bakari. He survived the sacking, but got transferred to the fumigation section, a department that had virtually no kickbacks. The corruption, embezzlement and theft charges against his superiors were so serious that the Large Room's manager was advised to take early retirement. He left with a brand new four-wheeled vehicle, a huge house in Mbezi township, a bar in Mwananyamala, two Toyota Hiace minibuses shuttling between Ubungo and the Post Office, and another house for his mistress in Buguruni.

The Chakacha dance was gaining momentum. Bakari could estimate about two hundred people crammed on the open air grounds of Biafra. The wooden stage was in the middle, made with pillars that rose up supporting a tarpaulin covered roof. The stage was at the front, and the background was made in

11

the design of a hut, where the group that played drums, guitars, percussion and accordions sat. Spotlights of different colours mesmerised the stage, and in its midst two young male dancers were kneeling, facing each other. They had plastered their faces with powder, their physique looking frail and pliable, and their short feet appearing as if they lacked vital vitamins in their bodies.

The young men wiggled their waists in a provocative manner. Bakari had shoved his way to the front and had a full view of the dancers. Watching them performing like that made Bakari feel squeamish, even though for a while they made him forget the troubles he faced. He had used most of the day and evening thinking of how to make extra money, and no solution had come to his mind. When a man finds himself in a situation where he feels he is losing control of circumstances governing his very existence, he is prepared to forsake his principles and do something that his conscience would otherwise preclude him from doing. Crime could be one of the options, but Bakari feared violence, and dreaded being sent to jail.

He would feel someone's back-pocket, and be tempted to insert his fingers to see if he could come out with a banknote or two. That option could prove very dangerous indeed, especially being done in an area where there were multitudes of people. If the victim were to scream 'thief', and had everyone turned on the culprit, then within moments he would be shredded into pieces. Bakari rubbed from his mind the possibility of engaging himself in such petty crime. He would rather think of more profitable deals such as shifting unattended stationery or tools from his workplace and go to sell them somewhere.

Bakari watched the two young men sweating, kneeling on the floor with their hands on the floor, twitching their buttocks towards the crowds. The artists were performing in order to make money and a living. Bakari sighed in disbelief, as he watched the eccentric dance. He convinced himself that he would be prepared to starve to death rather than make a living in such an ignominious manner. Not everyone standing and watching in the throng was appalled though. Someone standing next to Bakari was gasping in exhilaration.

'Inshallah, Inshallah,' a big bloke in a long overflowing robe, and a white cap over his head, squawked in excitement.

The boys drew closer to the crowds, lifting their buttocks up and down in peculiar movements. The gasping man took a five thousand shillings note and moved through the throngs waving the note above his head. He then stepped on the stage, collecting his robe on one side to avoid tripping over, and flashed the note in between one of the boys' buttocks, then finally tucked it under the boy's khanga.

'Yalaah, yalaah,' screamed another man with a light skin, beak nose and long curly hair. He lifted up his kanzu, took out a ten thousand shillings note and went to the stage. He approached the same young man, brushed the note between the young man's buttocks, kissed the note, and tucked it under his khanga, next to the other note.

'Why are they doing like that?' Bakari asked someone standing next to him.

'They are bidding for the dancer,' the chap replied.

'Why? Are the two gentlemen so much impressed with his dancing?'

'Not only the dancing part, there is something else they are competing for.'

'What, for the boy's khanga?'

'No, for his backside,' the man said with a smile.

'Is he queer?' Bakari gasped.

'Do I have to tell you?'

'Who are those two bidders?'

'I am not sure, but they appear like businessmen from beyond the sea.'

'Ah, I see, I am not surprised.' Bakari placed his hand on his mouth and thought.

There was no entrance fee for the spectators, but that did not mean the show was completely free. There were unruly boys who would go within the throng with a small flat basket collecting donations for the dancers and organisers. Otherwise, more money was usually organised through the agile fingers of numerous pickpockets prowling through the crowds.

Bakari was not getting much entertainment from the dancers, and the useless comments that accompanied them. Bakari detested the way the two so-called island businessmen kept on moving to the stage to place their bids. Bakari had got more entertainment on the same grounds, two months earlier, when one political aspiring leader was addressing multitudes of people, asking them to give him their votes in the coming multi-party general elections. The short man, wearing a tie and jacket in the Dar-es-Salaam heat, was promising to build each Tanzanian citizen a house to live in, a car for each of the fifteen million adult citizens, and bank accounts from which each person could draw according to the person's needs. The promises were enticing, but Bakari wondered why the vocal politician failed to get even one per cent of the votes.

Bakari thought of going home, but the time was still early. At quarter to nine the landlord could still be at the yard dozing a bit, or slapping himself repeatedly, attempting to kill the mosquitos hovering over his body. Sometimes he would slap himself even if there were no mosquitos. He had got used to it and it had become a habit which he could not quit. What his eyes would not miss, even as he snored from a light sleep, was the sight of his female tenants making their way to and from the toilet.

Mwajuma too, would be waiting for Bakari. She had a bit of nagging to impart to her husband. Today, she would not be staying awake to make her daily complaints about the lack of commodities in the house. Mwajuma was not bothered any more with stories that her husband had been seen drinking with another woman at a bar. Her concerns were with her younger sister, and the stories he had been telling her. The younger sister had always complained to Mwajuma about the landlord's advances to her, and the monotonous comments he would utter whenever she moved around the compound, but Mwajuma felt that the issue was beyond her ability to solve. They had to keep up with the landlord's filthy behaviour as long as they wished to stay in house number eighteen. It was also useless to tell her husband, because Bakari had no nerve to confront the broad-shouldered fisherman.

The story that Bakari had threatened to throw his sister-in-law out of the other room and have her pack her bags to her parents' house in Mtongani, disturbed Mwajuma. Mwajuma's sister worked at a bank in town, and it was nearer for her if she stayed in Kinondoni. In addition, Mwajuma wanted to keep an eye on her sister and saw no reason why her husband should wish to expel her. Ever since Bakari got transferred from the money wells of the Large Room to the dry fumigation section, it was Mwajuma who practically became the breadwinner for the family. Her small businesses of selling buns and samosas in the market, and sometimes second-hand clothes in town, netted more income than what her husband brought at the end of the month. It was therefore impossible for him to make all the decisions in the house.

# CHAPTER 2

The November heat and humidity in Dar-es-Salaam makes a person feel as if he is in a boiler room. This condition is exacerbated at night, especially when it rains a bit. Besides the humidity and mosquitos, the consequence of the rain makes it a nightmare to walk at night in the unlit streets of the shabby townships. There are also times when the streets get out of control owing to hooligans preying on lone figures walking at night, especially tipsy characters. The hooligans will remove whatever the victim wears, give him a clap or two, and let him wander home in his underpants. Bakari always walked looking in all directions, ready to dash for his life if any obscure individual closed near him.

It was another of those windless nights. Bakari choked at the swarm of mosquitos at the doorstep of house eighteen, and pushed open the tin door. It was half past one in the morning, and the landlord had long retired to his room when Bakari stepped in the corridor. There was not much noise, except for the snoring of one or two young men who slept on the corridor. The house he rented had ceiling boards, a marked improvement from other houses in the Swahili areas that were deprived of this infrastructure. When Bakari walked in the corridor he would not be heard by other occupants in other rooms; thus the chances were very small that the landlord would know that Bakari was in the building.

Bakari sneaked along the corridor, having gained enough experience of manoeuvring past the numerous human obstacles without stepping on anyone's legs. About five or six young men were renting a sleeping space on the corridor that night. It wasn't the peak season, otherwise close to twelve youths could be paying to sleep there. This was more so when natural disasters struck a region of the country, and there was an influx of people to Dar-es-Salaam. Relief aid to regions that are always overlooked by the government, or whose infrastructure render them inaccessible, usually takes time to reach the natural disaster victims. The affected people partly solve the problem by migrating to the capital itself, thus reminding those in authority of their plight. It would not be difficult for the authorities to notice the effect of the influx, as the number of petty criminals would increase; house breaking incidents would be prevalent; and an extra contingent of women roaming the streets would be noticeable.

The youths took turns sleeping on the corridor and the veranda outside the house. Six men would sleep on the corridor floor from ten up to two in the morning, then alternate to the veranda to spend the rest of the night. Those who had been braving the swarms of mosquitoes outside would then move in and spend the three hours behind a closed door on the corridor. They would abandon the corridor before six in the morning, to avoid the stampede from close to twenty residents of the house, rushing for the only toilet available in the compound. The corridor boys were allowed to use the toilet to respond to natural calls, but not allowed to take a bath in it. They would not be having water anyway even if there were allowed to bath, as none of the occupants would lend them their buckets. The boys' bodies would be cleaned by nature, unless they stumbled into a river or an obscure · water hole somewhere.

Bakari shoved the door of room number three, and quietly stepped into the room. He did not put on the lights, as he could move relatively easily in the room. He had stayed there for three years and knew very well the position of the furniture and each item in that cramped room. Even when he had been drinking he used to walk within his room at night, without the lights on, to go the toilet. Mwajuma had been protesting when Bakari put on the lights on his way to the toilet, and so he perfected the art of prowling in the darkness.

Bakari returned the door gently and released the latch without much noise. There was only a faint howl emanating from somewhere within the compound. Bakari stopped to listen, but nothing else could be heard. The yowl must have come from someone being seized by a demon in his sleep, Bakari was thus convinced. As he took off his shirt to hang it on the nail by the door, Mwajuma stirred, sat up for a moment, then went to switch on the lights.

'You will wake up the children,' Bakari complained.

'They are awake anyway, what is your worry?' Mwajuma replied.

'What do you mean?' Bakari's voice was still in a whisper, as he placed the shirt on the nail.

'Ho, I mean, how do you expect the children to sleep?' Her voice was slightly raised.

'But they are now asleep.'

16

'They are not asleep, they have fainted out of hunger.'

Bakari looked at Mwajuma, acknowledging the furious image on her face. When he first persuaded her to go out with him she was a really pretty woman. Her physique was what actually made Bakari use all his time and resources to go after her. When he finally conquered her and discovered her womanhood, Bakari felt as if he had entered into the golden gates of heavenly bliss. But the ecstasy was to wear off, once he started failing to live up to the standards he had set to her before. When the rent went unpaid for three months, a kilogram of meat appearing once a month, and Mwajuma failing to sport the latest khangas in fashion, the bliss turned into hell.

He took back the shirt from behind the door and put it on, without fastening the buttons.

'The children have not eaten for the whole day, and you are only busy getting drunk,' Mwajuma charged.

'I am not drunk.'

'I can see today you are not drunk of beer, only drunk of the prostitutes in town!'

'Don't talk to me like that, Mwajuma!'

'Talk to you like what?' Mwajuma's voice was highly pitched. 'What value do you have for me not to talk to you like that?'

'Shut up!'

'I won't shut up!'

Someone stirred in the other room and coughed. The cough was from a grown-up man. Following the coughing was a faint sound of a radio. A tenant must have been trying to tune to a distant station at that time of night. No radio station in Dar-es-Salaam was still transmitting at that time. If he were lucky he could get one of those noisy overseas stations. Otherwise, on hearing the noises, the tenant might have thought those were thieves, and put on his radio as a signal to them that he was well awake and listening to the programme.

Bakari hushed down his wife, fearing the noise might wake up the landlord and make the night even worse for him.

'I won't stop talking,' Mwajuma ignored him.

'Shhh, we will talk over these things tomorrow.'

'No, tell me now, what is going on between you and my sister?' Mwajuma was holding his skirt.

'Wait a moment, I hear something outside.' Bakari was releasing Mwajuma's grip.

'Hear what?'

17

Bakari opened the door, and quickly stepped out of the room. Mwajuma tried to follow him, but she stopped at the door. She saw through the faint lights in the corridor, her husband making his way past the human bodies on the passage. As she always slept early and woke up long after everyone had cleared the passage, Mwajuma lacked the art of sifting past the sleeping young men. If she was to follow her husband, with the anger that had gripped her, she would surely have stumbled over the sleeping bodies and caused mayhem.

'Big adulterous,' Mwajuma sneered as she shut the door of the room, and returned to her bed.

She was also wearing only a single khanga knotted on top of her breasts and it was impracticable to leave the room in that state and go to the veranda.

Bakari went to the veranda, stepped into the street, then stopped to hear if there was anyone following him. After a few minutes he was convinced that no one else had taken any interest in the minor squabble. He turned and stepped on the veranda again. The noises of a woman and man squabbling within the compound or in the rooms were a common occurrence. None of the tenants bothered much unless the wrangle extended into an exchange of blows, wild screeching of furniture, and sizable noises from the warring partners' children. In such a situation, the neighbours would wake up and try to mediate. If things went out of control they would call the cell party leader, or the police, to bring peace within the warring parties.

He squeezed himself between two dozing youngsters seated on a shaky wooden bench. Bakari searched his pockets for some cigarettes, then remembered that he had left them on the table in the bedroom. He really craved for a cigarette, but he could not see anyone smoking in the vicinity. It was something like half-past-two in the morning, and the switch-over between youths sleeping on corridor and those on the veranda had already taken place. Those who had just come to the veranda were still having a sleepy hangover and would not talk or smoke.

Bakari had two twenty shillings coins in his pocket, and decided to walk to the chip sellers along Kinondoni road. There were still a couple of persons having some chips and chicken, served on fat-infested plastic plates. Some were dead drunk, hardly managing even to put the food in their mouths. The chips friers would take advantage of these decapitated individuals, overcharging them or even going to the extent of sifting a note or two from their pockets. There were stalls selling cigarettes at the edge of the chips tables.

Bakari walked back and crossed again to Sekenke Street. He put the cigarette between his lips, took a long pull, then blew the smoke through his nostrils. Bakari cleared his throat and spat on the street. The thought of Mwajuma's words resurfaced in his mind. He was alarmed that the issue with her sister was further aggravating his volatile relationship with Mwajuma. Bakari was still convinced that his sister-in-law was to blame for the fallout they had, because of her habits at house number eighteen.

Two weeks earlier, on a Saturday evening, she had put on a mini-skirt, and was picked up by a Somali-looking chap in a dark Mercedes Benz. The young woman had only pitched up the following day in a taxi, at two in the afternoon. Bakari had fumed with anger and rebuked her. He had reminded her of the dangers of men: the possibility of falling pregnant, and worse, the looming dreaded disease whose cure had not been found. Mwajuma was not impressed with her husband's concern over her sister. Who was he after all, to part parental advice to her sister?

Mwajuma was convinced that her sister had found a good man with plenty of money, and things were promising. The fact that she slept out was not a big deal; who was a saint anyway? For a woman to hit it out with a rich and generous man, she had to make some sacrifices. Her dear sister was treading on the right paths. Her star was shining on her and she had the body assets to lure the rich and famous; why should she spoil her chances? Mwajuma could not understand her husband's motives.

Bakari's concern was prompted by jealousy rather than concern over Mwajuma's sister. Naturally, Bakari shuddered in desire whenever he saw his sister-in-law's big behind wiggle in her tight khangas, though he had not dared make advances at her. He had no money or guts to do that. The girl's stance and her attitude made it obvious to anyone who wanted to make a move on her, to do that through a medium of money. She would clamber onto a Daladala microbus to work in the morning out of necessity, but many times on her way back from work in the evenings, she would be dropped at Sekenke Street by a variety of those expensive cars prowling the streets of Dar-es-Salaam.

The children in the neighbourhood who liked to play a game of counting cars, screaming 'that is mine, that is mine', had lost count of the brand names of motorcars that served as good samaritans in bringing Bakari's sister-in-law home. The woman herself was childishly arrogant. She was at odds with the wife of the landlord, owing to her carefree style and Western ways of dressing. The landlord's wife had long suspected her husband was offering her gifts and money. The latest gossip going around the compound was that the landlord had bought Mwajuma's sister a pair of high heeled shoes and an expensive handbag. The elder woman had thus wanted Mwajuma's sister kicked out of the compound, complaining that she would mislead their teenage daughters into adopting her sleazy behaviour.

The behaviour of Mwajuma's sister of dashing out of the bathroom wearing only a single, flimsy khanga, barely covering her curved body, prompted the married women of house eighteen to call a meeting. The landlord's wife was at the forefront, especially when she observed the reaction occurring on her husband's body whenever Mwajuma's sister crossed the compound to her room. But as it is said in Kiswahili, a faraway stick never kills a snake, so the elderly women's grumbles were ineffective. The young woman continued sporting outrageous hairstyles, wearing tight fitting skirts and trousers, changing men at will, and pitching up at the house at any time she felt convenient.

Bakari squeezed himself on the bench again and stretched his legs. He took a few puffs on the cigarette, and coughed. The coughing might have been prompted by the hunger he was feeling, or stress. He was a professional smoker, who began smoking cigarettes more than twenty-five years ago. A puff of smoke mistakenly going to his windpipe was not supposed to make him cough and provoke tears from his eyes. Someone who had been sleeping on the veranda floor sat up and asked Bakari if he could have a puff.

'No, sorry,' Bakari answered.

'Please Mzee, you may even leave me a bit at the stud.'

Bakari kept quiet and coughed again.

'Oh Mzee, don't you even remember me?'

'Who are you?'

'I am the one who warned you that the landlord was coming for you last Sunday at the bar.'

'Where?' Bakari asked absentmindedly.

'At the Vijana Bar, Mzee, last week.'

Bakari hesitated for a while to recall the event. He was aware of the Swahili's tendency of purporting to a person to have done him this or that favour, or claiming to know him from somewhere, before asking him a favour. When Bakari used to visit his birthplace at Kisarawe, all the old people he met and greeted would stop him and beg for a five hundred shilling note, reminding him of how they took care of him when he was a child, or citing an incident in Bakari's life in which they would claim to have played a crucial role. Five years had passed since he last went to Kisarawe, a mere fifty kilometres from Dar-es-Salaam. Some elders in Kinondoni had warned

Bakari that the long absence from his birthplace might have contributed to his present state of misfortune.

Bakari took a long pull, tapped the cigarette and extended his arm to the chap on the floor.

'Simba and Yanga are playing tomorrow,' the chap on the floor said as he struggled to puff the little piece of cigarette sandwiched between his fingers.

Bakari just stared at the figure on the floor, without saying anything. He leaned his head backward, and swung his hand in the air, attempting to crush a couple of mosquitos hovering on top of his head. The chap was talking about soccer, whilst Bakari's head was preoccupied with so many issues. Bakari wondered how a poor and helpless chap like him occupied himself with soccer rivalries, professing to be a diehard fan of this or that soccer club, whilst he had no food in his stomach, or was not sure where he would sleep the following day.

Bakari had an assignment he thought of executing on Monday, at work, that could earn him some money. He had already removed five plastic drums of fumigating chemicals from the warehouse, and hidden them in an old container near the Port's gate. They had been loading stock from the store to a truck supposed to go and fumigate coffee beans at the coffee depot. Using the skills he had acquired in the stores, five drums left the storeroom but were not loaded in the truck. The skill of hiding the drums that passed in front of the store's officer and were inspected by the loading supervisor standing next to the truck, had to be traced to Bakari's dribbling talents as a former soccer star in Tanga.

The requisition for the whole consignment was issued by Bakari, the clerk in charge, but the one for the five drums was later clandestinely withdrawn from the files and torn to pieces, so no record of the five drums remained. At his convenience, Bakari moved the drums to the container near the gate, and liaised with the driver of the rubbish removal truck to pass near the container and load the drums together with a heap of rubbish to be found there. The consignment was to be taken straight to Kariakoo and off-loaded at a predetermined shop. Bakari sniffed and slapped his arm as the elaborate income generating scheme oozed in his mind.

Time was moving slowly, and the humidity was high. There was a distant light in one of the more affluent houses on the other side of town. It was a security light designed to impede any intruder from coming close to the door. The owners of the house could afford to keep the lights on for the whole night, signifying they could afford to buy a LUKU electricity card regularly. Bakari remembered about the contributions for LUKU card, and he was aware that a further delay in contributing would prompt the landlord to charge into his two rooms, remove the bulbs from the sockets and leave the family without a source of lights. The landlord would also storm into their rooms from time to time to make sure the family was not using their tape recorder or any other electricity consuming appliance.

A screeching noise made Bakari stir from the light sleep he had finally succumbed to. His eyes quickly got a glimpse of the huge car parked in front of the veranda. The door opened and cabin lights came on. A young woman quickly moved out of the car and walked out towards the house. The smooth purring sound of the Mercedes Benz hummed in Bakari's ears as it made a U-turn on the muddy road. Bakari's eyes quickly alternated between the woman as she pushed her way past the door, and the oblong tail lights of the luxurious vehicle.

'That is Mahmood Issa-Mahid, the owner of Rashdashan Hotel,' the chap on the floor commented.

'Which hotel?' Bakari asked absentmindedly, still baffled and trying to recover from the initial pain and shock of seeing his sister-in-law coming out of the German-built sedan.

'The posh restaurant in town,' the chap repeated in a raised voice.

'Oh yes, the Rash . . . shit!'

'The man sometimes drives the latest Range Rover as well,' the young man on the floor said in his scratchy voice.

'Mmmh, that is interesting,' Bakari said.

'He also owns a fleet of Fiat trucks.'

Bakari looked at the talking figure in the darkness, and his nostrils could still feel the strong scent of perfumes the girl wore. Tonight she stepped on the veranda wearing high heels and an outrageous short dress. Bakari's heart ached when trying to think what she had been doing with the Mercedes owner for most of that night. A man to accumulate so much money and own such property must have substantial business outlets. Bakari could not think of any business he could do to earn him money to buy even a second-hand car, or own a modest house for himself. Why does the Almighty God favour other people and give them more and above what they needed, and leave the majority of people with little? Seated on a wobbling bench amidst a mosquito-infected veranda, Bakari could not come to any solution to his problems.

'Let me light another cigarette for you, and I want to hear more of this Issa-Mahid.' Bakari struck a match and held the cigarette for the chap on the floor.

'Thanks, Mzee.'

'You are welcome.'

A heavily-sounding truck was passing along Kinondoni road, bringing vibrations all the way to Sekenke Street. Its faint lights were visible from the veranda, and it was clear that the truck belonged to those transporting goods using unregistered vehicles that were not roadworthy. They took advantage of moving late at night to avoid the traffic police.

Bakari had to wait for the noise to die down before continuing talking to the young man.

'So Issa-Mahid always comes here to disrupt my family when I am not in?' Bakari lamented.

'Sometimes he sends his driver to pick her up.'

Bakari listened as the chap kept on narrating in a heavy slanged tongue. The chap seemed to know lots of details of the rich man.

'What time normally?'

'Around half-past six, seven, after she comes back from work and changes into those short skirts of hers.'

At that time of the day Bakari would not yet be at home. He would have passed the hours in Kariakoo, either seeing his friends or loitering in a bar somewhere.

The dark night was slowly thinning away when Bakari stirred again. He glanced at his watch, and tried to focus at the position of the arrows. He made the time to be around four-thirty in the morning. Bakari had at least managed to catch an hour and a half of sleep and he felt slightly refreshed. He stretched his hands and scratched his cheeks, feeling the place where one of the many mosquitos had bitten him. There was a slight lump on his upper lip. Bakari reached for his sport shoes under the bench, and simultaneously shoved his feet into them. He stood up, stretched his hands again, and yawned. A foul smell emerged from his mouth. The smell, coupled with the pungency from his armpits and socks, made him feel lousy.

Today, he had to take a bath by any means before he left Kinondoni. That meant he had to make his way to the makeshift bathroom before everyone else woke up. It also meant that he had to brave his bedroom again. Mwajuma should be asleep at that time, or would not be in a mood for shouting again. If Bakari could search his memory, Mwajuma slept soundly when it was about to be dawn. He could easily remember that, because he always came late at night, most of the time drunk or dead tired. The only time he would be disposed to perform his marital duties would be at those early hours of the morning, but Mwajuma would be very drowsy and unwilling.

23

Bakari shoved the door and moved into the room. He had determination in his mind that a simple woman was not going to push him around. He rented the rooms; as such no one could deny him entrance. He was a man and was not supposed to be afraid of his wife. If she were to decide to impede him this time he would show her who was the head of the family. Mwajuma could scream whatever she liked, but he would turn a deaf ear to her. He got concerned about her recent behaviour of snapping useless words at him. He knew that his income was not contributing to the wellbeing of the family, but he considered himself the man in the house.

Bakari had watched with awe at the items Mwajuma brought into the house, which surely were above the income from her businesses. Bakari had refrained from asking how she afforded them, because he also shared in their use. He even kept himself far from the gossiping mouths of his neighbours to avoid overhearing news that would make him jealous and humiliated. As long as he didn't catch a man in his room, Bakari would pretend everything was normal with his wife, even though it was quite a while since he last had conjugal relationships with her.

The miaows of a cat near the window were the only sounds that could be heard as Bakari shuffled into the room. He took off his shirt and hung it on the wall. Bakari felt for some sandals on the floor, and approached the corner of the room. A pot fell and clanged on the floor.

'What is going on with you?' Mwajuma growled.

Bakari was all along aware that Mwajuma was alert that he had entered the room.

'Where is water for bathing?' he said in an affirmative tone.

'We had no money to buy much water yesterday,' she answered after a lapse.

'I need water to bathe.' Bakari sounded more forceful.

'There is only half a bucket to wash the utensils.'

'Where is the soap?'

'Ah, there is a piece on top of the door frame.'

The corridor had partly cleared as Bakari made his way to the toilet. Some of the young people had long left to go roaming the streets looking for early morning opportunities to make some money from any item left unattended somewhere. Others were shy to be seen sleeping on verandas, as they had boasted to their friends elsewhere that they come from affluent families, or were renting houses of their own.

Someone coughed from inside the toilet and Bakari paused at the door.

'Darn it, who can this be now?' Bakari showed disappointment, fearing the person was going to delay him outside the toilet and end up being discovered by the landlord.

After five minutes, a dark, thin man emerged with an untidy white sheet wrapped around his waist. His eyes were round and clear, as if they had been glued to his face. He cleared his throat and spat out heavy sputum on the floor, before brushing past Bakari. The man was leasing room number five down the hallway, and appeared arrogant. Bakari did not like him. Sometimes when Bakari greeted him, or attempted to enter into conversation with him, he would simply walk away. The chap had not agreed to lend even a shilling to Bakari, yet he seemed to be able to afford to give lots of money to the scores of girls he brought to his room.

The dark chap had left an unbearable stench in the toilet. Bakari spat several times, but he had to bear it, otherwise if he had to wait outside someone else could get into the toilet. Bakari used both his hands to lift the water over his head, making sure that as much water as possible fell back into the bucket. He carefully clutched the little piece of soap in his fingers and rubbed it over his face and hands. As the toilet was used by twenty or so members, each person had to bring some water and soap. The landlord had instructed that a maximum of half a bucket of water could be used by each person in a day, to avoid filling up the pit latrine.

There was hardly any house in the vicinity that had a toilet with running water. Bakari recalled hearing a political party candidate, whose party Bakari did not bother to know, blaring at the market that if the people gave him their votes he would install running water in every shack and house in Kinondoni. The overweighed aspirant was himself not residing in the township, but wanted votes from people he did not associate with. The candidate should have come and wash his massive body with three litres of water, to get the actual feeling of how the people lived in the constituency he wished to represent.

Bakari felt as if he heard movements near the toilet, so he coughed to make his presence felt. The door of the toilet was still to be fixed, and only a piece of gunny bag hung on the toilet in the meantime. An absent-minded individual could just come stumbling in. It was necessary for any user to make it possible for any one approaching to be aware that there was someone inside. Some other users would whistle throughout the time they were inside, or women who were very concerned would hang a khanga outside to keep everyone a considerable distance away.

He had not remembered to bring a towel with him, so Bakari used his hands to squeeze the water from his body and shook off the remaining droplets. In earlier days, Mwajuma would undertake to prepare the bucket of water whilst her husband was still asleep, put out a bar of toilet soap and towel, and make sure no one occupied the toilet until her husband moved in. If Bakari took a bath much later in the evening, when the toilet was not in great demand, Mwajuma would also walk into the toilet, wearing her single khanga, and assist her husband in scrubbing areas of his body that he could not easily reach. Mwajuma would get hold of the towel, rub it over his back, and help her husband shove in his sandals as well. All this time, Mwajuma would be whispering soothing and encouraging words behind her husband's ears, making him feel he was the only one in her life. Those were the good old days, and Bakari sighed when the thoughts appeared in his mind.

Bakari entered room number three and put the bucket on the floor. He looked around the room, lifted a wooden lid on the side of the bed from where he took a shirt, and searched for a pair of socks. He dressed, took his red shoes and put them on. At five in the morning, it was still early for people going to offices, except for those working in hospitals and hotels, who worked shifts. A number of buses had already begun whizzing in the streets competing for the early commuters. Noises from the turn-boys publicising their buses' routes could be heard as far as the Sekenke house.

Bakari was ready to move, and he took the little notebook from his other shirt. The folded white paper fell from the notebook again. It was the same warning letter that seemed to be continuously haunting him. His role in the problem that resulted in him getting the letter was minimal, but he ended up being punished in the same magnitude as the others. Bakari reckoned the Swahili saying: 'If one fish in a pond is rotten, then all others tend to be rotten as well', to have applied to him in this case.

The scandal began when accusations were hurled at Bakari and two other men working at the mechanics section for having sabotaged the company's commuter bus. Whenever the commuter bus, ferrying workers to work from home, was out of order, the authorities at the Port would contract a bus belonging to Kunjabis Transporters to do the commuting until the company's bus was put right. Kunjabis Spares, a sister company to the transporters, were also responsible for supplying all the spare parts used at the Port's mechanical section, and servicing a fleet of about thirty-five vehicles. The fleet comprised trucks, buses, tractors and saloon cars. The Port's buses would usually run for a maximum of a week in a month, and break down again, prompting the authorities to turn to the alternative transporters.

Rumours had reached the authorities that two of the mechanics had poured a peculiar chemical into the engines of two of the buses to make them stall, thus giving a chance to Kunjabis to put their buses into service, and supply some spare parts. Gossip circulating within the company indicated that the mechanics were on the payroll of the manager of Kunjabis Enterprises. Bakari's role in this scandal was the delivery of the five litres of chemicals to the mechanics. He did not pour the contents in the engines, and was not even part of those to benefit from the transporters' kickbacks. Bakari simply got a one thousand shillings note from one of the mechanics, for bringing the chemical. The Port's authorities had to send warning letters to all who took part regardless of a person's participation.

The authorities themselves would not be too hard to Kunjabis, as their managers were good friends of theirs. Once in a while the Kunjabis management would send presents to their counterparts at the Port, especially when it was time for renewing the transportation and spares delivery contracts. The Land Rover Discovery driven by the Port's Maintenance Manager was said to have belonged to one of Kunjabis' owners a while ago, and it is said to have been sold to the manager at a give-away price.

Thoughts of the activities at the Port made Bakari shake his head. When will there be equality in this world? he asked himself. But even if equality was impossible to come along, there should be at least some fairness or justice. Bakari was still talking to his mind as he arranged the notebook and papers in his shirt pocket. He had to go to Kariakoo to make some final arrangements for the chemicals' business deal. He needed to call in at his friend's tea room as well and see what could be gained from there. Bakari had not eaten anything since yesterday afternoon, so he needed some tea that morning, and at least five fat buns.

When Bakari had no money like today, it took him a little over an hour to walk to Kariakoo. He would need another forty-five minutes to reach the Port. He therefore had at his disposal, half-an-hour for breakfast and business.

'What shall I tell the landlord?' Mwajuma broke the silence in the room.

'Don't even bother talking to him.'

'He will come knocking at six this morning.'

'I won't be here by then.'

'Why? Are you afraid of him: a man like you?'

'I am not afraid of a weary donkey like him.'

'Then why are you running away so early in the morning?'

'I have business to attend to, and please don't probe me, Mwajuma.' Bakari turned to look at his wife.

'Probing you, we need to pay the rent, otherwise we will be evicted!' Mwajuma spoke at a shrill.

'I'll be bringing some money in the evening.'

'What about the debts at the market, butcher . . . ?'

'I said I will come with something,' Bakari said as he prepared to leave.

It was slightly windy in Sekenke Street. The sun had not pierced the horizon, but there was enough visibility to enable a person even to read the morning newspapers.

# CHAPTER 3

Clouds of dust bellowing from the wheels of a huge truck making its way past the narrow streets, precipitated on the fat buns sold on the pavements. The sellers did not seem to care about that health hazard on their products, supposed to be for human consumption. They could at least cover them with a piece of newspaper, although they argued that by covering them the clients wouldn't be able to see and appreciate the buns. The buyers themselves did not seem to bother about the layer of dust clinging on the thin strip of fat around the buns. Their decision to buy was merely prompted by the price and size of the buns. 'Who has fallen sick as a result of eating the buns, after all?' the sellers would contend. 'You consume more dust through your nostrils anyway.'

Bakari closed his nose until the dust settled down, then pitched a long spit to the road.

'I wonder why they allow huge trucks in Kariakoo,' Bakari said in disgust.

'They are delivering sand to that construction site over there,' Omari said, pointing to the end of the street.

'What are they making there?'

'A building for a football club.'

'Football in this country has floundered.'

'You know why, Bakari?'

'Tell me, Omari.'

'The management is eating all the money.'

'Ah, everyone does that in Bongoland.'

'It is worse in soccer, I tell you, Bakari.'

A young woman passed across the street, and simultaneously, the two men glanced at the way her skirt was slit at the back. The men had paused the conversation so as not to miss the scenery and form opinions in their minds. They did not say a word, but glanced at each other with faces of disapproval. The next moment, a group of three boys passed by, walking slowly, swinging their hands and shuffling their feet on the dusty road. Two had shaven their heads completely, and both had earrings on one ear. The other boy's hair was tied in dreadlocks. He wore earrings on both ears. When the youths talked, they did that with gesticulation of their hands.

Bakari looked at his friend and laughed. Omari was not amused, he was busy shaking his head.

'These boys are out of their minds,' Bakari said.

'You know where they are coming from?' Omari was still shaking his head.

'From playing chakacha, I suppose,' Bakari laughed.

Omari joined in the laugh, and cleared his throat.

'No, I doubt that; these are the stealing type.'

'But one of your sons has dreadlocks, Omari.'

Omari thought for a while, took a bite at a fat bun, then lifted his cup of tea and took a long sip. He looked up and scratched his chin.

'Ah, forget about those hooligans, Bakari.' Omari seemed not prepared to talk about his family.

Bakari reckoned he had asked his friend an embarrassing question. It was easy to talk and criticise other people and their children, but when it came to self-criticism, few people were prepared to stomach it. The stories of Omari's sons and daughters were as dramatic as his own life. The eldest son was desperately wasting his life consuming drugs with a certain musical group in town, in which he was supposed to be a drummer. Two other sons, each from a different mother, had dropped out of school and were busy roaming the streets picking fights on every street corner. His eldest daughter was the only offspring of his who looked promising. She helped in running the restaurant Omari owned, and helped her parents at home as well. Her younger sister, on the other hand, had begun wearing mini-skirts and coming home late, making her father very concerned.

Bakari glanced at his watch and then his friend. It was time for him to begin the second leg of his trip to his workplace.

'OK, the consignment may reach here around two in the afternoon,' Bakari said.

'Make sure not during the lunch hour, too many people are around at that time.'

'The truck will stop right at the back entrance of the hotel as usual.'

'How big are the drums this time?'

'The usual twenty-five litres,' Bakari said as he rose to leave.

The heat had already intensified, although it was only five past seven in the morning. A low flying aircraft droned above the tin roofed houses of

Kariakoo, reflecting the sun's rays on Bakari's face. Some women were busy fanning charcoal stoves on their verandas, ready to prepare some tea or porridge for their children before they left for school. These were the lucky ones; the perpetual difficult economic condition facing a majority of the people meant that a lot of other kids left for school with empty stomachs. Bakari was more fortunate; his stomach felt better following the two cups of tea and five fat buns he consumed at his friend's place.

Bakari belched and gazed at the end of the road. Sweat beads formed on his brow owing to the humidity. The big truck had turned and was coming back again, after off-loading its cargo. Bakari thought of changing streets in a hurry before suffocating in another cloud of dust, but something else came into his mind. He turned and headed back to the restaurant.

'Omari, I need to ask you something.' Bakari coughed as a result of the dust clogging over his face.

Omari frowned and looked at his friend of over twenty years. They had first met in Tanga when Bakari was a star with Coastal United football club. Bakari was a local celebrity who became a role model to the other youth at the municipality. Every young man at that time wanted to be associated with the famous man. Whether he became a role model in misleading the youths into hooliganism, womanising, and excessive drinking, was to be observed from the kind of friends he chose and kept. Bakari and Omari got on well because they both hailed from Kisarawe and had similar interests. They were both drinking heavily, but whilst Bakari ended his nights with a woman in his room, Omari would be drowsy with the sticks of bhang he used to smoke incessantly.

Omari had since quitted the bottle and become committed to religion. His rediscovery of his faith came about in the mid-eighties when a sudden surge of new and diehard believers seemed to be sweeping the country. This popular passion saw Omari joining other religious militants in breaking bottles of beer, condemning women wearing indecent clothes, and other habits they thought to be unsuitable in their society. Omari attended to his five prayers every day, and went to the evening prayers whenever he was in town.

Bakari returned to the restaurant while Omari was thinking of preparing himself to go and buy some malaria pills to be sent to his senior wife in Kisarawe. Every week, he had to spend at least two days in Kisarawe, where the elder wife lived. He had come from there yesterday, and had left her in bed with the ghastly disease, and had decided to send her eldest daughter to see to her mother. Omari's younger wife stayed with him in Kariakoo, helping at the restaurant in frying samosas and kebabs. She did not leave the house

31

much, but would sit at the yard in the back of the house next to her charcoal stove. Logically, Omari would not allow her to stray away from his eyes for a long time. At twenty four she was still attractive, and most of the time her husband would show jealousy, especially when she talked to younger men coming to the tea room.

'You were saying something, Bakari?' Omari looked at him, with the frown still on his face.

'Yes, I wanted to ask if you know a certain tall man, known as Issa-Mahid.'

'The man with lots of money, of course I do.'

'Driving a brand new Mercedes five hundred?' Bakari asked as if he did not believe Omari's assertiveness.

'That man is very hard working, industrious, and very pious.'

'That man is busy driving a wedge in my family!' Bakari seemed not impressed with the picture of Issa-Mahid as painted by Omari.

'Don't tell me he is after Mwajuma?'

'No, but her sister!' Bakari gulped in emotion.

'Why should that bother you then?'

'Bother me? The sister is like my daughter, and I have to be concerned over her wellbeing; I can't sit by and see a hooligan destroying her future.'

'Besides his good qualities, Issa has one weakness: he is crazy about women.'

'We have to put a brake on this chap.' Bakari was still showing a concerned face.

'I have warned my teenage daughter to be aware of him.'

'Does he come to you house too?' Bakari jumped in as if wishing to get support in his concern.

'He is still young and parts with lot of shillings, that is why these young girls flock to him; otherwise he is a powerful entrepreneur.'

Bakari stood from the wooden folding chair, and collected his plastic bag ready to leave again. He was finding it unbearable to hear Omari complimenting a chap he disliked. Bakari himself could not think of the main reason that made him dislike the Somali-looking chap that much. It was strange as he had not even seen him closely or talked to him to find out what type of character he was. If he were a mere hooligan, thinking only of making love to women, how did he manage to make so much money at a relatively young age? Bakari left his mind boggling over this issue as he crossed the road to the other side. He placed his left hand in his pocket and looked back at Omari, who was making his way into the restaurant.

'Omari, we have to fix this playboy,' Bakari said as he hurried down the street.

'Mind you, he is a very cunning man,' Omari cautioned his friend.

Bakari was sweating profusely as he dashed down the gate of the Port. The sun's rays refracted intensively on the surfaced floor, sending the heatwaves upwards. He managed to sign his name on the register when it was four minutes to eight. Ahead of him passed the fat telephone operator, always carrying oily paper bags full of snacks. She would sit at the huge telephone switchboard, a relic of the last world war, and spread open the bags. From them she would pull fried cassava, fish pieces, and half-cakes and eat perpetually. Once a while she would pause only to answer phone calls with a mouthful, using her oily fingers to move the switchboard buttons up and down. Bakari hated her, as he learned from his friends that the fat lady was responsible for telling the authorities that she had seen him taking a gallon of chemicals to the mechanical section.

Bakari had to unbutton his shirt to allow the perspiration on his body to dry. The store's assistant manager had today assigned Bakari, together with two other clerks, to check on the expiry dates on the chemical drums in the store. The three men were supposed to isolate those whose expiry dates were due, and list them in a registry book. In his stammering voice, with hands on his waist, the manager had shrieked the command to the men, exposing his brownish teeth and red eyes. He seemed to be drinking a lot, evidently shown by the huge puffs below his sickly eyes. He gave short instructions whilst walking, and did not give a chance to his subordinates to ask questions. The manager believed the act of questioning his instructions tantamount to insubordination, a practice he would not tolerate in his department.

Bakari looked at the assistant manager as he walked away, and sneered at him. The medium-built man was also not among the people Bakari held in high regard. The junior manager was responsible for sending all the unfavourable reports regarding Bakari's conduct to the higher authorities in the personnel department. The assistant manager hailed from the mountainous areas in the north of the country; Bakari thought the manager disliked him because he was from the coast. Bakari felt isolated in the stores section, having the illusion that every one disliked him and had bad intentions against him. He had no godfather to take care of his interests in higher circles. Bakari was convinced, as was the case with most other junior workers, that a person could not advance in his career, or even have stability at work, without an uncle, aunt, or a man from his tribe in the upper echelons of work.

The heat in the store had intensified, and even the pieces of paper on his hands were getting wet with perspiration. Bakari and his friends had listed more than half of the consignment in the stores in their registry books. It was, however, soon to be time for the half-past ten tea break. That was the time the rubbish truck moved around the compound to collect its load. Bakari had to be near the container to oversee a successful completion of his clandestine operation. Within and around the old container were all types of scrap: old furniture, utensils and rotting electrical equipment. It was therefore relatively easy to conceal anything in that confusion.

Few people visited the old, forty feet container in the first place. There had been rumours of the sighting of a huge green mamba slinking within the junk. The night watchmen on each shift had confirmed the news of mysterious noises emanating from the old containers at night. According to the eldest of the watchmen, there were other nights when pieces of junk would be flying all over the container, clanging violently on its walls, accompanied by shrieks.

'There are evil spooks and devils in the container,' summarised the sixty four year old watchman from Kilwa Kivinje, an area revered for voodoo casting and cleansing.

He had thus warned everyone caring to listen to him, to avoid the container for the safety of their lives. Most of the people at the Port were convinced by this advice from a man supposed to be brimming with experience of life. No one would attribute the mysteries to the tens of stray cats mating at night. Even Bakari had to solicit all his guts to approach the container when placing the drums. Yet as has happened innumerable times in every corner of the globe, the quest for money prompted men to undertake risks in whatever form. Men do realise the dangers of breaking into a house with the owners sleeping inside, but they would still clasp a machete, or an aging Makarov pistol, and unbundle the grills of a window somewhere.

Bakari squeezed past the heap of drums and boxes piled at the door of the store. As he moved past the door, a box fell and tins of liquid stuff opened and rolled on the floor. Luckily, as the caps were sealed, none of the contents spilled out. Bakari moved back, took the box and straightened it. He replaced the card box partition in the box and proceeded to place the tins in their respective slots in the box. On one of the tins he observed the expiry date. More than a year had already elapsed. Bakari just replaced all the tins, folded together the lids of the box, and placed it back on the rack.

Out of the room he met one of the men he had been working with in the store. Bakari did not want to lose any time talking to him, so he hurried past the man looking on the other side. The chap however asked for a match. Bakari paused, took out a worn matchbox and handed it to the short chap with uncombed hair.

'The job that silly Kibosho gave us is really backbreaking,' the chap said as he struggled to strike the match.

'Yeah, please hasten up, I am rushing to meet my relative out there.' Bakari was extending his hand to collect his matchbox.

'Jeers, the match won't light,' the man mumbled with the cigarette sandwiched on his lips.

Bakari took the matchbox, struck a match and extended it to light the man's cigarette.

'We are not supposed to light matches here, by the way,' Bakari said.

'Ah, why should you bother?'

'There are chemicals near here.'

'Never mind, they have all expired.'

The chap puffed his cigarette, and a car passed by near the two men. All the windows of the shining saloon were heavily tinted, so that it was not easy to see inside, or know how many participants were in the vehicle. The two men had stepped aside to let the car zoom past. Bakari seemed to have taken a rather strange interest in the car.

'Why should they hide themselves like that?' Bakari commented.

'Those are ruffians selling drugs, that's why they hide their faces,' Bakari's companion responded.

'Why? Are they coming to sell drugs here at work?'

'You shouldn't be surprised, but most likely this time they came to pinch someone's wife.'

'You mean so that no one can see her with them.' Bakari nodded his head.

'Precisely, and they would take her during working hours so that her husband would not suspect anything,' the chap disclosed as he extended the piece of cigarette to Bakari.

'Swahili women, you just cannot trust them!' Bakari said as he placed the cigarette on his lips and blew the smoke out. 'I wonder why they can't be satisfied with one man?'

'Money, my friend, money; they are crazy for good things: gold chains, perfumes, and the latest gizmo – cellular phones.'

The thought of his mate's words had reminded him of the plight he faced with his sister-in-law, and the negative feelings he experienced from his wife. If married women were cheating on their husbands in this cruel manner, what guarantee was there that Mwajuma was not doing the same thing to him? Maybe when he went to work, Mwajuma wandered into her lovers' dens, entertained them in perverted ways, and fulfilled their fantasies. This feeling of apprehension made Bakari shudder, and a desperate sensation of resignation gripped his whole body.

'Tell me, my friend,' Bakari said, rather absentmindedly, 'you said all the chemicals had expired.'

'Sure, are you surprised?'

'How can they have expired so soon whilst they were brought in only a month ago?'

'Don't you know of their plan? Right now we are supposed to be putting them on the side so that they can be taken to be thrown away.'

'Where will they dump them?' Bakari asked curiously.

'Dump them? The bosses are going to exchange them into shillings.'

Bakari's body shuddered again. The chap was talking as if he knew of Bakari's own plan. There were similarities, but the modes of execution were different. Bakari and his poor friends normally stole three to five drums in a fortnight, bearing the risks of hiding the drums and smuggling them using a rubbish truck. The managers, at a stroke of pen, would declare three quarters of all the consignment in the store unsuitable for further use, and order it to be disposed of. They would use the company's trucks and labour to dispose of the consignment to a predetermined warehouse somewhere in town. The chemicals would then be filled into new containers ready for resale. The manager responsible for ordering outdated chemicals would not be made to account for his deeds, but would be rewarded with a share of the loot, and most likely get promoted.

The siren for workers to resume work went on. Bakari was still sitting alone on the pavement, some twenty metres from the main gate. The refuse collecting truck was still far inside the terminal's yard, and had not come to collect from the heap of rubbish next to the old containers. To continue sitting alone on such an obscure place that was avoided by most workers could raise suspicions, especially at a time he was supposed to be back at the stores. A man who sits alone and appears to be meditating in an area known by everybody to be infested with devils and spooks, could very easily be misunderstood as to his intentions. If any person in Bakari's department fell sick, and the ill-equipped hospitals of the city fail to diagnose the disease, the Swahili might point a finger at Bakari, claiming he associated himself with devils and bewitched the sick colleague.

Bakari could not wait much longer at the pavement. He moved down the road to get closer to where the truck was parked. From a distance, Bakari saw the driver and signalled at him. The man behind the wheel saw Bakari and raised his hand. Bakari pointed to the direction of the gate. Although Bakari could not see the driver's face clearly, he thought he saw the driver lifting his hand, and was convinced that the driver understood the message.

Back at the store, Bakari found the logistics assistant manager standing at the door. The manager, whose tummy was progressively bulging out, glanced at his watch then at Bakari's face. The store's clerk noticed a sinister glow in his manager's eyes. They created an atmosphere that did not necessitate asking questions or explanations. The expression on the face spoke one language: the language that was certainly devoid of compassion or love. Bakari did not look at his face much longer. There were no long beautiful eyelashes or lush rounded lips on that middle-aged face, to have justified a man to keep on staring.

Bakari quickly brushed past the manager and went into the storeroom to resume his work. The manager had turned to look at Bakari as he took his registry book on his hands. Without lifting his eyes from the book, Bakari could envision the sheepish smile his boss wore at that moment. He knew the smile was not compassionate, but had cunningness written on it. Bakari's eyes moved to inspect the rest of his workmates and realised that each had accumulated in his corner a sizeable quantity of drums, already recorded in their registry books. The few drums and tins in Bakari's corner bore evidence that his concentration at work was minimal, and his mind had other priorities outside the Port's vicinity. The deputy manager had also taken note of the discrepancy regarding the performance of his clerk in his files, and was due to upgrade his observations into his seasonal report to the higher authorities.

While working for the Amboni Group, Bakari had confrontation with one of his supervisors, and their relationship had gone so sour that one day they had a brief exchange of blows. He was still young and energetic; the two or three punches from him had left a proportionate number of lumps on the soft face of the sluggish assembly line supervisor. The supervisor had gone around the complex, startled like a maniac, as a result of pain and humiliation. The two men were summoned to the disciplinary committee, forced to stand side by side, each giving his version of events leading to the scuffle. Bakari was a famous person by then, and any misbehaviour from him was bound to be overlooked by the management. The head of personnel was a staunch supporter of Coastal United football team, and it was not easy for him to administer punitive action against one of his team's brilliant stars.

Bakari had escaped with a mere counselling spoken to him in a soft voice.

Today, he would not dare clench his fists at his superiors even if provoked. As a simple clerk at the Port, no one recognised him in any special way. Bakari was just one of those numerous workers forming the statistics at the personnel office, and who at any moment could be made redundant whenever there was a need for cutting costs. None of the top officials at the Port could match him physically with his name, let alone remember he had ever kicked a ball in his life.

At five-thirty the workers boarded an open truck that would take them to Mnazi Mmoja and from there they would disperse into different directions. The two buses Kunjabis Transporters offered for a week were used to ferry more senior staff. The Kunjabis management had made it clear that they would not wish to have their buses overcrowded with people, otherwise the Port's authorities should hire more buses from them. The Port did not see the need to incur more expenses for the low-ranked staff. The rest of the workers could easily be sandwiched on the open tippers used to carry sand and construction stones during the day.

The account books of the transport manager would show that four buses were hired, and a cheque for hiring the buses for four weeks would be paid to Kunjabis. The accounts chief at Kunjabis would be prudent and evaluate the expenses of the fictitious buses, put a third of the amount of money into an envelope, and have it ready for the transport manager to come and collect. The two officials worked amicably in this manner and wished each other good luck in their endeavours.

The truck ferrying the workers rumbled over the narrow pothole-infested street joining the road to the Police Station. Bakari was seated on the truck's drop-side at the back. The truck went past the corner, past the railway terminal, and turned towards the main road. A big crane was still moving along a newly constructed building. The construction workers were still working at that time. A new shift had taken over and would continue up to eleven at night. Five stories were already constructed and steel ends were pointing upwards over the fifth floor, signifying that the building was to continue further upwards.

As he sat watching, Bakari saw the chap who had asked him for a matchbox at the store. His face was blank, signifying that nothing substantial was rotating in his clogged mind. He was poking his teeth with a little stick: a sign of desperation, as he did not know what awaited him at home, or what would his future be tomorrow. His shirt was unbuttoned, as half of the buttons had fallen off. Bakari stared at him, the chap saw Bakari's inquisitive face and moved closer to where he was seated. He asked Bakari if he still had matches.

'We will smoke together,' Bakari said as he handed him the box, which had two or three sticks remaining inside.

'That time you came late, the boss had been snarling at you,' the man said as he puffed the cigarette, with a match smouldering out.

Bakari watched as his mate curved his chapped lips, talking with a cigarette on his lips. He had round patches on his chest, indicating he was suffering from some sort of skin disease. He stayed somewhere in Kiwalani. There was no running water in that neighbourhood, so water for bathing was a luxury to a majority of the inhabitants.

'What did the donkey say?' Bakari asked.

'Kibosho just asked where you were.'

'And what did all of you answer this Kibosho bum?' Bakari looked at the smoking man with suspicious eyes.

'Well, someone joked that you were in the toilet, with a running stomach.' The man laughed, and coughed.

Bakari was not amused, though. He gently moved his foot on the floor of the truck and held tightly on the drop-sides as the truck swerved on a corner. The springs of the truck creaked and the body jolted. The speed of the truck was moderate; there was no danger that the truck might tilt over and drop the workers on the tarmac. Such an incident had happened a week earlier when a truck of similar type bound for Mbeya had lost control and plunged into a river killing fifteen people. There was concern from the press, and the government promised to carry out full investigations, as they had promised on several occasions when overloaded buses had reduced people into flesh mingled with twisted metal on the road to Morogoro.

The Port's truck stabilised itself on the road and Bakari reduced the rigidity of his grip on the drop-sides. He then received the cigarette from his mate.

'You know what the assistant manager said then,' the man said with his red eyes flickering.

Bakari just tapped the cigarette and placed it back on his lips. He nodded his head to allow the chap to finish what he wanted to divulge to him.

'Kibosho said he was preparing such a bitter medicine for you, that will give you a running stomach for the whole week.'

Bakari turned the cigarette and examined it. It had no filter at the end, and the saliva from his mouth had wetted the thin paper that wrapped the tobacco exfoliates. He normally smoked Sportsman, and when times were good he would prefer to have a full packet in his shirt pocket at all times. In times of distress and uncertainty, even a Nyota-Kali served him well. He did not realise how strong and pungent it was at that moment.

He looked at the solar operated clock at the roundabout popularly known as the clock-tower square. The truck was by then moving slowly as a result of a traffic jam, and Bakari could easily read the clock. It was quarter to six, still clear but the sun had set.

'Did the assistant manager say anything about the chemicals?' Bakari asked after a long silence.

'Not anything I can remember. I only overheard him lamenting over the phone that he suspected some rats of having swallowed drums of chemicals.'

'Did he say brats?' Bakari asked curiously, his eyes fixed at his friend's face as if he distrusted him.

'No, rats – mice; he said giant rats.' The chap was extending his hand to collect the small piece of Nyota-Kali from Bakari.

On the left side of the road was another new building which seemed to have been left unfinished. The project might have run short of money, or the contractor had taken the money in advance and absconded before completing the job. With defrauding being a fashion in town, Bakari was convinced that everything was possible, and one had to be extra careful in what one did. It was not strange for a person to approach a victim, promising for instance to sell him a radio. The defrauder would say to the victim: 'Give me money in advance then I will go and fetch you that radio from that shop at half the price they are asking; just wait here; I am coming now,' and the victim ended up waiting for hours with no one appearing.

Bakari recalled hearing of a case of a defrauder who managed to sell the same plot of land to three different people, giving each of them false documents, and later having the three men at each other's throats. It was a shame that the defrauder was a responsible officer at the lands department, and Bakari was surprised that the individual still kept his job and position.

Next to a wired fence were three kiosks, fashioned according to Dar-es-Salaam's taste, with cardboard on the sides and two or three corrugated metal sheets at the top. The sun's rays normally put a heavy toll on the attendant inside the kiosk, and the heat would cause the quality of the products to degenerate. This did not seem to concern the owners. They expected the clients to understand their dilemma and the impact of the weather, and bear it with them.

The truck dropped the workers at the usual open grounds at Mnazi Mmoja. Bakari was now heading to Narung'ombe Street. He was walking fast on the recently tarred roads of Kariakoo, his plastic sandals slapping on his heels.

Most of the shops were closed at that time, except for a few tea rooms. He walked next to a plush complex selling ice-creams, fruit juices and freshly baked bread. He glanced at the young people talking gaily as they licked ice-cream on cones. Bakari was convinced that they belonged to a class of the rich and powerful, who lived in an island of prosperity in a vast sea of poverty and desperation.

A street ahead, he passed through corridors of shabby vendors selling similar loaves of bread as he had seen at that complex, but in this case, dust and flies hovered over the bread. The customers for these street vendors were those people who found it difficult to walk only a block away to the complex and buy at the source. They also served people who were indifferent to living in a filthy compound, and were no longer finding satisfaction in being served from a clean sophisticated counter.

A Volkswagen Golf, driven by a young Asian-looking man, zoomed past Bakari and splashed some dirty rain water from the street. Bakari jumped onto a pavement by the side of the street, but was too late, and a sizeable amount of soiled water splashed on his feet and lower parts of his trousers. His mouth let out an uncontrollable insult, and he tried to run after the car to pay his dues to the driver for soiling him. He had collected some saliva and sputum in his mouth, hoping to reach the car as it approached the corner, and spit at the driver. Bakari's efforts were frustrated and the Golf pulled into a tarred road and sped away. Bakari had to discharge the contents of his mouth on the street, and continued hurling insults at a car that had long disappeared from his sight. People who overheard him speaking on his own as he walked along the road thought that he was drunk.

Bakari crossed the Uhuru Road into a narrow street passing between mountains of open receptacles woven from coconut leaves. There was a strong stench of a concoction of rotting tomatoes and fish. The area was a land port for the popular Nile perch and vegetables from Mwanza. On days when Bakari passed there when the consignment was being off-loaded, he would get the opportunity of buying a Nile perch at a good price. Mwajuma would nonetheless not be happy when he arrived home with that giant fish on his hand. She preferred fish from the sea. 'Why don't you go to the Ferry area and buy a nice kingklip, instead of these mud tasting lake monsters?'

Women were very funny creatures, Bakari thought as he eyed a group of young women laughing loudly and clapping their hands. He could not see anything in that vicinity that appeared funny enough to make six or seven women laugh so loudly and simultaneously. Bakari always believed that when Swahili women laugh harmoniously like that, they must have mentioned something silly. From the group of women, Bakari was left with only a few paces to enter the Narung'ombe Street. From there Bakari waved at a shoe repairman fondling a shoe at the pavement whilst some visibility was still there.

He reached the restaurant and went around the house to the back, as the main door was closed. Bakari knocked at the wooden door and waited for an answer. No one came to open the door. Bakari waited, and was surprised that Omari had closed the place that early. A while ago when he had his father sick at the Muhimbili Hospital, Omari used to close his business early in the evenings and visit him with his children. Omari was doing that so as to get the blessings of his father, whom he believed possessed mystical powers that Omari could absorb and get protection and prosperity in life. After three months in hospital, the old man had got well and left for Kisarawe. Omari had not informed Bakari if the old man was sick again, so his suspicion that Omari closed early to go and visit the hospital was not valid.

After fifteen minutes, Bakari turned to leave. He was filled with apprehension. Where could Omari have gone? Maybe he had decided to go to his second house in Tandika. Bakari decided to knock at a house of a neighbour, and a slender, red-lipped woman came to respond at the door.

'I tried to knock at your neighbour's door, but all is quiet,' Bakari said to the woman.

'I have not seen anyone this afternoon,' she said, biting her lower lip. Her eyes appeared like a sick or drunk person.

'Didn't you see any truck here today?' Bakari asked.

His eyes searched the woman from head to toe. She was not attractive and had nothing on her physique to make a man look at her twice.

'Truck? I don't recall seeing a truck.' Her face was blank and she was staring at Bakari as if he were bizarre.

'A red litter lorry?'

'I haven't seen a red lorry.'

Bakari was getting frustrated talking to a person who seemed not to be aware of what was going around her.

'Don't bother, thanks for your help.'

'We have some drinks for sale,' she spoke quietly to Bakari as he was leaving.

'What drink?' Bakari asked without much concentration.

'The African hot stuff – lion's tears,' she executed a weary smile on her face.

'You mean Chang'aa?' Bakari's mind discovered the euphemistic names used for the illegally distilled spirits made from molasses.

She nodded her head, the jaded smile still plastered on her pimpled face.

Bakari just waved his hand and turned to step out to the pavement. The woman was still leaning on the crooked pole that made part of the door frame of her shabby house.

'We also have nice women inside,' she cheered Bakari as he stepped into the street.

Bakari paused to digest the meaning of the words spoken by the woman, and without turning to face her, he continued along the street shaking his head.

'Where have morals gone to in this city?' he asked himself as he quickened his steps.

If he had two hundred shillings in his pocket he would have taken a fast Hiace at least up to Muhimbili, and finished the rest of the distance on foot. His feet were already feeling heavy, and he had only reached the junction near the fire station along Morogoro Road.

When he was a young boy growing up in the grey sandy soils of Miembeni, his uncle used to take him to tap coconut trees to extract coconut sap that made the famous coconut brew. The beer was popular throughout the coastal region. It is intoxicating if taken in large amounts, but not deleterious to the body and health like Chang'aa that is becoming a problem for many people. Drunkards' livers are getting shredded to pieces as a result of the hot spirit, and yet people continue consuming it. Boozers claim that they need only one or two glasses to get high, whilst to get kicked with the coconut beer you had to consume at least six calabashes.

Bakari used to watch his uncle scaling tall coconut trees with a curved tin behind his back. Bakari was always too scared to scale the trees himself, and preferred to remain on the ground kicking and dribbling premature coconut seeds that fell on the ground. It was from there that he developed his soccer skills that later made him a star in Tanga. After tapping five or six trees, the uncle would then cut a few green coconuts and throw them on the ground. He would then take one or two, shave the pointed edge carefully, and give it to his nephew to drink the juice. When Bakari had drained the liquid from the coconuts, the uncle would use the blunt side of his knife to carve out coconut flesh from inside the shell and hand the coconut back to his nephew.

# CHAPTER 4

Days had passed in Kisarawe and Bakari grew up to become a man and encountered the challenges of adulthood. The older he grew, the stiffer the challenges of life became. At Tanga he had owned a Honda motorbike and used to zip through the popular streets with a girlfriend in a short dress at the back-seat. That used to make people's hearts throb and quiver with envy. According to the acceptable Swahili norms, a woman riding on a motorbike or bicycle was supposed to clasp her legs on one side, and not to sit with her legs spread on both sides of the motorcycle or bicycle. Second, wearing a revealing dress was not tolerated because it provoked men, making them think of love affairs all the time, instead of concentrating on productive, national building activities.

Besides his strict Swahili upbringing, Bakari used to enjoy watching how men turned their heads to look when he zipped by. He acknowledged the jealousness plastered on their faces, knowing that there was little they could do besides grumbling to themselves. In Tanga, Bakari was also a part owner of a guest house situated in the popular Sixth Street. The business gave him considerable income and popularity in the municipality. At a relatively young age, Bakari had thought his life was already accomplished.

Yet tonight, Bakari was walking uphill along Kinondoni road, with sweat clinging on his shirt and trousers as if he had a bucket of water thrown on him. His feet burned, but he moved on until he approached the famous street passing beside his home. Bakari buttoned his shirt to appear presentable, and extended his hand to reach for the door of house number eighteen. There were people at the veranda as usual; Bakari disregarded them and pushed the metal door open.

The metal door creaked open and Bakari placed his foot in the compound. His bluish and exhausted face gleamed with shock as he saw the landlord seated right ahead of him. All his thoughts were with Omari, and he had totally forgotten that there was someone waiting for him at home. If Bakari had met Omari and got a share of their business deal, he wouldn't have been so alarmed at meeting the big man in shorts seated on a mat in the middle of the compound. Bakari could have even afforded to be arrogant and drop a ten thousand shillings note on the floor and watch the old fisherman squat on his knees to pick it up. Today, Bakari had no leverage, and it was now too late for him to hide or turn back to the door.

'I want my money now, Bakari!' the landlord snarled.

Bakari pretended to be searching his trouser pockets, and patting his shirt pocket. He forced his face to portray an image of a very concerned and alarmed person.

'Gosh, where is my money?' he was asking himself.

'Bakari, don't play with me, I say give me my rent or I am kicking you out right now!' The man was furious, with his lower lip vibrating up and down.

'I . . . I am trying to find where I put the ten thousand note,' Bakari stammered.

He bent to search the folds of his trousers, then stood up and cautiously eyed the man who stood ahead of him panting like a savage.

'Bakari!' The man screamed hysterically and vigorously shoved Bakari on the chest.

Bakari fell on his back and struggled to come to his feet. The feeling of apprehension was now leaving him; in its place anger was taking over. As he staggered to his feet, the landlord went on him again, this time pinning Bakari to the wall. He was now tightly squeezing Bakari's neck.

The only other time Bakari had found himself in such a precarious situation was a couple of years ago when he was returning to his in-laws' house in Mtongani around two in the morning. He had spent the evening with friends at a local bottle store, enjoying the fine Tusker beer from Kenya. Those were the days he still worked at the Port's Large Room, and had enough shillings even to offer his friends a round or two. A man who had the ability and generosity to offer rounds of beer was popular with people, and gained lots of friends in Dar-es-Salaam. Goat's meat was also being roasted in the vicinity, and for those who were drinking more than four beers, free soup made from goat's offal and blood was given.

By two in the morning Bakari had staggered into the road leading to the Bahari Beach hotel. It was a festive season. Bakari had every reason to celebrate and be happy. He had left the main road and joined another street going past some cassava plants. Four youths had appeared from nowhere and surrounded him. The youths had quickly made it clear to Bakari their intention of blocking his path. He was hesitant to take out the few shillings that were still in his pockets; as a result, the youths had to coerce Bakari into complying with their demands. One of the youths grabbed him from behind, squeezing his neck till he thought it would break.

This evening at house number eighteen, the landlord was also getting close to breaking Bakari's neck. The fisherman's rough hands were twirling around his victim's neck, and the weight of his smelly body was increasing the frustrations facing Bakari at that moment. The only difference from what happened six years earlier was that today, only one man was working on him, wetting his face with a flurry of sticky saliva that flowed incessantly from his uncontrollable mouth. During the assault at Mtongani, as one youth throttled him, the other youths were busy taking off his trousers, shirt, shoes and watch.

The landlord tightened his grip on Bakari's neck and was now banging his head on the floor. Each time his head banged on the cement floor a noise like that of a coconut being broken emerged. Bakari had to think of something fast. In the past episode at Mtongani, after the hooligans had taken from him what they wanted, they just gave him some few slaps, and kicks on his tipsy body, then they ran away. They had left a man in his underpants and a potbelly to wander unsteadily to his home. This evening, the landlord was tramping hard on Bakari's feet as well. Sharp pain was surging up Bakari's spine and he thought he was going to pass out. When all seemed to be coming to an unbelievable end, Bakari sent his long fingers into the wide open eyes of his attacker.

The five young and elderly men sitting outside by the little laundry at the corner of house number eighteen preoccupied themselves with issues that ranged from soccer to people's wives. In many communities, notably African societies, the topics of women or sexual styles that men fantasised about were restricted to men of the same age group. Such topics scarcely involved groups whose members had age differences of twenty or thirty years. On that Dar-es-Salaam street that evening, a sexagenarian man with a white cap on his head was amusing a group of young men with his sexual experiences. He divulged details of his bisexual career spanning three decades, ranging from the notorious slums of Mombasa to the southern coastal town of Kilwa. His listeners were so much absorbed to his stories, marvelling at the number of women and gay men he had conquered, that they hardly paid attention to the scuffles that were taking place inside the compound of house eighteen. Even if one of them heard the thuds or shuffles, he would have thought someone was moving heavy furniture or struggling with a bag of maize on the corridor. That was of course before Bakari's fingers had found their target on the crimson eyes of the lumpy landlord.

The landlord yelped in pain and loosened the grip on Bakari's neck. At this point the keen listeners of the boorish accounts of the old man left him with his mouth still bubbling out more obscene words and rushed past the metal door of house eighteen. There, on the compound, they found a blinded landlord with his hands moving in the air, yelling and shouting all types of insults. Bakari took the opportunity of the open door to dash out of the compound.

The landlord staggered after him, still not able to see properly. Bakari was about to step out of the veranda, but the landlord had reached him again. He held on Bakari's shirt, attempting to grab his hands. Bakari turned around, and to free himself from his grip, he sent a flying header that found its target on the landlord's wide mouth. The impact sent the fisherman sprawling to the floor. Bakari pushed through the throng of people who were now gathering to witness the commotion, and left the veranda.

Many people throughout Dar-es-Salaam liked to witness events that attracted crowds. Scandalous occurrences pulled crowds even from distant locations. People wanted to witness things they could talk about at work, in the market, or with their friends in other localities. Talking about other people's lives, especially their scandalous anecdotes, fashions the Swahili's obsession with life. They have an attachment to this habit, and the language itself is enriched with the appropriate vocabulary to ameliorate the resounding meddling. Bakari's prime concern at that moment was not with what the neighbours might be thinking of him, or what they would talk about for the next few weeks; he was primarily concerned with his safety.

He ran up Sekenke Street towards the market. Bakari was confused and petrified. The way events had turned that afternoon gave him reason to be very concerned about his well-being. He was running around the market, not knowing where he was heading to, and not sure of the situation he left behind. When the ugly incident happened to him in Mtongani those days, at least he ran to his in-laws to get solace and comfort from Mwajuma. When she saw that he was naked, she had quickly covered him with a khanga right at the door before he stepped in, quickly ushering him to their room. She had acted promptly and cleverly, such that hardly any one else in the house knew of the incident. She had boiled some water and used a warm cloth to soothe the areas of his body that had swollen as a result of the beatings. Tonight, Bakari had no one to comfort him, or to lead him to a place he could experience warmth and peace.

Bakari stopped and stood still as he reached the Biafra grounds. There was some music playing from afar, and Bakari tried to concentrate his ears

47

on it. The music sounded familiar, like those usual Lingala numbers being played every day on the radio. He could not tell the name of the number, as it was fading away, and he could not hear the music any longer. Bakari looked around himself and listened again to the slight wind that was blowing. Some cricket sounds emerged from the single tree that was in the vicinity.

From a distance he could hear the noise of cars moving along the Morocco Road. A belated fear gripped his body, even though the gale of wind was refreshing his face. Bakari had left behind a revengeful and angry man sprawled on the floor. Worse of all, he left his family in a hostile environment, to face the unpredictable wrath of the landlord. Bakari had only saved himself from the hurtling monster by running away, but he quickly realised it was a temporary solution as he did not know what was going to be his fate. The thought of his children at the mercy of a berserk, nose bleeding man, made Bakari think of turning back and going to face the consequences whatever they might be.

Bakari hesitated. During the commotion, Mwajuma had not even bothered to come out of her room to find out what was going on with her husband. How could Bakari tell which side she had opted to take? During the time a couple make pledges in front of families and friends, they normally vow to support and care for each other till death parts them. It is not strange though to hear now and then of a spouse killing the other out of jealousy, money or heritage. Some wives went to witch-doctors, got vile drugs and came to bewitch their husbands, exterminating them so as to remain with their house, car, and furniture.

For those more sophisticated, a husband would take a life insurance cover for his wife, then after a period of time, would stage a fatal accident that would get rid of the wife. With tears flowing over his wicked face, the husband would go to the insurance firm whimpering to be compensated for his spouse's departure. He would take the money and go to spend it with a newly found lover. Trust had become a very rare item these days, Bakari thought, as he moved around the Biafra grounds.

There were some deserted makeshift kiosks that were being used during the daytime to sell second-hand clothes. Bakari moved to one of them and sat on a long bench. He felt totally alone and isolated in this world. Mosquitoes swarmed around him, but at that moment he did not care about the tiny amount of blood they took with them. Bakari gazed at the open sky: it was partly cloudy on the sides of the huge round dome. Through the light provided by the half-moon, he appreciated how fast the clouds moved in the sky, sometimes appearing as if it was the earth that was moving, leaving the

48

clouds where they were. As he gazed, he began hallucinating weird images formed by the clouds. Bakari envisaged two huge bulls with horns curving upward ramming into each other. On the other side of the horizon, he envisioned rocks that were falling from a cliff and burying everything on the ground.

Bakari had stayed at the bench for three hours; his buttocks were strained and he made his mind to move. The first step he made as he left the bench brought him in contact with life for the first time since he arrived at the Biafra grounds. The obscure figure stirred and lifted his head from the bench he was sleeping on: another of those shabby structures.

'Who are you?' A sickly voice came from the veiled face.

'And who are you?' Bakari tried to put a more imposing voice.

'From the police, isn't it?' he asked in a staggering tone.

'What is your problem, have you been up to crime?' Bakari was now more confident.

'No . . . no, I have done nothing wrong, sir.'

'What are you having there?' Bakari's voice was louder and firmer.

'Just . . . a bag of mangoes . . . nothing more.'

'You stole them, isn't it? Let me see them.'

'I just found the bag here, sir, I didn't steal . . . you can have some, sir!' The man was ushering Bakari to the receptacle on the floor.

The hunger that was overpowering him made Bakari do what he wouldn't have done under normal circumstances. He collected five or six mangoes from the receptacle and left the vagabond in his hideout. Before leaving, Bakari warned the vagabond not to repeat what he did, otherwise he would collect him and dump him into the police cells. The man apologised to the person who introduced himself to him as a member of the secret police, and was relieved that he settled for a couple of mangoes before leaving him in peace.

At two in the morning, Bakari thought the situation might have quietened down at house number eighteen, and no one would be expecting him to turn up. There were long rows of houses and verandas where people slept, so it was relatively easy for Bakari to sneak from house to house until he approached his own. Apprehension gripped him so much that he could not concentrate on where he was stepping. For the third time he had placed his feet in the sewage waters, along the dirty unlit streets. His feet were only protected by the worn-out rubber sandals he always wore to work. Even when drunk, Bakari would normally manage to manoeuvre around the sewage streams, and rarely stepped in them.

Bakari felt queasy as he felt the greasy stuff between his feet and slippers. Normally when he went out in the evenings, he would put his turkeys on, but that evening he had left the house so much in haste. As Bakari drew closer to the veranda of house number eighteen, he could feel the pungent smell from his feet, coupled with that of his perspiring body. At the veranda there were people as usual, mostly youths who spent their nights sleeping there. Bakari made a stealthy move, stepped on the veranda and sat on the floor.

In his disguise, Bakari penetrated his eyes in the dark and tried to figure out the limping bodies along the veranda. His eyes were rewarded by the sight of the chap he offered a cigarette the night before, slumped on the opposite side of that rectangular veranda. Bakari slithered to the floor, moving on his hands and knees until he reached where the man was slumped. Bakari's shirt covered only half of his body; he was dirty and stinking, so no one would have recognised him. On normal days, even during this season when Bakari was going through severe financial difficulties, he appeared relatively smart in comparison with other common people in Kinondoni. Bakari had left the compound so hectically that evening that no one could have believed he would come back so soon. With that fact at the back of his mind, Bakari was confident to approach the chap.

Bakari knelt next to the man and tapped him on his legs. He did that cautiously so as not to astound the chap into waking up alarmed and hysterical. It was no secret that the youths who spend their nights on the verandas included mischievous ones who waited for their friends to doze off before sliding their fingers into their pockets to feel for anything worth taking. It was the case of the destitute stealing from another destitute. There were also cases of rape. It happened in more isolated houses, and the victims were mostly younger boys who were new in Dar-es-Salaam. In all verandas, nonetheless, the youths were always on guard, preferring to sleep with their backs on the floor to safeguard their assets from easy access from creeping homosexuals.

The young man stirred from the tiring sleep he had succumbed to, and tried to focus on the tramp kneeling in front of him. The chap growled at Bakari, thinking he was a leper from the streets trying to solicit him for some money. Bakari hushed down the startled youth and ushered his face closer to the young man to make himself recognizable.

'Gosh, Mzee, it is you?' the chap gasped.

'Shh, lower your voice.' Bakari spoke in a heavier tone than usual, to disguise himself.

'The landlord and his sons were looking for you!'

'Where are they now?'

'I don't know, but he had an axe in his hand, and blood was coming from his nose.'

'And what was he saying?' Bakari realised their voices had risen a bit and he tapped the chap to scale down his voice.

'He was hurling all insults you can think of. His sons were clutching knives, they were insulting too.'

Bakari paused and listened to the shuffle of feet coming from the entrance. He hoped that no one had discovered his presence and gone to alert the landlord and have him and his sons surround him. If they were armed with such lethal weapons they could reduce him to butchered meat if they laid their hands on him. Bakari was relieved when it happened to be one of the boys sleeping on the veranda on his way to pass water in the street.

'The worse thing is your wife,' the chap continued, when Bakari tapped him on his knee.

'What happened?' Bakari quickly asked.

'The landlord evicted her with the kids.'

'Evicted? To . . . where to?' Bakari had raised his voice in alarm.

Someone sleeping next to the two men stirred and looked up, but he later lowered his head again.

'The landlord had burst into their room shrieking, asking for you.'

'Did he think I was still inside?' Bakari was astonished.

'Yes, he then began throwing items from your room into the corridor.'

'And the kids?'

'They were thrown out!'

'Where did they go?' Bakari's voice was now trembling with remorse.

Confusion was seizing him. He felt pity for his kids and sensed that he was wholly to blame for their plight. His pulse had now increased so much and his knees were failing him. Bakari decided to sit on the floor to absorb the shock that gripped him at that moment.

'Do you have a cigarette?' the man asked.

Bakari had no energy even to reply to him. He badly needed a cigarette himself, but had nothing left in his pockets. He had grabbed half a packet from Omari that morning, and penuriously smoked them throughout the afternoon. When they ran out he was left nibbling his fingers. It was an adverse habit he had developed that not only made him look clumsy in front of other people, but was damaging to his nails, threatening to produce infections on his fingers.

The two figures kept quiet, having nothing else to say to each other. There was a faint sound of scratchy music a block away. The radio would periodically die down and suddenly surge to life again. Bakari's ears tried to concentrate on the faint sound to help him divert his thoughts from the tormenting moments he was going through. He felt as if his legs had swelled. It might have been from all the walking he had done that day.

Bakari had his own peculiar ways of prophesying on what was about to occur to him. He got the messages through different reactions in his body. That afternoon he had been having strange feelings in his mind and his hands were shaking. He felt chilly, and suspected he was catching a bout of malaria. After two hours the ill effect disappeared, and in its place, his eyes strained as if they wanted to dip from their sockets. The funny feeling disappeared again after half an hour. Bakari then began suspecting something. Bad luck was once again coming to visit him. Last time it came, he was taken to Bagamoyo, and the oracles had cast it away before any adverse effects occurred to him.

His mistake was that during the days he worked at the Large Room and earned a lot of money, he had forgotten the people who took care of him. Bakari did not send a khanga or kanzu to his aunt and uncle in appreciation of their efforts to send him to be cleansed. Bakari invested his money in bars and entertaining his friends. Bakari was still biting his nails as he tried to recall at least one of his friends whom he could turn to for assistance and consolation. He had offered so many beers to so many mouths, but at that moment not a single name came into his mind.

He began feeling hot; so hot that he felt as if he was sitting on a charcoal stove. Something was moving in his body, causing a turbulent reaction. During his time at primary school, he was told of the story of a person from a destitute country who was given food and assistance to go to a faraway country to learn the secrets its inhabitants used to gain development and wealth. The person was expected to return home to share and impart the knowledge to those he left behind. It happened that when the person reached the distant country, he became so overwhelmed by the luxuries and easy life the country provided, that he decided to stay there and forgot his people back home. After some years a terrible hunger gripped the country he had migrated to. Starvation and diseases were the order of the day and many people died. The fugitive person was so destitute that he collected the little energy remaining in his limbs and made his way back to his original home. When he reached the border of his home, they did not allow him into the country. The people he found there did not recognise him and refused to offer him assistance. As a result he perished of disease and hunger, at the margins of his own country.

Bakari suddenly sprung up and went to the entrance of the veranda. He paused for a moment and listened. His mouth was dry, his stomach rumbling, making him feel as if he was getting a running stomach. He stepped out of the veranda and ran down the road. Bakari was not sure why he was running, but he kept on running till he reached the corner of the street. He then remembered something and stopped. Someone running down the street at that time of the night gave rise to suspicions from everyone. The scores of people on the numerous verandas would only conclude that he was either a thief or a sorcerer. Both were feared and hated by the public. It needed one lone voice to shout 'thief' and he would have the whole of Kinondoni descending on him with stones, sticks and knives. The numerous young men wasting their lives on the verandas would have a place to offload their frustrations. At least some reasoning had come to Bakari at that fearful moment of his life.

Bakari could not go to any of the people he knew at that time of the night. He had to think of a place to put up until at least five in the morning. He recalled a particular time during his youth, when he would be invited to any house and given a warm welcome. The time Coastal United won the Tanga region's Club Championship League, Bakari was a special guest at weddings, Eid-el-fitr celebrations, and even on government's official holidays in the province. He was celebrated, gracing children's anniversaries, and women sang his praises.

He was now in shambles looking for a place to sleep. He had created a commotion at house eighteen that evening, and he feared to remain at the veranda. Someone could notice his presence there and sneak into the house to inform the wrathful landlord that the fugitive had defiantly turned up at the house. His wife and children having been forcefully evicted and his rooms ransacked, Bakari found no reason to hang around the place any more. He painfully realised that it was an end of a chapter for him with house eighteen. He would not dare return to Biafra grounds either. He was not sure who would be there at that time. Hooligans planning early morning raids on nearby houses could be camping there preparing to launch assaults at their targets.

An idea came into his head, and Bakari headed to the Kinondoni cemetery. Even if the landlord and his companions were searching for him in the whole of Kinondoni, they would not go to the cemetery. Most thieves kept away from there as well. The only thieves that prowled the area, came to strip dead bodies of their jewels, shoes and clothing. Even these prowlers came to the place filled with dread. A slight movement of the grass would see them stretching their necks, with their hair standing on end. Despite the villainous courage the criminals harboured, their minds were constantly occupied with the obsessed illusion that a ghoul might come out of a shallow grave and gobble them. If the thieves appeared whilst he was there, Bakari would pretend he was a demon and send the rascals fleeing for their lives.

The plight of his family touched him intensely as he stretched himself on some soft grass next to a short wall of bricks. Bakari remembered his young kids and wondered how they were coping wherever they were. He was lonely, and the place he laid his body to rest that night made him feel more isolated. In that vicinity no one talked to him; no one moved.

Bakari sat on a bench at the personnel office, his head slumped and feet crossed. The room was large, and on the walls were old wooden shelves sagging in the middle by the weight of files piled on them. The files were worn out at the edges, and most were covered with dust. Files that belonged to workers were relatively free from dust because they were frequently used, especially when salaries were paid. On the other end, files belonging to ill-fated members like Bakari were always dust free, but worn because of the frequency in which they were being consulted. The air-conditioner on the wall made a large rattling sound, compelling whoever was entering the personnel office to raise his voice in order to be heard by the husky manager. Incidentally, it gave an opportunity to the burly man to shout back, thus exercising his authority and fulfilling his fantasy for intimidation.

The only pleasant item in that office was a vase with a single red rose, and a card wishing the manager happy birthday on his fictitious forty-ninth anniversary. The official retirement age being fifty-five, crafty officials like the personnel manager would not sit idle and be taken by surprise by the retirement monster. In retirement, he would lose many times more than the hundred thousand shillings he had to offer at the migration to have his age on the new passport reduced by a decade.

In that dusky room that Tuesday morning, the two men sceptically eyed each other as the plastic wall clock, a quarter of an hour ahead of correct time, wryly ticked on. Bakari was purposelessly twisting his mouth sideways whilst the manager tapped his pen on the worn-out register he had opened and closed several times since Bakari stepped in his office. The weather was cloudy, but the heat was already intense. Noises from the cranes at the container terminal could be heard a distance away. The manager cleared his throat and again eyed the tired looking man seated in front of him.

'The chemicals theft could have landed you in jail,' he said.

'I assure you, sir, my involvement was minimal.' Bakari's voice was trembling.

'The problem with all you chaps, is that if you are left without supervision, even for a second, you steal.'

Bakari was quiet, looking at the manager.

'I don't know how the country can progress with all the pilferage!'

'I am not that bad, sir,' Bakari said in a low voice.

'Let me repeat, you are still under investigation; and I warn you, if you are not careful you may spend up to seven miserable years behind bars!' The manager's voice was rattling around the room.

Bakari looked at him and did not say a word again. Fear gripped him, but it was diluted by the anger he felt for the people he thought were responsible for putting him in this mess. Bakari sniffed, put his fingers in his nostrils and rubbed them. He then looked at the puffed cheeks of the man seated behind the oval desk. The greyish beard that stood prominently out of his chin was nearly an inch and a half long. Whenever the manager spoke, he began by opening his mouth before words came out.

'We are going to put you on suspension in the meantime; you will continue working, but receiving only one third of your salary until the investigations are complete.'

The manager then shooed Bakari out of his office.

Bakari walked back into the fumigation stores and went to report to the assistant manager. He met the manager's half open eyes gazing aimlessly at the window, his brownish teeth chewing on a matchstick. The assistant manager's sick eyes were then trained at Bakari, and the silly smile he always wore flashed on him. Bakari could detect the wickedness on the man's round face, and from his bulging stomach he envisioned the corrupt and selfish ingredients that filled up the tummy. How many items had he misappropriated, embezzled, and stolen, yet he walked scot free?

'Hey, why are you staring at me . . . Am I new to you?' the assistant manager croaked at Bakari.

'I have come to report, as instructed by the personnel.' Bakari sounded as if it were his first day at work.

'You mean he allowed you to resume work here?' The manager appeared unconvinced.

'Yes.' Bakari nodded his head.

In a brief inaudible period, Bakari seemed to be moving his mouth sideways as if he was chewing something, whilst the assistant manager's eyes blinked repeatedly, succumbing to the heavy toll of being devoid from rest. He spent many and long night hours in bars. The two men had temporarily forgotten what kept them looking at each other at the door of the stores department. It was only after Bakari let out a loud sneeze that the manager recovered from the temporary lapse of memory.

'What are you doing here then? Get back to work and help the chaps to load the drums in the truck,' the manager wheezed amidst a medium of a stench of alcohol.

The assistant manager appeared as if he had no idea of Bakari's predicament as he moved into the store. Bakari was not sure who was behind the plot that had led to the discovery of the five drums of fumigation chemicals next to the containers. He had now been incriminated by the Port's authorities for attempting to misappropriate the Port's property and was under suspension. Bakari was resolutely convinced that his bosses had been diverting whole consignments of the Port's property over the years, and instead of being punished they got promoted. At that very moment, they were loading three trucks full of supposedly expired chemical drums to be disposed of to a destination known only by the managers.

Bakari picked up the register book, went to the loading zone and began ticking the consignment that was being put on the trucks. One of his colleagues gave him a sinister look, whilst two others were talking about things he could not comprehend. From their ludicrous laughs Bakari could tell they were making fun of him. He suspected his story had filtered even to the rank and file, and the two laughing men were seeing him as a criminal.

Bakari did not care much what other people thought of him at that moment. He consoled himself that a majority of the workers were not looking at him as an evil person. His only concern was with the verdict of the personnel department that he should work as usual, but receive a fraction of his salary. Working in such conditions as most of them did, and under the perversive leadership of their superiors, a large number of workers would sympathise with him. With the meagre wages received, one had to steal to survive. Bakari always shared the little he had with his mates, and some saw him as their Robin Hood. Their superiors, working in air-conditioned offices, drove past the stores with expensive four-wheeled vehicles. The managers' official salaries for twenty years would not be enough to buy them even a second-hand scrap car, but no one spoke about that. Even at that moment as Bakari ticked on his book and loaded the expired drums into the truck, he was ostensibly an unwilling accomplice to a daylight theft being executed by his middle level managers.

If he were the only one stealing around that place, then the management would have swiftly punished him severely. Bakari was aware that because he was not alone, the case against him had to be handled at a low level and finished quietly. The management was cognizant that a prolonged enquiry would raise many questions.

An investigation team would have gone to the stores and prowled around the whole place, insisting on checking stock sheets and inspecting all corners. They might have questioned the reasons for such massive quantities of chemicals having expired so quickly without being used. Some probing officials would have liked to be briefed about the procurement procedures of the logistics department, and the reasons for their preferences of the most expensive quotations. Worst of all, wandering eyes of sharp investigators could have landed on obscure corners of the stores department and discover some illegal and prohibited powdered material imported from Colombia, belonging to some big fish in the establishment.

It was rare for the noble to get caught in the net of the law. If miraculously they got netted, they fell with a lot of those belonging to the rank and file. It reminded Bakari of the old kings of many African tribes: when they died, several people would be buried alive with them. A war could also break out resulting in the death of many innocent people. The anger of the deceased king's henchmen could provoke them to move into villages hacking down defenceless peasants, accusing them of harbouring the devils that took the life of their beloved ruler. Those days the wretched of society had no stand to air their grievances.

Even today, Bakari had no platform to air his grievances. He had had three warnings already, and now a suspended sentence. Any wrong word from his mouth might be met with a severe retribution. An accident might occur in the stores' department, whereby a forklift would drop a box on him and break his legs. Otherwise, he might be beaten by unknown people on his way home from taking evening walks. Bakari had heard of the fates of workers who dared cross the paths of their superiors, and he dreaded even to recall the ordeal they went through. The gates of the Ukonga Correctional Centre were always closed and heavily bolted; yet it was surprising how swiftly could they be unbolted to guzzle in a victim deemed to be a threat to the rich and famous. For the meek and weak, the safest option was to keep quiet and pretend everything was normal.

In his heart, Bakari did not see himself as a weak person. He had not regarded himself as a person deemed to spend the rest of his life relinquished at the receiving end. Once in his life, he had stood proudly in society and got the recognition he deserved. In his youthful days, whenever he walked into a group of other young men, they would all acknowledge the presence of a celebrity amongst them. The beer he ordered was a recommendation. His behavioural patterns, the way he walked, paused, and how he yanked his sunglasses off his face, biting the stem, was a model for the others to imitate.

Bakari considered what was going through his life at that moment to be a temporary occurrence. He was confident he would live through it, and walk in town again with his chin elevated. He would be able to walk into the house of Mahmood Issa-Mahid, who was presently harbouring his wife, sister-in-law, and children, and knock the hell out of his head. Bakari placed the blame on his sister-in-law for having taken Mwajuma to Issa-Mahid's house. Bakari understood that his wife was in a predicament following their eviction by the landlord, but of all places should she have gone to Issa-Mahid's place? He swallowed as these thoughts passed through his mind. The thought that his wife was on the loose made him feel even more puny in society.

He was now penniless, and he himself had taken refuge in a small room belonging to his friend Omari, in Temeke.

The trucks were ready to move out. The drivers of the privately owned truck company hired to help with the disposal were summoned into the manager's office for a briefing. In the meantime, Bakari and his mates dispersed out of the storeroom to gain fresh air outside, and organise themselves some refreshments. They sat at the makeshift kiosk and Bakari took a bottle of Sprite on credit and claimed to be given his bottle cap. He took the cap, peeled off the inner plastic cover, and peeped under it. It was clean and spotless. He considered himself as having no luck. He had not won any of the prizes that were being advertised by the bottle companies. What he did not recall was that he only drank soft drinks once a while, and whenever he had money he would settle for a beer. His chances of winning a radio, bicycle, or watch from the cap of a soft drink were therefore very remote.

After a while, the drivers emerged out of the assistant manager's office with smiling faces. One of them was still folding a five thousand shillings note and placed it in his pocket. One of the Port's workers loading the trucks who saw the note being tucked away, approached Bakari and tapped him on his shoulders.

'The drivers have been given their rewards for being cooperative,' the man said.

Bakari was about to respond, but hesitated when the stomach of the assistant manager emerged from the office. He lifted his pair of trousers that always appeared as if it was falling from his waist. The trousers were also too long, and the manager always dragged the hem over the dirty floors. It was easy to know in which direction of the department the manager was, owing to the pungent smell he left whenever he moved. The abundant beer he drank, and ample cigarettes, gave him a characteristic pungent smell.

The assistant manager came to Bakari and asked him for the register book. Bakari watched the man turning and heading back to his office, shuffling his feet on the floor. Bakari thought the man was so lazy that he was unable even to lift his feet. Rumours were rife at the Port that he was going out with the fat woman who talked incessantly, and worked as a telephone operator. She was married and so was he, but they enjoyed the intriguing passion of cheating on each other's spouses. They both had a weakness of lacking moderation on things they adored. She had virtually no control on her eating habits, and he could not control the amount of alcohol he consumed. Their bonds of intimacy were forged on the threshold of their weaknesses.

The manager disappeared behind the door and the chap who was talking to Bakari earlier came to him.

'I am sorry for what happened to you, man,' the chap said.

'Just forget it,' Bakari said, while hushing him down. 'Since when did a thief catch another thief?'

'They have been monitoring you guys all along.'

'Do you mean the assistant manager?'

'The head watchman at the gate had been a double agent all along!'

'What does that imply?' Bakari said, looking at the man leaning next to him.

'The watchman was eating from you guys, then he would go and report your activities to the managers and get a tip out of it.' The chap let out a cracking laugh followed by a sickly cough.

'How did you know that?' Bakari quizzed the man.

'Oh, we drink Chang'aa with him at Vingunguti, and when he gets carried away he bubbles out everything.'

'Why didn't you warn me before?'

'I . . . I did not have the nerve to approach you . . .'

'Or was it because the watchman was buying you Chang'aa with the tips?'

The man remained silent and looked on the floor.

'The silly bastard, does he think those managers will hesitate to fire him whenever they get a whim to do so?' Bakari raised his voice.

'He gets extra tips for allowing them to pass their loot. Like this consignment we have just loaded, you may find that it is not even registered at the gate.'

Bakari frowned his face and wanted to say something nasty, but the assistant manager was coming out again. The manager's eyes appeared as if he was reading their minds. He then dispersed Bakari and his friend, instructing them to return to their respective areas of work, and not to congest the driveway. The manager took upon himself to hand over the documents to the drivers.

# CHAPTER 5

Bakari was seated on a small stool sorting out bags of bread flour. The flour was to be distributed between the main restaurant at Narung'ombe in Kariakoo, and the newly opened tea room at Temeke. Bakari was running the Temeke operations. Omari came from the main corridor and eyed his friend, busy weighing the flour. The temperatures had soared that afternoon, and both men were bare chested with sweat streaking from them. Men work bare-breasted in Dar-es-Salaam; otherwise they get so wet out of perspiration and shirts would cling uncomfortably on their backs.

When the two friends lived in the Swahili cultured town of Tanga, and Bakari was relatively prosperous, Omari had survived out of his friend's generosity. Bakari had taken care of Omari financially, entertaining him, and bailed him several times from the police stations. It was normal for Omari to be picked up by the authorities for being found with stolen property, beating up someone in the ghettoes, or in possession of a couple of bhang sticks in his pockets. Omari lived most of his younger life on the wrong side of the law.

Omari did not embrace that life out of choice; circumstances and his upbringing relegated him to that position. At the tender age of three he was roaming the dusty streets of Kisarawe, begging, and survived the harsh and uncertain life of a street child. Someone had sired him, but instead of caring for him like other children, the person had sacrificed him to the streets to fend for himself against the tide of hardship, abuse, hunger and despondency. His mother was too poor to provide the necessary care a child needed, no matter how much she tried. Yet, he survived the streets and staggered through life to become a man. He then moved to Tanga where he met Bakari.

Now Omari had reached middle age, and whatever he did, whether legal or illegal; swindling someone or handling smuggled material, he would do that in an experienced way. He had friends in many important areas that would advise him on proper action to take when faced with danger or uncertainty. If he felt sick, there was a medical officer at the central hospital to give him special attention. In case a stolen car was found hidden in the backyard of his restaurant, there were security officers at hand to destroy evidence and cover up the case until it was struck off. He also had henchmen who would tip him if a rival gang member was planning an attack at his premises in revenge for a business deal that went faulty. On the softer side, Omari had his faithful aunts who took tea for free at his restaurant, in return for their assistance in organising him fifteen-year-old schoolgirls.

On that critical afternoon, Omari had been tipped by his accomplices that the chemicals deal which Bakari was organising from the Port had gone awfully wrong somewhere. Omari had closed his shop earlier than usual, and retreated to Temeke. If the police were laying a trap, they would have found his shop closed and him out of the way. Even his neighbours at Kariakoo knew how slippery Omari was, and it needed some more efficient authority than the poorly paid policemen to nab him down.

Things had calmed down over the chemicals issue, and Omari had already organised with his contacts in high authorities to disassociate his name from any issue pertaining to the chemicals misadventure. Now Omari was planning a new business strategy, and thought his friend could be of use.

Omari had approached Bakari to find out if he had thought over the proposal he had made to him earlier on during the week. He sat next to Bakari and smiled at him.

'They say, Bakari, if you can't beat them, join them.'

'No, Omari, if you join them they will assume you are defeated.'

'It is better to accept defeat, and benefit from it.'

'How is that, Omari?'

'I mean, otherwise you may still get defeated and remain worse off.' Omari was smiling, showing his uneven teeth.

Bakari just looked at his friend and showed no expression on his face. They were of the same age group, though Omari looked a lot older, owing to the abundant grey hair on the sides of his head. His face had taken the toll of life from the countless blows that had landed on it from his different adversaries. He was still alive today because on all occasions that necessitated him to exchange blows, he happened to be the one who inflicted more damage to the other contestant. Omari was now taking care of Bakari, and offered him a little business to run. Bakari had begun running the tea room a month and a half ago, after storming out of the Port, following a fierce exchange of words with the assistant manager.

Following the fallout with his assistant manager that included an exchange of obscene insults, Bakari realised it was worthless to go back to work again.

He had consoled himself that he would consult a religious guru, and have him read some sacred verses from the divine book that would result in the early death of the assistant manager. Bakari fulfilled that vow and was now keeping his ear on the ground to hear if the manager had been knocked down by a car, or fatally stabbed by a mugger in the streets. Despite the Swahili saying that the blows of a dwarf can not knock down a giant, Bakari remained convinced that he would have his revenge one day.

It was not the assistant manager that Omari was asking Bakari to join, but another foe Bakari had vowed to rub off from the face of the earth if given a chance. Omari was asking him to accept an offer given to them by Issa-Mahid for a joint business deal. If they cooperated with him, Issa-Mahid promised them the business would turn out to be very profitable. Omari was trying to make Bakari see reason.

'Bakari, you were simply risking your life last Friday, when you went to confront Issa-Mahid,' Omari said.

'But the fool was sleeping with my wife.'

'No, he is only interested in your sister-in-law. Your wife just followed her there to seek refuge.' Omari talked with a softer voice to his friend.

'I doubt if I can work for him, Omari.'

'You will be losing the chance of a lifetime.' Omari was sounding very convincing.

Bakari took a moment to analyse his friend's words, and especially the mention of money. Like most men, the word money would make him pause to think. It is money after all that makes the world tick. With money he could solve the problems he was now facing. If he had enough money he wouldn't have had his wife yanked from his hands and land in another man's arms. Omari was still talking to him:

'Your wife Mwajuma has already left Mahmood's house now, you don't have to be alarmed.'

'When did she leave?' Bakari felt embarrassed that he had to get such vital news from a friend.

'She went back to her parents' home.'

'To Mtongani? How did you know, Omari?'

'I am sometimes in contact with Issa-Mahid's assistants; now listen, Bakari, in the new business it does not mean you will be staying next to Issa-Mahid, you will be travelling a lot.'

'Where to?' Bakari sounded surprised.

'Come here, my friend, let me talk to you,' Omari said as he hushed Bakari to the pavement next to the kitchen.

The kitchen contained three charcoal stoves, two of which were furiously burning with yellowish blue flames. On top of the two stoves were oval frying pans sizzling with fat buns, samosas and kebabs. On the other pan, placed on slow heat, a round chapatti was slowly baking. A petite woman was seated next to the stove, sweat streaking below her colourful headgear. She was rolling wheat dough with a curved roller. She alternately dipped her thin fingers in a bowl of fat and smeared the fat on the rolled dough, before placing it on the rolling pad again. On the other side of the compound, a bare chested young man wearing a pair of shorts and plastic sandals was peeling and slicing potatoes.

Omari called the young man and instructed him to go and fetch a beer and soft drink from the restaurant. The young man returned and placed the drinks in front of the two men. He then stood to wait for further instructions from his boss. Omari dismissed him to go back to his work. Before the young man left he exchanged glances with Omari and Bakari noted that.

'A faithful assistant of yours, eh?' Bakari asked.

'A very good boy,' Omari smiled with a twinkle in his eye.

'He is the one who always escorts you when you go to your farm in Ruvu.' Bakari was also smiling.

'Yes, but don't listen to those Swahili people speculating silly things – there is nothing going on between me and him.'

'I know you, Omari: a jack of all trades.'

'Oh, come on, I am a straight man, Bakari.'

'Actions speak louder than words, my friend.'

'Well, after all, why are people so much interested in digging into other people's affairs?'

'It is part of society's preoccupations, Omari.'

A neighbour's radio was in full blast transmitting the day's proceedings from the parliament in Dodoma. The hot issue of the day was the new bill aimed at promulgating the new value added tax. The two men in the compound were not paying attention to the tax debate, although Omari constantly lamented every time the tax man came to visit him at his premises.

The two men were talking serious business, and Omari was still trying to convince his friend to embark on the new business venture, that entailed travelling to different places of the world and learning new things. Omari assured Bakari that he looked presentable, and if dressed in a suit and tie, he would really be regarded as a respectable businessman wherever he travelled.

'At least once a month you will land in Holland, Colombia, or even as far as Thailand in the Far East.'

Bakari's face was beginning to brighten up, and he coughed a bit as if to acknowledge the words passing through his ears. He brushed his hands to remove a little bit of flour that still clung on his fingers. He then moved his hands to rub the little beard on his chin. The beard had turned grey on the sides, signifying he was well into his middle age. He had stormed out of the Port without knowing where he would sleep and eat, and without a prospect of getting another job. But he was prepared to suffer rather than to have his dignity violated by a lousy assistant manager who always came to work drunk and expected to be respected and revered.

Bakari was prepared to listen to Omari as he was the only one keeping him afloat, by at least offering him a chance to sell buns at a tea shop in Temeke. They had done several business deals before and shared the proceeds without hard feelings. On four occasions, the chemicals smuggled by Bakari from the fumigation stores using the refuse truck had been successfully off-loaded at Omari's backyard in Kariakoo. Omari had made the arrangements to sell them to a private fumigation company, based somewhere in Kariakoo. If Omari had such ingenuity in carrying out business deals, it was worthwhile listening to him, as he spelled out the grand scheme.

'Issa-Mahid will pay us well, and offer us commission on every successful deal,' Omari emphasised.

'Where is the house Issa-Mahid mentioned to you?' Bakari's voice was lighter than before.

'He said you could use the house at Sinza.'

'How is the house?'

'Three bedrooms, sitting room, interior kitchen, and toilet,' Omari said in quick, clear voice.

'And will I use it all on my own?' Bakari's voice was showing disbelief.

Bakari had lived in such houses before, but with three or four other families.

'With that one, Mwajuma will immediately return back to you!'

Bakari's eyes were oscillating from side to side, and his jaws moving as if he were chewing bubble gum in his mouth. He raised up his arms and brushed his hair backwards. A slight smile was about to escape from his face.

'You said, when can we see Mahmood?'

'Even tomorrow – especially in the evening, at his petrol station in Magomeni.'

Clouds silhouetted the sun for a moment, briefly reducing the toll on the heads of the pedestrians walking along Narun'gombe road. The momentarily relief from the sun's rays did not help to reduce the heat that blistered the faces of the young boys walking home from school. They clutched their bags on their shoulders, some having fans made from grass twigs in their hands. The pupils crossed the road to the other end of the street, chattering incessantly. Bakari mentioned something concerning the standards of education in schools these days, shaking his head. Omari agreed with him, asserting that pupils learnt very little and spent most of their days dodging classes and playing games.

The radio from the neighbour continued blaring the proceedings from Dodoma. An opposition member of parliament was busy denouncing the government's new tax policy. The man was not offering any new ideas or alternatives, but simply mumbling words. He wanted his constituents to appreciate and recognise that he had been contributing something in the parliament.

Bakari walked down to Uhuru Street and boarded a Toyota Hiace to Temeke. He paid for his fare from an advance he had got from Omari. His friend was very happy that he had accepted the business offer. The minibus negotiated the corner next to Tazara Station, and took the Port Access road. Through the window of the Hiace, Bakari watched two men standing on scaffold frames painting the Tazara railway terminal. The Chinese-built structure was beautiful, but had been starved of fresh paint for a long time. At long last there was someone who had remembered to give it a facelift. The paint they were applying did not appeal to Bakari, as he would have preferred the structure to be painted in light blue or light green, instead of the darker shades. If he had his way, he would have preferred the edifice to be anointed with yellow colour with a boundary of green: the colours of his beloved team.

The mini-bus stopped a short distance from the railway terminal. A transit police officer in his characteristic snow-white uniform had waved down the bus. The officer demanded the papers of the bus. The conductor moved a short distance from the minibus for a private chat with the officer. After a while he ran back smiling to the bus. 'He was hungry,' the conductor said. He banged the side of the bus and it proceeded. The mini-bus dropped Bakari opposite the Majembe Auction Mart, and he walked for fifteen minutes to the little house.

He had a huge Marlboro bag on his hands containing bread flour and other items. Very few people knew him in Temeke, so Bakari moved fairly fast, not having to stop and speak with other people. He alternately exchanged the bag between his hands, when one arm could not bear the weight any more.

Bakari decided not to open the tea room again that evening. He only opened the door to allow the boys frying chips on the pavement to collect their equipment and stoves. Bakari then retreated to his back room. He prepared a bucket of water, took it to the toilet and had a deserved bath. The house he was occupying was tiny and in a remote area compared to house eighteen at Kinondoni, but there were fewer occupants and less commotion. The best part of all was that there wasn't a landlord to come shouting at him, and spewing saliva on his face.

He placed the bucket next to his bed and sat on a small stool. All the furniture belonged to Omari, as Bakari had very little with him. Most of the items from his previous house had been collected by Mwajuma, who took them with her to Mtongani. Following her eviction, Mwajuma had turned up at Kinondoni the following day, with Issa-Mahid standing next to her. The landlord had had to open the rooms, succumbing to Issa-Mahid's insistency, and Mwajuma collected her belongings. Issa-Mahid had then tossed a ten thousand shilling note on the floor and made the landlord slither on the floor to collect it. Issa-Mahid had then left house eighteen sneering. He had his hands on his waist, mumbling that people with no money always behaved in such inhuman and uncultured ways.

The downgrading and humiliation of the landlord was the only part Bakari liked about Issa-Mahid. He wished he had the guts like those of the shrewd businessman to go and force the landlord to lick his shoes then toss him some money on the floor. But Bakari reckoned he did not have the resources to back him in such an adventure. To be arrogant and authoritative, one needed to have money and the right connections with the upper echelons of society. In the absence of such might, one is susceptible to the possibility of being disgraced and bossed. Being broke and powerless, Bakari had to depend on other men to sort out his personal problems for him.

On hearing that Mwajuma had gone back home, Bakari had taken a bus to Mtongani to plead with her to take him back into her life. She had not even bothered to see his face. Her words were transmitted to him at the door by a neighbour who happened to be at Mwajuma's home. 'She asks you to leave,' those were the words she had for her husband. Bakari had felt forsaken, and pleaded with the neighbour to go and tell Mwajuma that he really loved her, and cared about the children. After ten minutes, the neighbour had come back to the door and sulked at Bakari.

'She asks you if you are going to put her and the children to sleep in the street?'

The only positive courtesy he received from his in-laws' house whilst standing at the door, was a small parcel of his little belongings wrapped in an old newspaper. Bakari was not even entertained with a glass of water, although it had been sizzling hot that afternoon.

That sad misadventure had occurred nearly three weeks ago, and the pain and embarrassment had subsided a bit. Bakari was seated on his bed and it was about seven thirty in the evening. He had three hot chapattis, with some gravy and a mug of tea. He also ate some fried fish he had bought on his way from Kariakoo, and he felt quite satisfied. Bakari had no one to talk to in the room and he judged that it was still early for him to go to bed. In addition, ever since Mwajuma left, he had not had the comfort of a woman.

Four thousand shillings were in his pocket, and as it is said in Africa, a man with food in his stomach and money in his pocket thinks of nothing else but a woman. Bakari thought of restraining himself until his financial condition improved before indulging in entertainments, but he could not hold himself back. After all, life was short and no one could foretell what could happen the following day. He put on his shoes and stood up.

There was music playing at a nearby bottle store, and the melody reached Bakari's ears. He took the shirt behind the door, and closed the door behind him.

The whole front wall of the little bottle store was painted with a huge bottle of Serengeti beer. Bakari preferred Safari beer, but as it was not available, he could settle with any type. All that mattered was the barley in it. He enjoyed the cold, bitter effervescent taste as it travelled down his throat. Bakari sat on a long wooden bench as the night settled in, and ordered a very cold Serengeti. It had been a while since he last had the satisfying experience of a cold beer. Bakari gulped three quarters of a glass, before lowering the glass on the table.

There were two other people in the bottle store talking to each other. They were not talking loudly, although Bakari could hear their conversation. He assumed the two men were still having their first drinks: that was the reason for talking at a low voice. The experience he picked from drinking places was that people talk louder as they consume more alcohol. When they are finally drunk they will be shouting at the top of their voices. He hated this behaviour but he had to keep up with it as he frequented bars and clubs whenever he had money.

The men were talking about the attempted coup plot in Zambia, and the political upheavals in Kenya. They seemed to be up to date with current affairs, and argued with each other over the facts. One of the men argued that the soldiers who made an attempt on Zambia were from the troubled port of Mombasa and simply skipped over the common border between Kenya and Zambia to carry out the coup. Some arrived in Zambia by boat, the man was trying to convince his friend. If they were arguing loudly, Bakari would have been convinced they were drunk, but he sympathised with them for their little understanding of geography.

Several people were passing along the main street, going in different directions. Bakari was not paying particularly attention to the passers-by, as it was dimly lit outside. Occasionally, he would stare at a khanga clad woman passing with her plastic sandals slapping on her dusty heels. Bakari could see even at that level of visibility that some of the women's khangas had gone for weeks without being washed. He understood the predicament and sympathised with them. In Uswahilini, as the shanty towns inhabited by the common people were called, water had long passed from being a necessity into a rare ornament reserved for the rich. Nature takes care of its beings though, and life goes on with people surviving on the little drops that are sold in plastic drums in the streets.

The thoughts that were to occupy Bakari that evening involved his debut meeting with Issa-Mahid. Bakari was filled with anxiety whose origin he could not tell. He convinced himself that he wasn't afraid of Issa-Mahid. Issa-Mahid was a man like him, and he even appeared to be younger than Bakari by a couple of years. One of the main differences was that Issa-Mahid moved in a top of the range Mercedes Benz, whilst he squeezed himself in a packed Hiace mini-bus. Bakari also took pains to admit that in their new business venture, it was Issa-Mahid who would be pulling the strings and he would be responding to his moves.

An eleven-year-old girl brought Bakari another beer, opened it, and took out the empty bottle. She quickly crossed the room and went past the inner door. Bakari understood why she had to make a quick departure from the room. His two companions had switched from discussing current affairs into an explicit language of their intimate lives and adventures. Their words were obscene and could turn off even an adult. Both men would be in their late forties and with grown-up children, but their mouths and habits did not correspond to their ages. If they abided by their African heritage, they should have known that grown-up men were supposed to be exemplary, and role models to the younger generation. Bakari cast a stern eye at the two men, implying to them that they should reserve the discussion of their fantasies to the privacy of their homes.

There was a rattling noise of a motorcycle going down the street. Following behind the motorcycle was a barking dog trying to catch up with it. The dog was running close to the rear wheel; then suddenly, someone apparently perturbed by the commotion the dog was making, threw a stone at it, and sent it yelping across the street with its tail between its legs. Bakari, viewing the incident through the door, laughed a bit, and took his wide mouthed glass on his hands. He lifted the bottle with the condensing water dripping on the floor and poured the beer into the glass. The streets were still visible thanks to the light supplied by a single lamp post along the veranda. There were no street lights in that street, and even those on the main road to Temeke had long stopped functioning.

Someone came to the entrance of the bottle store and stood at the door. She wore a Baibui dress that covered her whole body, except for the face, hands and feet. Her left hand was lifting one edge of the Baibui to her mouth. Her three fingers were decorated with different types of rings, and below her wrist were two or three bangles made of brass. Bakari looked at her with an expressionless face. She was not beautiful, yet her eyes were pleasant to look at. They appeared as if she had just woken from sleep. When she flipped her eyelashes, an appealing impression escaped from her eyes. She had her eyebrows cleanly shaven off and a thin, black pencil line formed a curve above her eyes. She seemed to be unconsciously appealing for something in the bottle store that no one could tell.

As the lady got into the room, Bakari made a gesture at her. She came to him and asked what he wanted to tell her. She frowned, and her mouth kept on biting the edge of her Baibui. Her voice was soft and her intonation very appealing. Bakari invited her to have a beer. The woman in her flowing black tunic reluctantly evaded Bakari's offer, mentioning that she had only come to the store to find out if someone was there. She then hovered her eyes around the room, only to be met by the sickly, repulsive eyes of the two other men in the room. The blokes were already drunk by now, and had switched from talking politics and passionate matters to witchcraft. They had dwelled for a long time on this topic and from the tone of their voices and expressions on their faces, it was obvious that witchcraft was a subject they dreaded and revered.

'I don't see the person I was looking for, so I am going,' she said to Bakari, biting her lips.

Bakari was not going to give up so easily. In addition, the woman's request for departure was not affirmative.

70

'I am going.' She lowered her voice, her eyes were betraying her.

'Let the attendant come and I will order you one Serengeti,' Bakari said, smiling at her.

From close quarters, Bakari realised that she had full legs and sizeable hips under her tunic.

After a few moments of indecisiveness, she compromised and said she would take only one glass of beer as her religion prohibited her from taking alcohol. She would accept the little glass so as not to appear rude to a good gentlemen who had been kind to invite her to share what he was consuming. According to proper Swahili habits, if someone offers you something to consume, even if you dislike it, at least you must accept and take a bite or a sip. The woman sat at a small stool two metres away from Bakari, as according to traditions, a respectable woman would not drink seated next to a man.

After she had finished four bottles of beer and the night had matured, Bakari suggested she should pass by his tea room, just to know the place. The woman reminded Bakari that her culture was against married women passing by homes of men staying alone. It was better if her counterpart was in the house; at least she would have reason to pass by and relate to her how nice and generous was her husband. The woman had nonetheless agreed to divert her way for a few minutes, to see the place, so when her counterpart arrived, she would know where to come and greet her. Moreover Bakari had promised the woman a bag of samosas which she could take home to her children.

The heat had started very early that Friday morning. At five thirty the sun had not come out, but sweat had begun dripping on Bakari's face as he fanned the charcoal stoves. Tea and hot buns had to be ready by six in the morning, to serve people who went to work early. Bakari had actually woken up at four in the morning and escorted his partner three streets away to her home. He had stopped a couple of houses before reaching the entrance of her house, so as not to be seen by neighbours or other early birds. Bakari remained standing behind a tree to see his partner safely entering the veranda of her house, then turned to head back to his tea room. The woman had insisted on leaving Bakari's room at four in the morning, so as to be at home before her kids and house mates woke up in the morning.

Bakari felt fresh, relieved, and revitalised with some new kind of energy. It was as if a load had been relieved from his shoulders. The woman had promised to come to his tea room again after five days. The other days she would be staying at home, as she expected her husband, who was a truck driver, to be back from delivering goods to Iringa.

Bakari moved to the main room and arranged the three tables in the room. He lowered the chairs that had been stacked on top of the table during cleaning. The young man who helped at the tea room came through the door and made his way to the yard. He greeted Bakari, wringing his hands. His short gritty hair was full of blanket dregs, his hands as pallid as if he had been working limestone.

'Is this the time to come to work?' Bakari raised his voice, as it was five minutes past six.

'I am sorry, Mzee,' the young man said with a trembling voice. 'The bus broke down along the way.'

'How does that help me?' Bakari retorted in a sharp voice. He knew the teenager was lying.

'Mzee, in addition my mother was away, I had to look after my little sister till she came.'

Bakari wanted to say something else but paused. A Swahili always has reasons for everything, he said to himself and shook his head.

'Go to the kitchen!' Bakari ordered him.

He looked at the boy hurrying to the kitchen and waited until he heard the noises of clanging utensils, then he moved to clear the glass cupboards that were used to display the snacks. He had a tray of fresh snacks that were to be displayed. Bakari thought for a while about the responsibilities attached to the young man who worked for him. At the age of sixteen, he was supposed to be taking care of his younger sister. The boy had told Bakari that his father had abandoned the family some time ago and gone to Mwanza. Where then could the mother have been to abandon the children to look after themselves at night?

What was the use of being born into this world if you have no one to care for you? Bakari's head formed these questions. A soul is brought to the world, sometimes accidentally, and exhorted to desperation and abuse. Cases of abandoned children, or those born from irresponsible and abusive parents, were widespread. Many houses in the vast Uswahilini zones had vivid examples of neglected children, who were being denied their right to grow up normally, attend school, and become responsible adults.

How could the fabric of society be allowed to deteriorate to such low ebb? Bakari searched his mind as he arranged some samosas in the bainmarie. All African tribes had, as their prime norm, the obligation of caring for children. Each individual in the community had the responsibility to care for the children collectively, without caring if any particular child belonged to that individual or not. When these different tribes moved to the city's shanty towns and formed themselves into the collective tribe of Waswahili, this norm seemed to have disappeared.

In his heart, Bakari felt guilty as these thoughts crossed his mind. Could he exonerate himself from being responsible for the escalation of children suffering? Where was Mwajuma at that moment? What guarantee did he have that his children were going to have a cup of milk that morning? Bakari shook his head and wished another topic could cross his mind and set him free from the torments of guilt. Maybe he should think of soccer, or ways of increasing the clientele of his tea room, so as to divert his mind.

Slight drizzle had started outside, without warning. Early that morning there had not been any sign that it might rain. Bakari paused to try to remember if he had left anything outside that could get spoiled by the water. After he convinced himself that everything was under shelter, he continued to prepare the tables. The teenager came to the room carrying a tray of sizzling fat buns. He left the tray at the counter and went back to the yard. Bakari moved to the counter, placed the tray of the fat buns at the edge of the table and covered them with a transparent lid. He then sat at a high stool behind the counter waiting for the customers to come in.

The early years of Bakari's life had been spent at Kisarawe. Life was not bad at all, as his father had a job in an office at Minaki Secondary School. His mother had a sewing machine, making clothes at the Kibarua Shopping Centre. At their home, situated at the outskirts of Kisarawe town, Bakari and his brothers were each morning assured of a bowl of soft porridge with a teaspoon of sugar. In the afternoons, they would have stiff maize or cassava pap with fish, and occasionally, rice with beans. In the evening, the children's dinner would include fried cassava, and anything left over from lunch. On at least one Saturday a month, his mother would prepare chapattis or pilau. On this precious day Bakari and his brothers and sisters would not stray very far from home. Smiles would be written on their faces as they played gaily on the veranda waiting for their mother to call them for dinner.

In the evenings, all the children would do their chores without being reminded or compelled by their mother. The children would tie two khangas at their ends, then tie one end to the eldest child. They would roll the khanga around the waists of the second and third born. The other end of the khanga would be tied at the waist of the youngest child. The children would then move their arms forward and backward, shuffling their feet on the ground, imitating the train from Korogwe that passed near the Pugu station. Bakari was the second on the line, his elder sister being the engine of the train. His other brother was immediately behind him, and their youngest sister always dragged from behind.

Bakari had since lost his eldest sister, the engine of the family train, in a road accident along the Wami to Segera road. His younger brother also perished, the victim of an armed robbery at his house in Tandika. With the loss of the two, Bakari was left with fewer people to lead him in life, and to give him a shoulder to lean on in times of trouble. The youngest sister had moved to Kenya, where she had married a teacher in Limuru. She rarely kept in touch with her family in Tanzania. The distance Bakari used to have with her as they played the train game, became even more apparent.

Bakari attended primary school at Kisarawe for four years. Back home from school he and his friends would pass near the Minaki Secondary School where his father worked. His father had told him on several occasions that he would join Minaki if he worked hard at school. Those dreams were shattered when his parents left Kisarawe and moved to Mwanerumango, near the city of Dar-es-Salaam. At Mwanerumango he was enrolled into another primary school that had from standard five to seven but with only two functioning classrooms. The three classes used to alternate using the two available rooms. Sometimes the local dignitaries would hold their meetings in one of the classrooms and classes would be suspended for that day.

Bakari got so confused with these class changeovers that he spent most of his time playing with a rubber ball on the school's fields. Later in the afternoons Bakari and his friends would wander into a river that ran about two kilometres from the school, and pass the afternoon swimming and hunting pigeons with their catapults. By the time he reached standard six, Bakari had decided to abandon school altogether, and went to join a musical group that was struggling to make it in the neighbourhood. The musical group failed to get off the ground owing to lack of instruments and sponsorship, and Bakari, a prospective drummer-boy for the group, was left out in the cold. All was not lost as that occurred at the time his football skills were gaining new heights, and in a matter of time he was to find fame and fortune in the coastal municipality of Tanga.

# CHAPTER 6

Someone walked into the tea-room and called for attention. Bakari came from the yard with two pots expelling steam from the gaps on the top lids, and responded to the man's greetings.

'Can I be of assistance to you?' Bakari asked.

'I am selling cooking oil,' the man said.

'What cooking oil?'

'Mtishe – good quality.'

'How much?'

'Five thousand each, I have three gallons,' the man said as he dug his hand in the big sack he was carrying.

'Too expensive. I am not interested.'

'OK, make it four and a half.'

'Where did you get them?' Bakari looked at the chap.

'Uncle, the Indians are selling each for ten thousand at the factory!'

'So you took the oil from the factory?'

'Uncle, everyone has to make a living; not only the Indians.'

'Do you work at the factory?'

'No, my cousin does; now Mzee, give me four thousand flat then.'

'I am sorry, I am not interested.' Bakari was heading back into the tea-room.

'Mzee, I need to eat – OK, give me three and a half for each.'

Bakari was holding the chap's hand, showing him the way out of the door of the tea-room. By the time the chap stepped out of the last step, he was asking for two thousand shillings per gallon. Bakari did not budge, as he had had enough bad experience with such illegal items. The drums of chemicals he had been smuggling out of the Port had brought him close to death when a man he had not seen before held a knife close to his neck demanding his money back. The man, fuming with anger, had actually pricked Bakari's neck, claiming that more than half of the consignment he had brought, which was supposed to be weevil killing chemicals, was actually dirty water.

A drop of blood had surged out of the little wound inflicted by the knife, and the sight of his maroon blood compelled Bakari to pop out all the money he had in his pocket. The man departed with Bakari's watch as well. When Bakari checked with his friend, Omari had assured him that the chemicals were intact at the time they left his shop. Omari said he suspected that the agents he hired to distribute the chemicals to the clients might have played a foul game and doubled the volume so as to make extra money for themselves.

That was not the first time Bakari had fallen victim to the contemporary wave of swindling, baptised as 'Utapeli' sweeping the country, especially the city of Dar-es-Salaam. He had once bought a straight of whisky from hot spirits agents at the Kinondoni market, and gulped three quarters of it without getting drunk. Bakari was amazed as his ears would normally start warming up after only three to four tots of whisky.

The last straw was when he fell sick with malaria, and swallowed close to twenty chloroquine tablets bought from a street vendor, but the fever kept on increasing until he was rushed to hospital in a critical condition.

Bakari had vowed that the next time a person did the Utapeli trick to him, he would make sure the person did not repeat the prank to anyone else. Concerning women who desert him in a bar after drinking a lot of his beers, Bakari had thought of a remedy for them as well. Next time they excused themselves with the pretext of going to the toilet, he would insist that they leave their handbags with him. In this case they would not sneak out of the back door and leave him stranded alone on a table with two half full bottles of beer in front of him. Bakari grunted and reckoned that the increase of Utapeli in the city was an outgrowth of a tendency of people wishing to get everything for nothing.

The slight drizzle was trickling down the window panes. Bakari helped the young man move the stove from the open area to under the corrugated sheets extending from the roof. Luckily, all the frying chores had been completed, and the fire was only needed for warming the tea and coffee. Two customers were already in the room and were seated at separate tables. Bakari moved to serve them with boiled eggs and tea.

More rain was now pouring outside the tea-room as the customers ate. Such rains were a blessing to the paddy farmers in the outskirts of the city of Dar-es-Salaam, and the adjacent districts of Ruvu. Peasant farmers would be soiling their feet in the paddy fields for long hours to produce Dar-es-Salaam's favourite dish. Those who didn't appreciate the hard work going into the production of rice were the first to criticise the quality of rice, comparing production from one region with the others. They would meander around the stalls in a market, pick a handful of rice from a pile, sniff it, take a couple of grains into their mouths and grimace.

'The rice from Mbeya is longer, smells better, and sweeter than this from Ruvu,' they would be heard saying.

The rains in the midst of the city were not welcomed by an overwhelming number of the city dwellers. Most of the roads would end up water logged, sewage blocked and inundations appearing everywhere. The street beside Bakari's tea-room would be filled with dirty water, washing down to the houses built on the valley where the street ended. Some of the pedestrians running away from the rain would get in the tea room. Most would not sit idly at the tables, but would warm themselves with a cup of tea. The sweet aroma of fresh buns and samosas would incite them to order a bite or two. In that way, the rain was bringing clientele. The pools of water on the other hand hindered prospective customers from coming. Bakari was further inconvenienced, not knowing how he could walk to the main road to catch a bus to the town centre without dirtying his trousers.

The meeting he needed to attend that afternoon was important. It was a briefing session of how he was to do his part of the business, in undertaking international trips. If he were to appear with wet, soiled trousers in such a crucial meeting with a person of Issa-Mahid's calibre, it would give Issa-Mahid a negative impression of his business associate. Bakari had heard that the first impression an employee gives to his superior nurtures the attitude that the superior will exert towards the employee in the future.

Bakari had a vivid example to verify this fact at the fumigation section of the Port. Bakari came to the fumigation section demoralised, and a victim of a disciplinary action that had swept across the corruption riddled Large Room section of the Port. He was an insignificant participant in the corruption scam, but was not spared from the purge. When the assistant manager saw a subdued man arriving at his section, the manager quickly formed notions of him. He had information that Bakari had got dislodged from the Large Room owing to unscrupulous and undisciplined acts. The manager had immediately begun distrusting Bakari, and kept special surveillance on him. Bakari was aware of the manager's distrust of him, and had long suspected that he did not have a secure future under the man the workers derogatively referred to as Kibosho. And when the final showdown between them erupted, sending shrieks and insults across the stores, Bakari knew it was a culmination of grudges forged over a long time.

Bakari was thinking of sending the boy to the main road to wave down a taxi for him, but hesitated. He was wondering if the drivers would stop if waved at by such a young teenager. The other option was to offer the assignment to one of his clients, and as a reward, exempt him from paying for the tea and snacks he consumed.

There was a prayer being aired on loudspeakers a few blocks from the tea room, and Bakari realised it was midday. The rain had subsided and he was expecting that soon afterwards it would stop altogether, so that he could make preparations for provisions for the night. In the evening Bakari would open the tea-room up to eleven, and supervise the young men frying chips at the pavement. Bakari was working hard, as he wanted to catch up with what had slipped out of his life. He was living with very little respect from the people. At one time in his life his name used to appear in the sports pages of major newspapers especially when Coastal United clinched the National Club Championship League. These days Bakari was having trouble reminding people that he had ever played soccer at a regional level.

Bakari attributed his loss of fame to the attitude of sports administrators and other personalities in authority in the country. Unlike other parts of the world, in this country, there weren't any sponsorships for sports events, except from one or two organisations. Players in the country were not fêted, held in high regard, or made into national heroes as were their counterparts in Latin America. They were not regarded as role models to give inspiration to the younger generation as was done in Europe and America. In those countries, major players would be called to preside over fund raising functions or charities. Bakari shook his head as this painful aspect crossed his mind. He shrugged at the unwillingness of local clubs to sponsor their players to go and play international football in Europe as was done by all the leading countries in Africa.

His family members in Kisarawe were respected and his surname was associated with the revered sheiks who acted as religious and spiritual idols of the region. Although Bakari was born in what was considered a modern era, he still underwent initiation in his village. His grandfather had taken him to the elders to be circumcised and taught the customs of the Wazaramo people. He learned the interpretations of the different titles that were acquired by the Wazaramo who contributed significantly to the betterment of the tribe. The title of a Maalimu was the highest, and was only achieved if a person averted major disaster from the tribe such as war or plague. Other titles like Mkongwe and Mwamba were attributed to wise people of the tribe and strong personalities who excelled in sports, especially in local wrestling matches.

Wazaramo girls were taken to their grandmothers, also for initiation. Their commencement to womanhood involved the very basis of being taught to be responsible women. Through the 'Unyago' traditional classes, the girls were tutored in the skills of taking care of children and their husbands. The girls were warned that failure to develop vital skills to hold on to a man meant losing him to other women. So the other major task of the grandmothers was to tutor their granddaughters on the types of seducing languages to speak to men; how to prepare mouth watering coconut dishes; and techniques of waist wiggling when making love, as a bonus to their husbands.

These thoughts brought the image of Mwajuma into Bakari's eyes. She hailed from Rufiji, but had spent her early life in different areas of the coastal region, and most of it in Dar-es-Salaam city itself. She was a Swahili girl, bred with all the characteristics of a girl raised up in the core of Dar-es-Salaam's shanty towns. She attended school up to standard seven at the Ukonga area. When she reached the age of sixteen, her father insisted she should be confined into the house in line with the Swahili traditions, until a prospective husband pitched up with the right dowry to ask for her hand.

Mwajuma's father was attempting to impose an outdated custom to a girl who had already spent many hours watching movies of life in the Western world, and sensational dancing artists from the Asian sub-continent. She had visited all the major show rooms and theatres in the city centre. She had sneaked out of the house many times without her father's knowledge, to listen to pop music and watch adult video cassettes at her friends' houses. She was only sixteen years of age, but her knowledge of the social aspects of life was well advanced. It was a daydream to keep in seclusion a sixteen-year-old girl, who had more than once absconded from home, and secretly attended all night orgiastic parties at a secluded beach frequented by tourists in the Kigamboni area.

Bakari had not found his future wife covered in khangas from head to toe in an obscure area of Uswahilini. He first picked her from a musical extravaganza performed by the famous Marquiz Original Jazz Band. Those were the days when the band was rocking the city with its 'Sendema' beat and every young person wanting recognition had to be at the formidable Lang'ata Centre, where the band performed. Mwajuma, having finally absconded from her father's home and taken refuge at her aunt's place in Magomeni, found the Sendema paces irresistible.

At the Lang'ata Complex, Mwajuma slipped into the arms of a flamboyant man who seemed to be spending shillings as if he owned a money printing machine. In fact, Bakari was at that time making money in droves at the Large Room, where he worked as a clearing clerk for the Port. After their first encounter came the second, and several to follow. He had shopped for expensive shoes, gowns and gold earrings for her. On each encounter, Bakari stuffed her black handbag with a pile of brown and blue bank notes.

Mwajuma had fallen pregnant and, unlike the other pregnancies Bakari had provoked in Tanga, he decided to keep Mwajuma as his wife. She was just eighteen at that time, and the type of girl he felt proud to walk with in town and show to his friends. Mwajuma's father was disheartened: not only did he forfeit the possibility of getting a dowry, but his pride was also undermined. Gone for ever were the chances of hosting a grandiose pilau session, and listening to the great sounds of the Mdundiko dance.

Mwajuma's mother had defended her daughter's position, saying that her daughter had found a man to meet her needs and expenses; arguably all that a woman wants from a man. Bakari on his part thought he got from her what he regarded was the best from a woman. Although she had missed the Unyago initiation she had perfected her skills of handling a man, probably from the numerous parties she used to attend, or from being lodged in the different guest houses in the city. As long as money flowed into the house, Mwajuma continued offering herself to him in the best way she could, and prepared mouth watering dishes.

A slight gale swept through the compound behind the tea-room, and brought with it dry leaves of an avocado tree growing in the neighbour's compound. A dry leaf fell into a basin of water Bakari kept there for washing utensils. He moved towards the basin and scooped the dry leaf from it. He moved back to his room situated on one side of the compound, opposite the kitchen. At the extreme end of the compound was a pit toilet that was also used by neighbours from adjacent houses. Bakari took the electric iron from his room and unwound the cable extending from it. He again remembered that he had not bought a plug, something he had told himself many times not to forget. He however took the three wire ends and using a matchstick, shoved the wires into the socket on the wall.

Normally he would not use the electric iron to press his clothes, but on this exceptionally important meeting, he reckoned it was unwise to attend with wrinkled trousers. As he was only pressing his trousers, the electric iron would not consume a lot of units from the Luku meter. Bakari remembered his wife when he was pressing his trousers. She used to do that for him, while he sat talking with his friends at the veranda.

It was at times like these when he really missed her companionship. Bakari knew, however, what was the source of all his unhappiness with Mwajuma. The popular Swahili proverb that fortune brings laughter and poverty tears, was genuinely revealed to him. When he moved to Kinondoni's house eighteen, life was fully jovial, and the rooms were filled with jokes and laughter. Bakari would arrive home in the evening and find five chapattis ready for him, with a delicious beef stew to accompany them. Mwajuma would coyly ask her husband for five thousand shillings to buy the latest khanga in the market with intriguing words emblazoned on it, and Bakari would actually dish her out a ten thousand note. All this changed abruptly when Bakari was kicked out of the money wells of the Large Room, and landed in the miserable and boring fumigation department. Money is what makes a woman, Bakari was convinced.

The boy working at the tea-room came and informed Bakari that there was someone to see him. Those days when Bakari had money, when told that there was someone to see him, he would ask for the name of the person, his description, and what he wanted. He would then pull himself slowly to the door, or wait for a while till he was reminded for the second time, that someone had been waiting for half-an-hour to see him. These days of hardship, as long as he was not owing anybody, Bakari would not mind seeing people for whatever reason they came to his place.

He flipped up the socket lever and pulled the three wire ends from the plug. Bakari put his shirt on and looked for his plastic sandals from under the bed.

'You said the man is at the door?' Bakari asked the young man.

'Inside the tea-room already, Mzee.'

'Have you collected all the cups and saucers?'

'Yes, but . . . Mzee, two saucers fell and broke.' The boy looked down in a timid manner.

'Two saucers have what?' Bakari heard all right but asked in disbelief.

'Broken, Mzee . . .'

'And you are proud of that, eh?' Bakari raised his voice.

'No, Mzee, I am very sorry. I won't repeat again.'

'Don't even bother, you may repeat it every day, because you will pay double the value from your wages.' Bakari was now almost shouting.

The young man was still looking down with his head bowed. He was expecting mercy from Bakari, but met his wrath. If Bakari was going to deduct all the items the boy broke in the tea-room, the young man would take home less than two hundred shillings. His income was contributing to a large extent to the expenses at home. His mother, a single parent, was finding it hard to keep the family going and had to remove her son from school to help contribute income to the family.

Bakari in the meantime, peeped at the door and saw the exaggerated forehead of a person he met in the streets the other day, and claimed he knew Bakari from the days in Tanga. Bakari had agreed to stop and talk to him because he was one of the few people who declared that they could still remember Bakari as a famous person. This morning, Bakari thought of retreating to the backyard and instructing the young man to tell the tramp that he was not in, but he realised he could make use of the man.

'Hoi, Mr Bakari, I wanted to know how you woke up this morning.' The man raised his hand.

'Go first to the main road and get me a taxi, then I will greet you.'

'And I wanted to hear how your sick aunt is getting on.'

'I said, go to the road!' Bakari said with his finger pointing out.

The man's plastic sandals slapped on the muddy water as he rushed along the street. A slight drizzle was beginning again after a brief period of sunshine. The drizzle continued and Bakari could hear it trickling down the corrugated sheets. A big Scania truck was coming down the narrow street spewing water on the sides of the street. Where it passed, it left tracks of mud that would make smaller cars struggle to pass through.

Some women walking on the sides of the road with baskets on their heads, preferred to hold their plastic sandals in their hands and walk barefooted. The market they were going to in Temeke was not as elaborate as that in Kinondoni. It had fewer vendor stalls, and sold mainly food and a few other items. On rainy days, the market would virtually be inundated with muddy water, and only goods displayed on top of the tables would survive being destroyed by it. At the Kinondoni market on the other hand, one could obtain foodstuff, utensils, clothing, hardware tools; and even services such as shoe shining and nail polishing. Women would walk into the passages where the beauticians had their stalls, extend their hands out, and for three hundred shillings have the young men apply nail polish on their nails.

Time was going past and Bakari checked on his watch. He was left with an hour and a half to be at the meeting. He also had to pass through Kariakoo to meet Omari. He wondered if the man he sent to look for a taxi understood properly what he was supposed to do. The road was only a kilometre away from the tea-room, and it would not take a person forty-five minutes to reach there. At most a person would spend fifteen minutes waiting for a taxi, not more than that. Taxis moved up and down the road all day searching for passengers. Maybe the man had found someone else who gave him two hundred shillings for carrying him on his back across the muddy road, and forgot about the first assignment. Tramps like him do gain some money by standing next to water-logged roads and offer services to passers-by who wish to cross the road without dipping their feet in the muddy waters.

The taxi was eventually at the door of the tea-room, and the tall chap jumped out and came inside. Bakari did not wait for the man to inform him that the taxi had arrived and offer his excuses for the delay; he went to the pavement and met the taxi. Bakari ushered the panting man to a table near the door to receive his reward.

'Offer him only one cup and one bun,' Bakari instructed the young man who served at the tea-room.

'And Mzee, we have just run out of charcoal,' the young man said.

'Darn it, you are only telling me now?' Bakari stamped his foot on the floor.

'I . . . I did not check in the store.'

'Now, do you expect me to produce the charcoal from my pockets?' Bakari's face had changed again.

The boy had no more words to say. Bakari had to leave for a meeting; suddenly his assistant tells him that the fuel needed for producing all the items sold at the business had run out. In other words there could be no more activities for that day. They needed charcoal to continue frying more snacks, warming the tea and coffee, and, more importantly, to prepare other snacks for the following day. Charcoal was available from the market, although Bakari preferred to buy at the Temeke charcoal stalls, three miles away from the market, to take advantage of better prices.

'Take an empty bag now, run to the market, and bring a bag over your head,' Bakari snarled at the young man.

'But Mzee, I need some money.'

'Oh my, I think I will have to deduct this from your wages too. We now have to buy charcoal expensively at the market because you did not alert me earlier!'

The young man took two thousand shillings from his boss, and quickly turned to head into the compound.

'And tell the man to drink his tea quickly as I have to close the place,' Bakari said in a raised voice.

The driver had turned the car and it was facing where it came from. He brought the car close to the pavement of the tea-room and opened the passenger door ajar. Bakari needed only to step from the pavement into the Peugeot. It was a little after midday, and Bakari had to be in Kariakoo in time to collect Omari so they might go together.

'How much to Kariakoo?' Bakari inquired.

'For you, Mzee, only three thousand.'

'Oh come on, since when?' Bakari had not recovered from the agitation he got from his servant.

'Petrol is expensive these days.'

'But I took a taxi for two thousand last week!'

'Those must be the unofficial ones.'

'What do you mean by that?'

'You see, Mzee, taxes are also up, licence fees . . . all things. Anyway, pay me two thousand five hundred.'

Bakari thought for a while and straightened his shirt collar in the mirror by the passenger's sun visor. The taxi wheels sliced through the water, skidding over the mud. Some pedestrians along the way jumped onto elevated stones to avoid being splashed with dirty water.

'These days everything is just taxes,' Bakari said.

'Don't mention, they require us to pay a hundred thousand shillings a year,' the driver quickly responded.

'I don't know where we are heading to in this place. Just look at these roads we are paying taxes for.'

'What are the politicians from the opposition parties doing about this?'

'Don't mention them to me,' Bakari said.

The driver saw the way his passenger shrugged his shoulders and got convinced he had a grudge against opposition politicians, or did not trust them. In his taxi hung a little flag of the DPCN party, and there was a sticker on the cover of the glove compartment showing the balding head of the party's leader. He noticed Bakari trying to scratch the glossy picture using his long nails, and wanted to tell him to desist from doing that. From his facial expression, the taxi driver realised that Bakari had no love lost for his political idol. His passenger was complaining about the government and at the same time disliked all the leaders of the opposition. The taxi driver wondered on which side of the political spectrum was his passenger.

The taxi took a turn into the Port Access road and the driver took the right lane. He was approaching the traffic lights at Tazara, when a big Landcruiser overtook them and suddenly stopped in front of the taxi. The taxi driver had to pump hard at the brake pedal, trying to stabilise the car. In the meantime Bakari was yelling at him to swerve to the left. The taxi, whose tyres had worn treads, skidded a bit, but luckily managed to stop. The driver hurled an insult at the owner of the four-wheeled vehicle.

'The fool doesn't have consideration for other drivers on the road,' Bakari said in exasperation, as he eyed the brown-skinned driver ahead of him.

'Yeah, simply because he is driving an expensive vehicle he thinks he owns the road,' the taxi driver said.

The taxi driver was not ready to forgive the culpable driver that easily; he hooted at him, and the Landcruiser driver turned to look back. A thick moustache was fixed below his long curved nose. The man gestured with his arms as if to ask the taxi driver what he wanted from him.

'Look at him,' the taxi driver sneered.

'His mouth is hidden beneath his moustache,' Bakari said.

'He really looks like a crook to me,' the taxi driver said.

'These are the ones making lots of money, but are exempted from taxes, while poor people like you are strangled out of breath,' Bakari said, gesturing at the driver.

'You are saying the right thing, Mzee. We wish we had people with insight like you to contest for our cause.'

'I am not interested in your lousy politics,' Bakari said after a few moments.

Bakari lit a cigarette and puffed, filling the cabin with white smoke. There was a white sticker on the dashboard with a picture of a cigarette between a red circle, with a transverse line crossing over the cigarette. The sign did not bother Bakari; having hired the taxi, he reckoned he had the right to behave the way he wanted. The hullabaloo of the anti-smoking campaigners was getting on his nerves. If they don't want to smoke themselves why infringe on the right of others? Bakari thought as he wheezed a torrent of thick smoke out of his nostrils. The driver sneezed, and Bakari looked at him. He was preparing his mind for an appropriate answer if the driver were to dare to make a comment about his smoking. Instead, the driver cowered from exhorting one of the rules of his taxi business.

The taxi went below a huge poster showing a beautiful girl drinking from a bottle of Coca-Cola, and took the Narung'ombe Street. Bakari noted that it had not been raining a lot in Kariakoo, and the streets were fairly dry. A pick-up truck with loudspeakers was going around town calling for a political meeting to be held at the Jangwani Grounds, by the supporters of the Demonstration Party. The party's leader was going to dress down his opposition counterparts over allegations of mismanagement of their party's funds.

'On Saturday they are meeting to sift out once and for all, all their grudges,' the taxi driver said.

Bakari was not paying attention to the driver's words. The crises taking place in political parties did not concern him. He wondered why the driver kept on bringing out these boring topics. Bakari distrusted the politicians, and was convinced that all their efforts and noises were aimed at making money. How can a poor, hungry man have the time and energy to stand on the podium and talk for five hours? Bakari was asking the driver, if these politicians wouldn't swindle their supporters when given a chance. Bakari had also indicated to the driver that he suspected the politicians had no rivalry, but colluded in the darkness to loot their poor supporters.

'Who does that?' the driver asked when he realised his passenger was talking to himself.

'The different parties; those who pretend to be fighting in public.'

'Are you sure of that?'

'What do you think yourself?'

'I think they are fighting to serve the poor man,' the driver said as he pulled up in front of a restaurant at Narung'ombe Street.

'Keep on thinking like that,' Bakari said as he came out of the taxi. 'Here is your money.'

'What about the rest?' the driver said in alarm as he shuffled the two thousand shillings notes.

'I told you two thousand, have you forgotten?' Bakari asked the driver.

'But we agreed on five hundred more!'

Bakari was already walking into the pavement leading to Omari's restaurant. The driver was calling him from behind, but Bakari would not turn to look at him.

'Go to Jangwani on Saturday, your heroes will give you the five hundred,' Bakari said in a low voice, and sneered.

Bakari cleaned his feet on the door mat and stepped into the room. Once he had passed through the door, he pretended to be admiring the carving placed on the corner, which had been there ever since he first walked into the restaurant three years ago. From there he listened to hear if there were any footsteps coming into the restaurant. The couple of people seated on two adjacent tables absentmindedly eyed Bakari as he admired the sculpture. He was talking to himself, cherishing Makonde works, and attesting that the country was fortunate to have an ethnic group with such ingenuity. At that moment he heard a car jerking and driving out. Peeping through the window gauze, he saw the taxi disappearing around a corner. It was safe now for Bakari to move around the restaurant and towards the back yard.

Omari was waiting for him and invited Bakari to the compound.

'You kept time, Bakari.'

'Like a European.'

'You seem to be interested in the joint venture, my man.'

86

Bakari slapped his friend on the back, and proceeded to sit at a short stool carved from a wooden trunk. He lifted himself up a bit and pushed the stool a distance from the flaring charcoal stoves at the middle of the compound. The fish that was being deep-fried in the pans would sometimes crackle, spewing hot fat that could provoke blisters. Bakari was not only afraid of the blisters, but of getting ugly dots on his clean blue shirt. The mud on the pavement had soiled his shoes a bit. Bakari looked for a small splinter of wood, scooped the mud, wiped the splinter on the ground, then repeated the same thing on the other shoe. He then tossed the splinter at a corner of the compound and brushed his hands.

'You are very elegant these days, Bakari,' Omari laughed.

'Not at all, who can I impress without money?'

'We have to think of making money, then no one will stand in our way.'

'With enough money, I may even get Mwajuma a companion in the house,' Bakari said with a smile.

'You mean an adversary?' Omari broke into a roaring laughter.

'Anyhow you put it.' Bakari also laughed.

'It is with us, Bakari, when a man makes it in life he should have at least a spare wife somewhere.'

'I think it is justifiable; noble men are a rare species, and women should appreciate them.'

'Maybe we should have some lunch before we leave?' Omari said.

'Good idea, my friend.'

The compound was filled with a rich aroma of rice cooked with coconut juice. The rice had cooked slowly with red hot charcoal placed on the lid covering the rice pots. Bakari and Omari moved to another room adjacent to the main restaurant, reserved for entertaining guests of the house or close family members. The girl who washed dishes in the yard was called to serve the two men. She bowed while receiving instructions from Omari and then left the room. She later returned with a jug filled with warm water, a towel and a little bucket. The girl moved to where Bakari was seated, poured the water over his hands and used the bucket to catch the dripping water. She then did the same thing to Omari. Afterwards she passed the little towel to the two friends to wipe their hands.

A big metal plate of cooked rice decorated with bits of cinnamon and cloves was placed on the little stool between the two men. On top of the rice was a thick gravy of tomatoes, onions, and several spices. On another dish were two fairly large fishes that had been deep-fried. The Swahili say you best enjoy a meal if you eat with your hands. The two men were frequently licking their fingers, as they shovelled the rice and fish into their mouths. During the religious festival seasons, the rice would be served on larger metal dishes and placed on a coconut woven mat. Whole family members would sit around the large dish and eat. There were laid down rules, that no one would take another handful before each member had had a chance to have a go at the dish.

A fresh beer was placed on the floor, and a cold Fanta for Omari. He had been trying to convince Bakari to leave alcohol altogether and embrace religion like him. Alcohol was constantly portraying him as a sinner and was going to destroy his chances of getting sanctification from God. Another issue Omari kept reminding his friend about was adherence to prayers and not to miss any of the eminent prayers required to be entreated in a day. Bakari listened to his friend's counselling, nodding his head.

It had been overwhelmingly humid in Kariakoo, besides the showers that had been pelting the corrugated sheets. The humidity and spices in the rice were making Bakari sweat, and he felt thirsty. He poured the beer in the glass and took a prolonged gulp. Bakari belched and confessed to his friend that he was finding it so difficult to kick the bottle. He confessed to Omari that it was easier for him to give up women and cigarettes than his cold beer.

At that moment the servant girl walked into the room and brought a bowl of spinach, prepared with ground peanut paste. It was also flavoured with black pepper and garlic. Omari complained to the servant for having delayed the spinach for that long. He then extended the bowl to Bakari to scoop a bit. Omari assured him that the spinach was so good and would renew his virility; he thus advised Bakari to take more of the spinach. Between conversations and mouthfuls of rice, Omari appeared thoughtful and was not eating as well as he usually did. Bakari had observed this issue and prodded Omari to relate to him the source of his unhappiness.

'My friend Bakari, I don't know how to put this to you,' Omari responded.

'What is it, Omari, problems with money as usual?'

'No, it concerns these children nowadays,' Omari said.

Bakari swallowed the food from his mouth, and listened to the wheezing noise as Omari drew some gravy from the head of the fish. He observed him plucking the eyes of the fish and putting them in his mouth. Bakari was able to eat all the parts of fish except for the bones and eyes. He leaned towards Omari.

'Children are now growing too quickly, they accompany the changes in technology and life,' Bakari said.

'Growing is not a problem, but when they begin shaming their parents.'

'What is new Omari, your boy has been fighting again?'

'Not the boy, it is my younger daughter.'

'The one you are always worried about?'

'Yes, and just now she wants to go and parade naked in front of the public.'

Bakari did not make any comments to avoid making his visibly disappointed friend more embarrassed. He just squeezed a sizeable ball of rice on his wrist, dipped it in the peppered gravy next to the half eaten fish, and placed the ball into his mouth. He chewed with satisfaction, then moved his hand to pick some fish flesh.

Omari was still masticating what he had in his mouth. He moved his hand and chased two flies hovering over their meal. Omari then moved the back of his hand to wipe sweat forming on his brow. He was balding progressively and had most hair on top of his ears and around the lower parts of the head. He preferred to shave it short, sometimes making it appear as if he was completely bald. When he was younger, people believed his head was as hard as a stone, following the destruction he caused whenever he delivered the deadly flying header to his enemies. His head had since become frail with age, and instead of using it to settle scores, he used it to make a living and manoeuvre his adversaries.

Omari belched a bit, and called the servant girl again. He asked her to bring him a glass of water. He then looked at Bakari and shook his head. Omari had the habit of shaking his head whenever he talked. This habit made people distrust him, because shaking the head is synonymous with refusal. Therefore if one promises a person something then shakes his head, it leaves the person confused. After Omari had drunk the glass of water and sighed in relief, Bakari decided to prod his friend about his concern over his daughter.

'She said she is to participate in the so-called Miss Dar-es-Salaam show,' Omari said.

'The beauty pageant?' Bakari asked.

'Yes, then she will have to undress in view of the whole city; even the television cameras will be there.'

'That is what these girls call modern, these days.'

'Modern? She may think it is modern, but it is her father who is going to take all the shame.'

Omari eyed Bakari and lifted from Bakari's trousers a piece of rice flake that had flown from his mouth as he talked.

'I understand you, Omari.'

'Her mother seems to be indifferent.'

'What does she say?'

'Nothing, she seems as if she is encouraging her into it!'

'Mothers have a special understanding of their daughters.'

'Understanding? She doesn't seem to bother whether her daughter ends up becoming a prostitute.'

'Omari, calm down, those pageant girls don't become prostitutes.'

'Bakari, what are you saying, our religion is firmly against that!'

'I know, my friend,' Bakari said as he stripped off the last bits of flesh on the fish's skeleton.

'Yes, and you know I am a religious councillor?' Omari's eyes were gazing out.

Bakari was now anxiously searching his mind for something to change the subject. There was still plenty of rice to attend to, and Bakari was determined not to provoke statements that could put in jeopardy the feast he was having. It had been a while since he had been entertained to such delicious rice and fish dish, and his appetite was insatiable. Prices of fish at the Kariakoo market were sky-rocketing. A normal kingklip would go for six hundred shillings. Bakari shared the popular thought that vendors had to push their prices up to compensate for the high fees they paid to the city council for renting the vendor stands.

There were rumours that the huge market was to be privatised. Many of Bakari's friends had expressed relief at the news, but he was sceptical. He had seen a lot of public enterprises being privatised, ending up laying off a lot of workers and selling their produce more expensively. What would stop the new owners of the huge infrastructure from fixing even higher vendor fees?

Omari lifted from the chair and moved to the door. Bakari followed, his stomach weighed down by the food he had eaten.

'Let me go and change so we can move,' Omari said.

Bakari remained in the compound. He stretched his hands up in satisfaction, and paced up and down on the cracking cement floor waiting for his friend to organise himself. He moved close to the wall with his hands in his pockets. The house girl was at the water fountain, scrubbing the pots. Once a while, she would splash used water into the small channel discharging water in the street. There was a nail protruding on a green, worn-out door on the compound. The nail was fixed to a broken splinter of wood.

Absentmindedly, Bakari extended his hand to play with the loose splinter, and maybe wanted to get a sliver to poke his teeth. He scratched the old green paint that was peeling from the door, and the movements caused the door to open. Two or three cockroaches ran across the newly lit room to find places to hide. Bakari's concentration was towards the moving insects on the floor, rather than the curiosity of wanting to see what was in the room. Owing to the force of gravity, the door had by now moved halfway open.

Avoiding stepping on the cockroaches and being entangled by the numerous spiders' webs, Bakari's natural reflexes directed him to shut the door the way he had found it. Incidentally his eyes caught sight of white plastic drums that had a blue band around them, written across in bold red letters. A dark green solution could visibly be seen inside the eight drums stacked in two rows, on top of each other. He blinked his eyes and shook his head in order to refresh his mind to recall where he had seen similar drums. Bakari then heard footsteps from the corridor. He quickly shut the door and moved away from it. He stopped at the centre of the compound.

One of the cockroaches that had wandered from the store was still staggering around the compound looking for a dark place to hide. The creatures were shy, fed only when it was dark, and were very destructive to food. The house girl who had all along concentrated too much on her chores to notice what Bakari was doing, saw the big maroon insect running towards the fountain. With one leap, she crushed it, using her bare foot. Bakari squirmed at the disgusting popping sound that emerged as a result. The sight of a maroon insect lying on a pool of white stuff made him feel queasy, temporarily diverting him from realising that the door had flung itself open again. Meanwhile, Omari's footsteps were getting nearer.

Omari appeared in the compound and joked to Bakari that he had not had enough rice, and wanted some more buns. Bakari laughed at his friend's joke. He looked at him, and observed how he fastened his trousers in the middle of his protruding tummy. This was a clear proof that Omari was eating well. Omari fastened the buttons of his long sleeved shirt, and told Bakari they should move.

Omari was stepping from the veranda, but seemed to have noticed something that he did not want to alarm Bakari. He ushered Bakari out of the veranda and told him to keep moving and he would catch up with him in a minute. Omari quickly got back into the compound. Through his agile ears, Bakari could hear a door being firmly shut followed by a click of a key. His inquisitive ears kept concentrating, and he heard Omari calling the servant girl in a low, yet harsh voice. Bakari could not hear more of the conversation, but he was sure he heard someone being slapped. Indeed Bakari could later hear faint groaning noises from the compound. Then Omari briefly raised his voice and that was all. Bakari quickened his steps down the road, not to be caught eavesdropping.

On the left of the road were a group of youngsters playing table soccer and making lots of noise. The tables were an investment for the owner of the little soft drink parlour, where young men would buy tokens for two hundred shillings, drop the tokens in the machines and have a game. Such machines were a new invention in the Swahili townships and were surely poised to change the outlook of the younger generation. This was also evident from the hairstyles which some of the youths wore. Most had cut their hair short with lines fashioned on the head, beginning from the forehead. There was a stream of dirty water crossing the street, overflowing onto most of the roadway. Bakari had to move to the edge of the road, and jumped on top of a pavement of a house to avoid stepping in the dirty water.

Bakari took advantage of a rough concrete slab to wipe from his shoes the little soil that had clung to them as a result of the sewage water. He then got back into the middle of the street, swerving a bit to avoid a bicycle that was coming down the street. The cyclist stopped next to Bakari and told him that he was selling fresh milk that was in the drum he was carrying on the back carrier. Bakari thought of having a glass, but changed his mind as his stomach was still full. He was also becoming wary of taking milk that had not been boiled, owing to reports of pockets of cholera in parts of the city. There was also the persistent threat of tuberculosis. Now he had a full stomach, he could afford to be aware of all health hazards.

Twenty metres down the road, Bakari saw Omari emerging from the door of the veranda of his restaurant. He waited for him and as he drew closer, Bakari noticed that his friend's face was crinkled with distress. Bakari looked at Omari and expected an explanation for the exasperated look on his face. Nothing was coming from Omari except for heavy breathing sounds and sniffs. As if not satisfied, Bakari took another look at his friend's face as if it were new to him. Bakari had seen the face growing, changing, and aging over the past two decades, yet today he seemed to notice something rather intriguing. Omari's cheeks had puffed up and made his eyes look narrower. The lines of his cheekbones were more obvious, and strangely extended above his ears. Sensing unusual behaviour from his friend, Bakari desisted from asking him what was going on.

They walked in silence along the road, and sweat beads accumulated on Omari's face. He moved by dragging his feet on the road, and it wouldn't take long for his newly polished shoes to get dusty. Bakari wondered why Omari had not bought himself a car, with all the business he was doing. A restaurant owner and trader of his class deserved at least an old pick-up, instead of squeezing himself with the rank and file into the crammed Daladalas. Bakari nonetheless was aware of his friend's many responsibilities. He had a number of houses to take care of, and there were those persistent rumours that he was keeping an eighteen-year-old girl somewhere around Kariakoo as his new mistress. Such young ones can only agree to go out with an elderly man if he shows them money.

Seeing his friend had completely dissolved himself into thoughts, Bakari saw it fit to lighten up the moment.

'Where was my sister-in-law today?'

'I beg your pardon?' Omari raised his face to face his companion, blinking his eyes repeatedly.

'I say, I didn't see your wife today?' Bakari had slowed down to allow Omari to walk past him.

'Ooh, I forgot to tell you, she went to Kigogo to her mother to collect some garlic. We have been given an order to prepare a lot of stewed rice, so we needed more spices.'

'What celebration is in the offing?'

'The daughter of the city councillor for Kariakoo is getting married to a businessman from Pemba.'

'The councillor is very influential, surely it will be a big bash,' Bakari said gesturing his hands in the air.

'The Pemba businessman is from a very rich family, his father owns a five-storey building here in Kariakoo.'

'Can't I help to make some of the order at the tea-room?' Bakari asked as a joke.

'No, I mean you will be travelling.'

'But we have not yet known that, we still have to hear from Issa-Mahid?'

'I know, but you are to leave soon.' Omari was speaking confidently in short sentences.

Bakari kicked a small piece of metal lying on the road, and it went clanging along the pavement. He was surprised as to how his friend was so sure of the programme schedule even before the meeting took place. As far as Bakari was convinced, Omari and Issa-Mahid were not close to one another.

The two men covered the rest of the distance to the Tigre filling station. Omari told Bakari to wait outside near the pumps, and he moved through the back door. After a while Omari emerged out of the door.

'Let us sit here at the bench, Issa will be coming soon,' Omari said.

From the bench, the two men could see a large section of the main street with numerous Daladala buses moving up and down. The buses created a considerable amount of chaos, hooting repeatedly. Most of them travelled with young shabby boys hanging at the doors shouting incessantly. The boys hung so carelessly at the doors, and on many occasions these boys would fall off and get seriously injured.

A glittering Sangyong Musso drove into the driveway of the petrol station and stopped on a clear area behind the office building. It was an hour and a half since Bakari and Omari arrived there. A tall light-brown man came out of the car, checked his trousers and without speaking to anyone headed into the building.

'There is Mahmood, today he is driving his wife's car,' Omari said.

'One of his wives?' Bakari said and chuckled.

'Cut it out, Bakari, and please be careful how you address him. He is a man of integrity.'

'I didn't mean to dishonour him, Omari.'

'Come on, let's go in to meet him.' Omari was leading the way.

# CHAPTER 7

He put his briefcase beside him and sat on the orange plastic seats at the airport's waiting lounge. The flight was scheduled for ten in the morning. Bakari glanced at the top windows and saw the bulging belly and shiny forehead of his friend. Omari wore sunglasses and waved at him. He was wishing Bakari luck on his debut trip overseas. Bakari had flown before, but that was as far as Entebbe in a club championship match, ten years earlier. He had not crossed the ocean and this trip to Calcutta would be his first as a businessman.

Bakari adjusted his tie and felt the bag again, as all the instruments of trade were there. He had been checking on his bag several times now, and wondered whether he was nervous or simply forming a habit of making sure he didn't lose his possessions. He felt like having a beer at the counter, but refrained from it, convincing himself that he had to learn to control himself especially on such important trips. He should not enslave himself to the extent that whenever he had money in his pocket, he only thought of beer or a woman. He urged himself to begin thinking broadly on progressive and intellectual aspects that could improve his economic life and enhance his status in society.

Bakari lit a cigarette and raised his head towards the top windows. He saw Omari again, but he was looking sideways. Omari looked fairly jovial today as he accompanied Bakari to the airport, and kept on wishing him a safe and successful journey to India. The sight of Omari reminded Bakari of the incident at his restaurant, when the storeroom door had swung open and revealed the white plastic drums. Bakari did not take much interest in the consignment, but related it to Omari's behaviour when they were about to leave the compound. After deliberating over the incident at length, Bakari came to the conclusion that Omari was hiding something from him in the store. This was the reason Omari had to punish the house girl for being careless and leaving the store un-padlocked.

The voice of the ground hostess came over the speakers informing all passengers of Flight 240 to proceed through gate number five ready for boarding. Bakari glanced at his boarding pass and raised himself from the chair. He glanced over the window and Omari was waving at him with his face beaming. Bakari waved back as it was the only place they would see each other before proceeding to the bridge to board the plane.

Emerging from the bridge, the passengers were struck once more by the hot, humid air that was characteristic at the airport. Perhaps the hot sun shining intensely on the long tarred runways provoked much of the heat. A couple of long-legged birds flew over the airport's buildings giving out peculiar quacking sounds. People with experience of nature and its habitat would have suspected that the birds had detected a snake or a rat on the grassy areas skirting the runways. Left undisturbed, the birds would make quick swoops down, pick up the creature with their long and accurate legs, and soar to a feast. Apart from the beauty and wonders of nature, there were two jets stationed on the tarmac, and a Cessna and a Twin Piper parked close to a hangar.

The scenery reminded Bakari of the days he used to live at Ukonga and would come with other kids to the old Dar-es-Salaam terminal, to watch the army's single Karibou plane taking off and landing. As most kids would feel at that time, he dreamt of becoming a pilot when he grew up.

The ground hostess meanwhile had led the group of passengers to a hissing jet. The jet was surrounded by a number of personnel tending to it in different ways. The long plane with blue and red stripes around its fuselage was on the tarmac with two flights of steps going up to its front and rear doors. Bakari got into the cabin and was assigned to a seat at the back, on a row that had three seats. He sat at the seat next to the corridor. In that section he was allowed to smoke. Going on a debut trip to a land he had not been to before, and to meet people he did not know, provoked some sense of apprehension. Being a smoker, that was the time he got the urge to smoke more often than usual. He had brought on board three packets of Sportsman, and these would keep him company for a while.

Bakari knew some little English, enough to enter into conversation with a stranger. He did not care about English grammar, and understood more when spoken to than the amount he could speak. He found the language really difficult, although he had been taught it at primary school from standard three to six. Like many other Swahili speakers, his tongue was heavy to pronounce English words properly. He also became nervous when compelled to express himself in a language considered by many to be of educated and sophisticated people. All over Uswahilini, if someone talked in English when the person's mother tongue was Swahili, people would say the person was proud. Only in bars, after people have had enough to drink, is one able to hear a lot of people talking in English. The drinks would have washed away any inhibition and nervousness from their faces.

As the plane gained attitude, the no-smoking sign went off; instantly Bakari reached for the red and white packet in his shirt pocket. He tore open half of the silver foil on the top and tapped the other part. Two cigarette sticks popped up; he pulled one out and placed it in his mouth. He cracked the little gas lighter and puffed. Bakari peeped at the window, a little distance from where he sat, but could not see much outside. His eyes returned to the cabin and he gazed at the blue carpet with green winding lines, running along the length of the aisle. The plane was taking a curve, tilting itself at an angle. After cruising for a few moments the plane regained its normal position again. The jet was now cutting through a pile of clouds provoking slight agitations on board.

Time was passing. Bakari rested his head on the backrest and closed his eyes. He was not tired, but he had nothing to preoccupy himself at that moment. The two men seated abreast of him were of different nationalities and Bakari could not think of anything to say to them. He doubted if they would understand each other in the first place. Besides the language barrier, instructions given to him by Issa-Mahid prohibited him from discussing the nature of his journey with anyone he met in the aeroplane and abroad. He was warned to stick to himself, look serious, businesslike, and confident.

His eyes were closed, but Bakari was not asleep. He felt hot, and reached for the little knob above his head to regulate the temperature. Bakari had earlier on seen another passenger seated ahead of him doing the same thing with the knobs. A cabin luggage door flung open on its own, and an air-hostess moved to close it. She stretched her thin, brown hand and made three attempts before the door clasped on the apparent loose hasp. The sight of a self unlocking door once again reminded Bakari of the green door at Omari's compound. If the drums of chemicals he saw in the store were the same chemicals they were smuggling from the fumigation section, how did Omari manage to get those extra drums to have them hoarded in his store?

Bakari had managed to smuggle out the chemicals on eight occasions, and got caught on the ninth attempt. On each attempt he would take four to five drums. Bakari took advantage of the confusion during the tea break when everyone was busy looking for an egg or some samosas, and would not be paying particular attention to a man collecting rubbish from the store and throwing it near a discarded container.

97

Omari was responsible for receiving the consignment from the rubbish disposal truck and storing it temporarily at his restaurant, before offering it to selling agents. The agents would collect the chemicals in whole drums or portions, according to their needs or orders they had realised. Omari would then collect the proceeds and offer Bakari his share. On all the eight occasions, Omari had reported to his friend that all the drums had been given to the distributors and left his premises.

On three occasions, Omari had told Bakari that some of the agents had disappeared with the money, so he shared with Bakari the little that was left. Twice, Omari had reported to his partner that some of the drums had been stolen outside the restaurant whilst waiting to be collected by agents, and had given Bakari only a portion of the money realised. At one time Omari claimed that by the time the drums arrived in Kariakoo, some of them had spilled out in the rubbish truck, such that hardly half of the consignment could be realised.

Bakari had always trusted his friend and took his word whenever he gave it to him. Omari did not mention the price he sold the drums to the agents, or the prices the agents sold to their clients. He had not mentioned to Bakari anything concerning dilution of chemicals or replacement of the chemicals with dirt and coloured water. Bakari always respected his friend for his business skills and ingenuity.

Bakari's mind continued to be preoccupied with the intriguing situation at Omari's restaurant. Where could the other drums of chemicals have come from? Failing to come up with an answer, he reached for another cigarette from his pocket. Bakari was convinced there were only two syndicates in the chemicals smuggling scam. Besides, his operation with the rubbish disposal truck was a bigger and more organised syndicate involving the assistant store's manager. Bakari was convinced that the two groups ostensibly knew of each other's existence, and were business enemies.

The assistant manager's syndicate, being more powerful and influential, eventually knocked Bakari's group out of competition, causing him to lose his job as well. Bakari did not know who were the assistant manager's distributing agents. Even Omari, a person who knew the sources and movements of most unsanctioned businesses in town, had confided to Bakari that he did not know the buyer of their rival's chemicals. Omari had earlier on calmed Bakari and told him not to be concerned with the competition Kibosho was creating in the market, as he knew better buyers all over town and would soon beat Kibosho out of business. The promise was made by

Omari on receiving the sixth consignment. A week later he was reporting to Bakari that the agent who was handling the drums had fled Dar-es-Salaam to a southern region. Omari had vowed to his friend that he would send his henchmen to track down the culprit and extort the money from him.

His eyes were again distracted by the very thin air-hostess as she passed along the aisle. She wore a skirt that was a few inches above her knees, revealing broad knees that supported very slender legs. Bakari always thought airlines only employed beautiful women as air-hostesses. The one he was seeing in front of him was way off any description of beauty according to Bakari's criterion. A woman Bakari could appreciate should have a big behind and full arms.

The air-hostess reminded Bakari of the first woman he met in Tanga, who had borne him a son. The son was not planned, but was a product of the reckless lifestyle he led during his heyday in Tanga. She frequented his place, and did not get discouraged even when Bakari clearly showed signs of ignoring her. Despite his numerous other girls, Bakari was not short of energy to meet her demands as well. She fell pregnant, and her father, a senior officer at the Regional Trading Company, came charging into Bakari's flat. He demanded that Bakari should marry his daughter or he would take stern actions against him. Taking advantage of being a revered celebrity in town, Bakari did not take the man's threats seriously, and was not even aware of the time he became a father.

The girl's father had gone ahead with his threat and charged Bakari in the local magistrates court. The summons was later withdrawn after the intervention of Bakari's godfather, a top official of the Coastal United Club and an influential regional party leader. The case was relegated to the traditional elders' council, who compelled Bakari to pay the victim's parents three goats as a compensation for damaging their daughter. It was only after the son had reached the age of three that Bakari prowled into the Mkwakwani suburb of Tanga to take a look at a little boy bearing much resemblance to him.

The second woman Bakari made pregnant, who bore him a daughter, was older than him by five years and had had two other children from different men. He had a relationship with her because she made him a shareholder in her guest-house business, situated right in the centre of Tanga town. The guest-house was popular with the municipality's affluent people, especially married men wishing to have intimate relationships with their girlfriends. The proceedings from the venture ensured Bakari a constant income, and money to have a good time in Tanga. He sometimes entertained his friends at the guest-house, pampering them with cases of beer, hot stuffs, and roasted meat.

As he allowed his eyes to wander in the cabin of that Asian airliner, Bakari thought of the son and daughter he left abandoned in Tanga and felt guilty. It was now almost six years since he last saw his daughter, and four years since his son came to pay him a visit in Dar-es-Salaam. What would he say to his now teenage daughter when he met her? Bakari's mother had urged him to go to Tanga and bring his children to Dar-es-Salaam to be under his care. Bakari was not sure if Mwajuma was going to accept the care of two teenagers not belonging to her, in addition to her own children.

His mother had volunteered to take care of the children in Mwaneromango; still Bakari did not bother to go and fetch them. When his mother was sick and ailing, she had called Bakari and pleaded with him concerning this issue. With her trembling voice and shaking hands she had whispered emotional words to her son: 'Their suffering and tears will fall on you and drown you one day,' she had told him.

Maybe the children's tears were responsible for the difficult period Bakari was going through. He had been taught in religious classes at Kisarawe, that God's graces came through children. The Almighty would channel fortune and good luck through tender and young human souls who are still pure and scrupulous. Little children do not tell lies and are open to express their minds as they see fit. If they saw something unusual they would not feel ashamed about it, but would speak out openly even in front of the public. Bakari had forgotten this important teaching. The time he went for initiation, the elders of his clan had cautioned him against being negligent to his children, counselling him that they were gifts from heaven. Neglecting them was like slapping a man who gives you food when you are hungry.

The announcement on board that the plane was preparing to land, eventually snapped Bakari's deep thoughts. He stretched his arms and yawned. He took the plastic glass from the table and extended it to the passing air-stewardess. The sound in the plane had changed and the plane was losing altitude. Bakari checked his seat belt and looked through the window. He could see clusters of corrugated roofs on a vast area of Calcutta town. It appeared like an industrial area, as there were several chimneys emitting fumes and smoke of different shades. There were further announcements on board, but Bakari was not paying attention to them. More air-hostesses were rushing up and down the corridor to help passengers straighten their seats and removing any obstacles in preparation for landing.

Bakari placed his fingers on his shirt pocket and pulled out a small envelope from a pile of other papers. He placed it on his lap and removed the contents onto his hand. He felt the texture of three broad bank notes coming out of the envelope. Bakari turned the notes around as if to study them properly, then replaced them in his pocket. There was another piece of paper, which Bakari unfolded and read its contents. It had street addresses, house numbers and names written on it. At the bottom of the piece of paper were code names and numbers he had to remember and use at his destination.

Issa-Mahid had grilled Bakari on this subject, shouting at him at the top of his voice when he failed to repeat a number correctly. With his eyes popping out, Issa-Mahid had jabbed Bakari's stomach, calling him names whenever Bakari confused the name of a town with that of a special agent:

'You are useless, totally incompetent; how can you become an international businessman if you fail to differentiate between the name of a country and its currency? The franc is not the name of a country, it is the currency of France,' Issa-Mahid had bawled at Bakari during the final briefing sessions.

Omari was all the time laughing in his heart when Bakari was being rebuked. He would not have dared laugh aloud as Issa-Mahid would have reprimanded him as well.

Outside the airport lounge, Bakari saw one of the peculiar cars he was directed to hire on arrival. These were the informal taxis that were to take him to the town of Bajiap. The taxi would drop him in a small inn at the outskirts of the town. All Bakari had to do was to make a telephone call and ask for the name provided on the piece of paper, and just mention to him that he was already at the inn.

During the briefing session at the petrol station, Issa-Mahid had pulled the telephone from his office through its long extension, and placed it in front of Bakari. He had asked Bakari if he was used to talking over a telephone. Bakari had nodded his head timidly, and Issa-Mahid had directed him to make a trial call to his other petrol station at Mwenge.

'Hold the receiver well under your chin and speak directly on the mouthpiece,' Issa-Mahid had instructed Bakari.

The taxi stopped at the gate of an aged inn and Bakari came out. He stepped on the worn out marble pavement, and moved to the big wooden door. There was a man standing at the curved door who did not move when Bakari approached the door. Bakari looked at the thin untidy man, and wanted to ask him to clear out of the doorway. The light brown man with a greying moustache blankly stared at Bakari's dark face as if he didn't exist. Bakari waited for a few moments, hoping the man would finally realise that he wanted to get into the inn. In the meantime Bakari checked the notice board on top of the shabby house to make sure it was the right address. He then attempted to draw closer to the door again. Realising that the man was not going to budge, Bakari decided to crouch and pass below his arm.

Despite the unconventional way he used to get into the inn, Bakari was relieved he was finally in the building and avoided what appeared as a possible confrontation. Bakari could not tell what prompted the man to behave in such a manner, unless he were mentally disturbed. He quickly regained his composure and decided to disregard the minor mishap, as he had more important tasks to perform. Inside the inn, he saw another man seated behind an old garnished table. Bakari placed his bags adjacent to the table and tapped on the table to draw the attention of the supposed receptionist.

'I need a room,' Bakari said in his accented English.

'In the basement, twenty dollar,' the man said.

'Twenty . . . what, rupees?' Bakari exclaimed.

'Rupees not for foreigners.'

'But I was told I could pay with rupees, and I brought some . . .'

'Take it or leave it, man, I don't argue,' the man said, facing the other side.

Bakari had nothing else to say, as he could not debate for a long time in English. He took two ten dollar notes and gave them to the receptionist. The uncaring receptionist then called a funny name, with his brownish teeth sticking out in an unpleasant manner. Suddenly the man who would not let Bakari past the door appeared, and with the same solid face, looked at the receptionist, waiting for instructions. The receptionist indicated to the man to show Bakari his room. The man moved quickly without saying a word and went along the passage. The receptionist instructed Bakari to follow the man going along the passageway. He quickly picked up his baggage and went behind, spiralling along some steps. It was dark as they continued downwards along the partly chipped and uneven steps. A foul smell filled the staircase, coupled with heat and dampness.

Eventually the guide shoved a door and pointed his dry finger into the room. Bakari looked in disbelief at the man as he turned to leave without saying a word. His big head rested above his raised shoulders as he began to ascend the steps again. Bakari was still standing at the entrance of the door listening to the attendant's leather sandals slapping hard on his heels as he continued ascending the steps. Bakari tried the slender bed in the room and it sagged in the middle. He wished to go to the toilet, and wandered from his room into another passage, trying several doors on the way, until he found a squat toilet that seemed to have been constructed a hundred years ago.

Besides the discomfort, Bakari's main concern was to make the important phone call. He made it at the reception, and this time he was allowed to pay in rupees. With the black telephone receiver on his hand, Bakari was not concerned if the attentive man at the reception heard the conversation. He only needed to ask for the person's name at the other end of the line, and spell out the sensitive code word. The other person acknowledged his identity, and also revealed his coded message. Bakari was to wait for his secret host outside the inn the following day.

After the phone call Bakari returned to his room. It was five in the evening, and not knowing the town or anybody else, Bakari stayed put there. The few people he had met already were unfriendly and he saw no reason to talk to anybody else. He thought of going out of the inn to take a walk in the neighbourhood, but the idea of meeting the guide at the door and having to stoop to get out made him change his mind. Instead, Bakari went upstairs and approached the receptionist again.

'Are there any entertainments at the inn?' he asked the receptionist with his best English.

'What?' the man replied.

'Any video, or TV to watch?' Bakari said.

'No drinking in the hotel; no mischief, hear?'

'I am not asking for drink, I need to watch news.' Bakari was alternately pointing to his eyes, trying to make the man understand him.

'If you are having eye problems, go to room three downstairs.'

'What is in room three?' Bakari asked in surprise.

'There is a Mafutah-Guru, he will pray for you.'

'I don't need prayers.'

'Then your eye problems will go unsolved.'

'How do my eyes appear?' Bakari was still showing surprise.

'I hope your disease is not infectious, we don't want epidemics at the inn,' the man said, staring at Bakari's eyes.

Bakari thought it was useless continuing talking to the man, who kept on responding to him as if he were a child. He went along the passage and down the stairs into his room. He stretched himself on the sagging bed and had a light sleep. Bakari was used to sleeping in uncomfortable conditions, but at least he would be able to socialise with someone. He reckoned that his face was too dark with a broad, flat nose that appeared strange to other cultures. His lips were thick, his hair woolly and curly; surely he must have been taken as belonging to the low caste. Most common people in the sub-continent would not associate with the outcasts; as such Bakari was not worth much to his hosts for them to talk to him.

It eventually became dark, and Bakari switched on the lights. The twenty or thirty watt bulb glowed only sufficiently for him to find his way into the room. He felt hungry. Bakari checked his rupees in his pocket and moved up the stairs to face the man with sickly eyes at the reception. The receptionist told him he could go around the corner, there was a restaurant. The receptionist however, indicated to Bakari that if he gave him the money and a tip, he would go and get him a nice meal. It was a better option for Bakari, as it would save him from more problems with the language. His problem was accentuated by the heavy nasal accent of the people in that town.

Bakari waited in his room. After a while, the receptionist, wearing a long shirt and baggy trousers that tapered at the bottom, gave him a parcel wrapped in brown paper. The man bowed and turned:

'I will be back with a drink, sir,' he said.

Bakari was taken aback by the quick service and apparent sudden change of attitude from the receptionist. He had left him a tip of twenty rupees, and the man was ecstatic. Bakari now realised the problem with his hosts, and became increasingly reassured of the incredible power of money. Money can bring respect where there is contempt. He now had a chap who earlier on considered him so worthless even to respond to his compliments, running over the staircase to serve him. Bakari had heard of the word 'baksheesh', but it had not made real meaning to him until that moment. If he had had five rupees in his hand when he was approaching the door of the inn that afternoon, he would have had a butler bowing for him at the door, and yanking the luggage from his hands.

The man returned to Bakari's room with a glass containing a brownish liquid. There was a comical smile on the receptionist's face as he handed Bakari the glass.

'Nice juice, try it.'

'What is it made of?'

'Molasses, don't worry.'

The man left and Bakari took a sip. He squirmed, and raised the glass to take a good look at the juice. He saw precipitates at the bottom of the glass. He placed the glass on the little table next to the bed. Bakari opened the brown bag and lifted the fried chicken, placed together with fried rice. He broke off a piece and placed it in his mouth. The taste was not bad, but after a few bites, his tongue started getting the message. Bakari was used to hot food, and actually enjoyed hot samosas, or chewing green pepper with roasted meat. The concentration of hot pepper in that chicken exceeded anything he had ever tasted in his life. His tongue was now burning as if set on fire, and he stuck it out to get fresh air.

He quickly went for the glass of brown liquid from the little table, downed the contents and coughed. Bakari scooped the rice and hoped it would appease his mouth. Bakari was hungry and had no choice but to persevere with the special dish brought to him. With his eyes closed and mouth wheezing, he kept on chomping the rice and chicken dish. Bakari went to the bathroom, and drank some more water. He also took off his shoes and washed his feet. He had stayed with his shoes for a long time, and the athletes foot infection was taking a heavy toll in between his long toes. Bakari returned to his room, wrapped the chicken bones in the paper bag, and placed them together with the glass outside the door.

He changed into a pair of shorts and loose T-shirt, and lifted the upper end of the bed-sheet. Before going to bed Bakari drew the curtain at his window and peered at the dimly lit surroundings. As the room was in the basement, he could not see much except for the windows of the other rooms on the other side of the building. Bakari could hear noises of people moving along the road that ran on the front part of the inn. There was nothing much for him to see, so he returned to bed and laid his tired body down.

Bakari felt relieved when the sun came up the following morning. He only needed to wait for four more hours before his contact person came to pick him from that unpleasant place. Although it was still early, Bakari could hear the transit outside and noises of people as they rushed to their different businesses. He felt isolated, and there was nobody else to talk with in that inn. Bakari remained in bed thinking.

Apart from the time he had spent at the Keko prison for beating up a colleague while working at the Large Room, Bakari had not found himself confined to such a limited area. At least at the Keko Prison he communicated with other detainees, despite the consistent brawls that occurred between the inmates. Bakari remembered that it was Mwajuma who came to bail him out of Keko after spending three days drowned in that swamp of mosquitos, lice and homosexuals. Mwajuma had paid three thousand shillings for the case to be withdrawn, and Bakari was set free.

The image of Mwajuma flashed before his eyes, and her long neck protruding on well curved shoulders. Bakari sniffed and realised he was going through the present troubles just for her sake. He was a man gripped with distress, and when engulfed in circumstances that made him isolated, the feeling of loneliness recurred in him.

Time moves slowly when one has nothing to do. Bakari looked at his watch; it was still quarter to eight, but the sun was burning fiercely already. The picture on the wall, on top of Bakari's head, showed five men in a canoe rowing with what seemed like oversized oars. The fading on the edges of the picture determined that it was taken quite a while ago. There must have been a rowing competition along a river somewhere in the country. Bakari was no stranger to boats; he had been in a fishing boat belonging to his uncle in Kigamboni. The uncle was trying to convince Bakari to follow his line and become a fisherman, but Bakari lacked the patience to spend long hours of seclusion at the sea to make a living. He preferred to be on shore where he could spend the same hours at an office, and live a better life than sacrificing in the seas.

He turned around in the squeaking bed and slept on his side. When Bakari used to spend long hours in bed at Kinondoni, his younger daughter, whose face was a miniature of her mother's, would come and open his eyelids. Bakari would smile at the child, lift her up and place her on the bed. At that time, Mwajuma would be urging her husband to leave the bed and have his breakfast. As they only had two rooms, the breakfast would be served in the room used by Mwajuma's sister and the other kids. The two beds in the room would be pushed to the sides, and a small table placed in the middle. On it Mwajuma would place an enamel kettle of hot tea, six tea cups and two plates with scones. The family would have its breakfast before dispersing to different activities.

At midday Bakari stood at the door of the inn on the lookout for the appearance of a blue Tata pick-up. His hosts had instructed him to be on the lookout for such a car, that would pick him from the inn. Bakari had left his keys at the reception. Before leaving, he extended his hand to the receptionist to bid him farewell. The receptionist had coldly avoided his gesture and only asked him if he had paid all his expenses. Bakari was surprised by the receptionist's ambivalent behaviour, but quickly realised that the effect of yesterday's tip had already worn off and the man was back to his old attitudes.

Bakari moved away from the door to some shade. Behind him he saw the unfriendly face of the doorman appearing from the passageway. The doorman had gone to Bakari's room after he had checked out to make sure everything belonging to the ragged boardinghouse was left behind.

He had to catch a flight back to Dar-es-Salaam the same day at four in the evening. Three hours were left to complete the business deal before checking in again at the airport. Bakari could not determine the distance from where he was to the airport, as the taxi which brought him to the inn had gone a roundabout route, and left him confused. He shuddered at the possibility of missing his flight, as he had little money with him and that was not enough to cover to expenses of an additional day in Calcutta. He leaned against the tree and played with the leaves of a branch that was bending over. He picked a tiny red seed and squeezed it on the palm of his hand. The liquid that emerged from it appeared like blood, and it spread on his hand. It reminded Bakari of the occasion at Issa-Mahid's petrol station.

The day they had a meeting with Mahmood Issa-Mahid, Bakari and Omari had to undergo rituals that Mahmood administered to them to ensure that they remained faithful and secretive about the whole operation. Bakari took the oath that if he revealed anything, then his fate would be determined by the sharp, doubled edged knife which Issa-Mahid had placed on the table between the two men. That had followed a long session of instructions given by Issa-Mahid, who at other times had banged the table so severely that its legs wobbled. At one instance Issa-Mahid had struck the knife on the table with such ferocity that it penetrated for a whole inch into that pine table. The two other participants in that meeting had shuddered in disbelief when imagining the blow being delivered to a man's chest.

Issa-Mahid had taken the knife, made a small incision on his arm and blood came out. He extended his arm to Omari first, then Bakari; both had to lick the blood. Issa-Mahid proceeded to do the same thing to the two other men. Both pulled their arms back in pain as Mahmood made incisions on them. They behaved differently from Issa-Mahid, who did not even twitch his eyes when he made the cut on his hand in the first place. Issa-Mahid had growled at them, accusing them of being scared like young women. To make money, one had to sacrifice, endure pain, and persevere in the most difficult situations. He expected strong and brave men from Omari and Bakari if they were to go ahead and undertake the business ventures.

Issa-Mahid had proceeded and ordered both men to lick each other's wounds. Mahmood had then licked both men's blood. Drawing his face backwards, Mahmood had stared at them with frightening and wicked eyes: 'The price of any deviation from our agreements today, will be death,' he croaked.

Issa-Mahid had also assured his accomplices that if they cooperated well, and were faithful to each other, there would be lots of money for each of them. Bakari was assured that if he made a successful run with the Calcutta trip, Issa-Mahid would allow him to go and look after the house at Sinza. The house had a master bedroom, and two other rooms for the children. It also contained a living room, kitchen, inner toilet, and a veranda. For the first time in his life Bakari would be able to occupy a house of his own. If the business went well, Mahmood had promised Bakari a chance to purchase the house. With all these possibilities at his disposal, there was nothing to impede Mwajuma from returning to him.

Issa-Mahid had finally ushered his companions into a small room in which the three men could hardly squat together. The room was weird and was filled with the smell of burnt skin and raw fish. There were shells on the floor, placed on some sort of greyish sand. On the walls were calabashes of various sizes and beads hanging from strings made of hide. Mahmood had cautioned them to keep quiet in that sacred room and no word was to be spoken. Cramped in the room, the three men sweated profusely, especially after Mahmood had lit the wick of an old lamp and a yellow flame emerged. They spent about fifteen minutes, then Mahmood shoved open the door and they came out. Bakari had wanted to cough, but had been warned not to emit a sound until they returned to the room they were seated in before. The initiation process was complete, and Mahmood had ordered the two men to report to his office the following day. They still had to work out other formal parts of their business venture. Mahmood did not explain to his companions the significance of getting suffocated in that mysterious room.

As these thoughts crossed Bakari's mind, he was not aware that he had been standing for a long time. It was only after an old rattling pick-up pulled up close to his feet that he stumbled and blinked his eyes repeatedly. A man came out of the faded blue vehicle and approached Bakari. The man flashed a smile below his curved nose, and revealed a set of darkened teeth. It was the first smile Bakari experienced in that distant land.

'I spoke by phone with your boss last night,' the moustached man said to Bakari in a deep voice.

'You spoke to Mahmood Issa . . . ?' Bakari asked.

'Don't use names here, just the codes.'

'I am sorry, Commandant Zero.'

'And you, who are you?' the short, slightly greying man asked.

'Agent Bongo.'

'One more thing: the weight of a hundred eagles?'

'Two elephants,' Bakari said without hesitation.

'Ask the question.'

'Ostrich with bent legs?' Bakari asked.

'A bat,' the man quickly replied.

'No,' Bakari retorted, 'Kangaroo!'

The man with a beaked nose smiled to him. All the coded messages were correct and the men had not mistaken one another. The man in tunics turned and moved behind the van.

'Excellent, now get into the back of the canopy.'

Bakari leaned over the half-door of the tinted canopy, and got inside the cabin. The driver then closed the door. Bakari saw him moving to the front and got behind the steering wheel. From that position Bakari could not see him any longer, but heard the car starting. It pulled out of the driveway of the inn into the main street and drove away. The car left the main town section and proceeded along a narrow road to a residential area. The car kept on moving at high speed, reducing speed only to allow other vehicles to pass, or giving way to a wandering cow.

A slight chill of fear gripped Bakari as the vehicle kept rattling on the stone built roads towards the unknown. Dust was bellowing from the wheels and some got into the cabin. Bakari was being taken by strangers to a destination he didn't know. He became aware that he had immersed himself into a hazardous game, and he had to play by its rules. The risks were immense; yet according to Issa-Mahid's philosophy, if a man wants honey, he has to risk being stung by bees.

Bakari had not began feeling the stings as yet, but was well aware that the bees were hovering all over the place. If any of the plans were to go sour, Bakari knew he would pay with nothing short of his life. Yet even the saints, and all those who attempt to live by the rules in this world, do also die. Innocent and God fearing people were losing their lives in accidents, or getting killed by robbers. Bakari's accomplices had tutored him to believe that it was better to risk one's life making money. If death eventually comes, it would not be in vain. 'Selling buns alone won't make you rich, Bakari,' Omari had encouraged him. As he sat in the rattling van, Bakari wondered if Omari had himself undertaken similar trips.

The car pulled up at a metal gate and Bakari could hear the gate's hinges squeaking. Then the car moved again. Bakari heard the footsteps of the driver moving towards the back, and heard the door of the cabin opening. The man ushered Bakari out. Bakari stepped out onto a paved sandy passage that led to a low house covered with creepers. The house was surrounded by different plants, that included banana plants and palm trees. Bakari was led to a couple of folding chairs placed under a tree. A man came from the house and joined the two men under the tree. The driver instructed Bakari to offer the man his briefcase. The two men left Bakari alone under the tree and retreated to the house.

Cricket sounds emanated from a small thicket made of short, scrawny leaved plants. The peculiar leaves were interrupted at intervals by little amber coloured flowers. A bee or two hovered over the round petals and frequently settled, flapping their wings on the long pistils.

The top was covered by clouds and it appeared as if showers were imminent. The young gum trees Bakari saw in the distance reminded him of the place he had grown up in Kisarawe. When he and his friends played around those trees they joyfully called each other names of different professionals. One of his peers was the doctor, and the other a minister. There was also a cook, a prisoner, a mason and a killer. Bakari's nickname was the policeman, because he always succeeded in finding his friends in their game of hide and seek.

# CHAPTER 8

At childhood he had a nickname, and today Bakari was moving with another nickname given to him by his new employers. With the new nickname of Agent Bongo, he was no longer involved in children's games, but real adult contests. He had to play by the rules, keep his eyes open, and put all his five senses to work. Issa-Mahid had honoured Bakari's request to undergo cleansing before he embarked on this trip. Issa-Mahid had given Bakari some money and two days off so that he could make a trip to Bagamoyo. Bakari saw the need of a consultative visit to the oracles at the old graveyards, to pray in them and leave some money and food in the main tomb.

Issa-Mahid, who had himself performed similar rituals a number of times, sympathised with Bakari's wishes. Issa-Mahid did not restrict himself to Bagamoyo; he had visited Kilwa, gone to the shores of Lake Rukwa, Ujiji, and his last pilgrimage was to Mbamba Bay. On each visit he had a different purpose and special programme he adhered to. If he had to go to the southern regions to purchase precious stones, he would first take a trip to a renowned necromancer to offer him directions. Issa-Mahid was aware that there were many swindlers who could sell him polished pieces of bottles in place of ruby. He was convinced that his businesses could not prosper without the right type of enchantment.

There were rumours that Issa-Mahid had taken part in the abduction and mutilation of a little girl for the purpose of obtaining body parts that would be used by a medicine man to work out a lucky spell for him. Many people were convinced that the cunning businessman was culpable, but no one came forward to establish credible evidence of his participation. Those who had witnessed his participation probably lacked the nerve to come forward and give evidence against him, or were otherwise hushed up with a couple of thousand of shillings.

The relatives of the missing girl had grumbled for a while, but the authorities had ruled out any wrong doing on the part of Issa-Mahid. The top brass of the security forces had also dismissed the rumours. They

111

ascertained that Issa-Mahid was a successful businessman of high standing in the society, who would not have stooped so low as to disembowel a little child. He was indeed a man of integrity, as he had on a number of occasions donated huge sums of money for the political campaigns of very important figures in the opposition. Mahmood had built a conference room in his two-star hotel at the disposal of VIPs who wanted to hold their discreet meetings, and had rooms at the disposal of executives wishing to entertain their friends.

Bakari was still under the tree shade in that suburb of Calcutta, waiting for the two men to come out. He wondered what his two companions were doing in the house. It again appeared to Bakari like the old game of hide and seek, where he would be left outside the door while the other children hid, then he had to find them. In this type of game, Bakari was the one to hide and avoid being detected by the same policemen, after whom he was nicknamed. They would, however, not detect him if he played smart and looked like the serious businessman he was supposed to be.

Bakari even carried business cards. He was a director of Spice and Deodorants Distributors company. The head office of the company was in Dar-es-Salaam with a branch in Zanzibar. There were two telephone numbers, a fax number, a cellular phone number, and an electronic mail address. The cards had a logo of Aladdin's lamp with fumes coming out of it. At the top of the card, the words: *'Importers of spices and deodorants from Asia, Europe, and Latin America'*, were written in italics. That afternoon, Bakari's business accomplices were preparing a sample of the products he imported, in a special briefcase which he brought along from Dar-es-Salaam.

A red tie hung uncluttered below his neck, and fell to his belly. Bakari's stomach had not recovered sufficiently from the tormenting months of hardship to begin protruding outward like that of most businessmen in Dar-es-Salaam. The braces that rose graciously over his broad shoulders and crossed at a leather patch at the back, at least gave him the appearance of an upcoming businessman.

Such finery on the former footballer corresponded well with his leather briefcase that was being hoisted by the two men as they emerged from the house. Before he left Dar-es-Salaam, Bakari had made a quick round to the shops using the allowance given by Issa-Mahid. He had purchased two new pairs of trousers, three shirts, a new pair of shoes and two ties. The shirt he was wearing now had just been removed from its packet before being washed.

The briefcase was however provided by Issa-Mahid.

It was dark brown, made of leather, resembling the type carried by English gentlemen. It was almost new and had the characteristic smell of leather. The briefcase had a flap shutting with a buckle on the side. It was slender at the top where a strong padded handle rested. The briefcase broadened at the bottom with a solid base, that allowed it to stand on its own when held upright. There were several pockets stitched on the two main divisions inside the bag. On one side of the divisions were elastic straps conveniently made for holding objects that would otherwise splatter throughout the compartment.

With his white shirt firmly encircling his thin neck, the driver placed the leather bag on a table outside the door of the house, and summoned Bakari to draw closer. The man had shaved his chin, shaving the hair on his neck as well. He appeared pretty hairy, as some of the hair on his chest protruded through his flimsy shirt. It was fairly hot that afternoon, and the only people who really felt comfortable were those wearing cotton shirts with tiny holes, and flimsy baggy trousers.

Bakari's tight shoes grasped his toes as he surged towards the table. On the opposite side of the garden he saw large, peculiar birds with what appeared like tiny horns on their foreheads. They looked like the guinea-fowl that were common in Kisarawe where he grew up. The only difference was that the guinea-fowl of Kisarawe had no horns. Bakari and his friends used to hunt guinea-fowl in the government protected forests near the Minaki School, and when succeeding in catching some, they would bring them and put them together with hens in the hen-run. On Sundays, the family would enjoy a lavish meal of rice and guinea-fowl relish. Bakari would be rewarded with one of the thighs as a compliment for bringing home such a feast. The bounteous feasts incidentally came to an end when an infected guinea-fowl put in the hen-run had infected the stock, causing the death of seven hens. Bakari's father had from that time banned the bringing of guinea-fowl into his compound.

The moustached man opened the briefcase, whose compartment was empty, and took hold of a metal tin that was being carried by the second man. The driver shoved his thin hand into the long tin and produced a clear plastic bag.

'Cinnamon,' he said with his croaky voice.

Bakari watched as the man strapped the bag containing grey granules in the briefcase. Then the man poked his hand in the tin again, and this time came out with another bag containing a yellowish powder.

'Garlic!' He spoke with a strong accent, emphasising the word. His eyes shone out.

Bakari observed the protruding knuckles of the driver as he shuffled several bags of assorted colours from the tin into the bag. By the time the eight different spices were stuffed in the bag, it bulged considerably. There was still some room for four small bottles of perfumes.

'I am supposed to have a folder with price lists,' Bakari asked.

'Be patient, I know what I am doing,' the driver said to Bakari without looking at him.

Bakari sneezed loudly, probably irritated by the aromatic dust emerging from the metallic tin. The driver stared at him with those callous eyes.

'Better be careful with your sneezing as you carry this bag,' he told Bakari.

'Why?' Bakari asked with a smile, taking the man's words as a joke.

'If you sneeze like that at the customs you might drop the bag, and splatter all the samples, and the business.' He spoke with a mean face, with his mouth crinkled.

'I promise I won't let out any secrets.'

'You better not, let the customs people and their sniffer dogs do the sneezing – not you. Am I clear?'

Bakari observed that the man had an absurd type of attitude. He appeared like someone who had experienced the rough side of life. His face personified a child that had survived the streets, who fought to get his bread. His dark fingertips insinuated those of a man tugging through obstacles and dangers to stay alive. His face was made of steel, and appeared not to be harbouring any emotions or feelings. Bakari wondered how many people he had hurt with the rough, brass ring circling his index finger. It was not easy to evaluate how much suffering his hairy arms had inflicted to humanity. Everything about his appearance, and the way he fumbled with the leather bag, depicted him as a person associated with villainy.

Bakari stood watching his package being prepared by the proficient hands of his host. The cooing of a grey feathered pigeon outside its nest made Bakari feel apprehensive as if it was disapproving of the activities being done at that oval table. Yet as the bird should be aware itself, food does not come to its mouth on its own. The bird has to leave its nest and wander in different directions in search of grains and insects to feed itself. In so doing, the bird takes risks, endures sufferings and is exposed to all types of dangers.

A man must also wrap his bags and wander out of his house, sometimes, travel to faraway places in search of food. For those bestowed with high education and skills, they may earn a living using the knowledge endowed in them. The unfortunate ones who having no proficiency in working and earning incomes that can sustain a life, have to think of other options. The options for those belonging to the latter group, who happen to be in the majority, are limited. They may be forced to retreat back to the villages and be forgotten by everyone. Otherwise they might embark on other means of survival. These means may sometimes be dubious and risky, but men are prepared to gamble on them. That mid-morning, Bakari was watching his business accomplices clutching the flap of the leather bag, and clipping it in its buckle.

'Not so heavy, isn't it?' the driver asked.

Bakari extended his arm wishing to feel the bag as well, but the driver lifted it and carried it on his side.

'Let us go,' he said.

Bakari pushed the chair that was in his way, adjusted his tie, and followed the two gentlemen back to the blue van.

The other side of the house was not as well kept as the front. Bakari could see shabby sheds, and from the smell that emerged from them, they could be for keeping goats and sheep. There were some old barrels that appeared to be used for capturing rain water for the gardens. On the other side of the house, Bakari saw some well groomed guinea-fowl splattering on soiled water. There was a dirty stream running down a narrow furrow and collecting in a huge pool of stale water. It was not easy to tell outright if the sewer water was to be used as a bio-gas project for generating energy, or if it was simply a case of neglect to the environment.

An hour and a half was left for Bakari to check in at the city's international airport. The van was rattling along a different road from the one they came from, and on every corner the car would turn and go in a different direction. Bakari was no longer gripped with apprehension as he knew it was for his hosts' own interest to take him to the airport so that he could carry the consignment to its destination. Despite the fact that the driver was moving around in circles, Bakari was convinced they were not taking him to be dumped somewhere. If they intended to harm him, they could have done it at the weird place they came from.

Apart from that self assurance, Bakari was quietly planning what he could do in case of an eventual emergency. He remembered the way the driver moved his finger across his neck as a sign of what could happen to him if he were to lose the bag. Maybe his hosts were moving in circles so that he would not be able to figure out where he came from. There was always the danger of the operation misfiring, and the authorities could coerce Bakari to identify his accomplices' hide-out. Bakari's only option as he sat at the back of the rattling vehicle, was to wait and see.

Bakari was convinced that he could handle the two men seated at the front of the van if they challenged him, as they did not look that strong. The problem would be if they took him to a place where he would be faced with a crowd of people desiring to offer him as a sacrifice to their idolatry gods.

Bakari was carrying with him the dark, hard seed of a plant he could not identify, that was fused with an enveloping seashell. The healer at Bagamoyo had told Bakari that the object, which the healer had baptised as 'Ndumba' would protect him from any inimical situation. Whenever he felt insecure or threatened he should just take it out of his pocket and grasp it in his hand. Bakari was now feeling its texture, and moved it on his palm. Mysteriously, it appeared bigger and warmer than when he first took it and placed it in his trouser pocket.

As the van turned into a much smoother road and moved at a higher speed, Bakari became more relaxed and straightened his legs. He now realised that he worked for a more highly organised formation than he originally thought. Two days prior to his departure from Dar-es-Salaam, Issa-Mahid had given him the last briefing. He instructed Bakari on how to present himself wherever he went, and especially in front of anyone he suspected to be working for the state or the security forces. Issa-Mahid had taken Bakari to his out-of-town office, and made him simulate an approach at an international airport's customs and immigration desks.

Issa-Mahid had made Bakari carry a similar briefcase loaded with bags of rice and sugar. 'Don't portray the face of a man from the village, please,' Issa-Mahid had bawled at Bakari as he approached the desk supposed to belong to the customs. 'And stop your habit of walking looking down like someone searching for a lost shilling!' What Issa-Mahid didn't know was that Bakari did not adopt the habit of stooping his head out of choice, but it was a culmination of a prolonged period of depression and helplessness from the day he got dislodged from the Large Room.

The Port's chemical deals that Bakari used to make with Omari earned them an average of twenty to fifty thousand shillings. At least that was the figure Omari pronounced to Bakari. That amount when divided by all the participants in the syndicate earned Bakari nothing more than ten thousand shillings; although he took most of the risks. If the chemicals' deal was airtight, involving only those benefiting from it, who then could have leaked the information to the assistant logistic manager?

The Tata van arrived at the airport lounge and the driver opened the door for Bakari. With his tight trousers clinging to his wide thighs, Bakari clambered out. The driver helped him, checked his tie, and straightened his braces. Bakari acknowledged that rare gesture from his host and looked at him in his eyes. Bakari could tell that the man was not used to being looked directly in the eyes. He quickly verified that the message from his host's eyes did not correspond with his gestures. They had a texture of ruthlessness and harboured distinctive wickedness.

The other man banged the door of the van and stood outside the car, looking at the two men as they talked. He had not opened his mouth since Bakari first saw him. He might be dumb, or programmed by his masters not to open his mouth until told to do so. Otherwise, he might have been disciplined to do whatever he was told and ask no questions. He could also be a bodyguard of the authoritative driver, accompanying him to make sure Bakari did not try anything funny along the way, or dispose the contents of the bag at a different destination from the prearranged one.

Bakari clutched his clothes bag and swung it on his back. As he waited for further instructions from his companions, he passed time watching the hangar of the airport building. There were two people standing on top of a scaffold structure with different tools in their hands. They were renovating the hangar, as one part of it was already shining with new paint. Owing to the heat around the airport yard, the men were wearing only pieces of fabric wrapped around their waists and around their legs. Their backs were dark, blackened by the punishing sun. They must have been at least fifty metres from the ground, and the way they stood, balancing on the thin metal pipes of the scaffolding, was really breathtaking. A small misstep could see them tumbling to their certain deaths. Perhaps owing to the abundance of people in that town, a single life lost was not such a big thing to the contractors hiring the two men.

Immersed in a culture that was completely alien to him, Bakari was relieved to depart from that city. The driver and his companion walked Bakari a few paces to the entrance of the airport lounge, then they stopped. Staring at Bakari, the driver lifted the briefcase and extended it to him.

'Is your passport with you?' the man asked in his characteristic rattling voice.

'Yes,' Bakari replied in a low voice as he moved his hand to accept the bag.

'And your ticket in order?'

'I have it with me.' Bakari felt annoyed being addressed like a little boy.

'Be careful,' the man said while still holding the other end of the leather bag.

Bakari virtually yanked the briefcase from his host, and turned towards the airport entrance. He was saturated by the garlic breath from a man who seemed to consider the leather bag more important than the person carrying it. Lose it, and you lose your life; that was what Bakari was made to understand, first by his new boss Issa-Mahid, and now by his accomplices. If the plane were to crash and he were to survive but the bag got lost, his associates would weep uncontrollably, probably forfeiting his life as well. Before he disappeared into the airport lounge, Bakari turned to eye the two men in their baggy trousers. They stood about twenty metres away, looking like statues.

There was a medium built woman at the check-in counter, with long black hair parted in the middle and knotted on both sides of her head. She had overemphasised red lipstick on her thin lips that corresponded to the red dot on her forehead. Bakari offered her his ticket, and she took it under the desk to match the name against those appearing on her list. She tore the middle slip and clipped a piece of paper on the ticket, her bangles clicking on one another. She handed the ticket back to Bakari with a boarding pass.

Behind him on the line were several other people of different nationalities. Bakari could not see any face that appeared familiar to him. There were two or three Africans, but he was not sure if they were conversant in Kiswahili. The people Bakari mixed with in Dar-es-Salaam were not the sophisticated type to be found flying between different world capitals. In Dar-es-Salaam, Bakari socialised with the working class and small business people. He did not drive a luxurious car to be noticed in town, or share a surname with any personality belonging to the rich and famous clubs. If by chance he were to meet another person of his class jetting across the cities of the world, the person would most probably be a carrier of a bag like his, with secret compartments.

Bakari left the desk, went to a chair and sat down. He checked his ticket again; its destination was Nairobi, from where he would catch a connecting flight to Dar-es-Salaam. There were advertisements of different products at the airport lounge, with the Coca-Cola board catching his eye. In every destination he had been to, Bakari had noticed elaborate posters advertising the famous drink. Below the Coca-Cola poster was another poster showing a child handling a pint of milk. The poster did not mention the type of milk, but Bakari guessed it would be powdered milk, as he did not see evidence of cows being milked during his stay in the country.

The aroma of spiced chicken emanating from one of the doors of the waiting lounge made Bakari feel hungry. He had no more rupees to spare, so he simply had to wait until he was on board to be served with food and drinks. The time had come to proceed to the immigration and customs desks. Bakari stood up, checked his braces, and followed a couple who joined the line ahead of him. He had his hand in his pocket, but removed it and let it move up and down over his left brace.

Bakari presented his passport to the middle-aged man behind the glass window. The officer in khaki uniform lifted his cap a bit and opened the little green booklet. He flipped the pages to check the necessary details, shuffled some papers on the desk and wrote something. He then took the stamp and pressed it on an open page. Nodding his head, he handed the passport back to Bakari. The furniture surrounding the glass window was made of tinted pine that had a gloss finish. Anyone passing by the window after having the passport stamped would feel the strong scent of mint that was used to polish the wooden pieces. The floor, made of shining white tiles, was slippery, and one needed to walk carefully to avoid slipping. The floor had just been polished, and there was a notice placed at the end of the hall, cautioning people that the floor was slippery.

There were other notices along the front side of the customs wall that cautioned passengers against carrying dangerous articles such as compressed gases or explosives. Some of the notices were written using letters that were totally strange to Bakari. He had seen similar letters on the wrappings of products manufactured in China that were abundant in Dar-es-Salaam. The thoughts of China reminded Bakari of the time he applied for a job at the textile factory with the prospect of being taken to China for training as a factory technician.

Bakari had logged his application and was called for an interview. The line of the prospective young men waiting to be interviewed extended for twenty metres, and by the time Bakari had his turn, the interviewer had almost run out of steam. Bakari, like the rest of the prospective applicants, went home waiting for a response. Three weeks later he received a light envelope with a paper inside having a few lines expressing regret that his application was not successful. It was not the first time he had received such a response, but at least on that occasion his application was acknowledged. Numerous other applications had gone unacknowledged and Bakari was not sure if they were even considered or were dumped in the waste basket straight away.

Bakari reached the customs desk, took a deep breath and placed the briefcase in the X-ray compartment before passing through the metal detector door. The briefcase emerged on the other side of the X-ray chamber, and there was an officer standing there.

'Any dangerous stuff in here: weapons, etc?' he asked Bakari.

'No,' Bakari answered in a low voice, looking at the white capped officer.

'Mind to open it, sir?' the officer requested in a normal voice, his hands wrapped with tight, white gloves.

'Sure,' Bakari said as he proceeded to unbuckle the strap and displayed the open handbag.

'What are these?' the officer said without touching the plastic bags of different colours in the bag.

'Samples of spices.' Bakari's voice was steady.

'Okay, thank you, sir, you may close your bag.' The officer was already facing another passenger in the queue, behind Bakari.

The roof of the room where Bakari and other passengers were waiting to embark was dome shaped with high windows that curved at the top of the dome. It appeared like a cathedral, although even with his limited knowledge of global issues, Bakari knew it was unlikely to find lots of cathedrals in Calcutta. He conceded that the artistic imaginations and ingenuity that combined to form such a masterpiece deserved praise. Several other buildings he saw in town were also magnificent, especially the age old temples constructed on elevated sites, gracing the overpopulated towns. The thirty minutes he spent at the waiting room were absorbed by thoughts of his two days stay in Calcutta with its enigmatic scenery. The announcements were later made for passengers to proceed to the boarding gates.

The plane that was crossing the Indian Ocean was wider than the one Bakari boarded on his way to the Asian subcontinent. The seats were also neater and more comfortable. Bakari noticed the crew were friendly and without hesitation, the stewardess had agreed to offer Bakari an extra dinner pack when he requested her. Bakari viewed the lunch packs offered in airlines as being too little to appease his hunger. The stewardess also brought him an extra bottle of wine. In total Bakari had three bottles, as the passenger seated next to him did not feel like having wine and offered it to Bakari.

There were five more flight hours, but with a full stomach and refreshment from the wine, Bakari lowered his seat to induce a deserved nap. The classical music from the microphones was not the type he adored. He flung the instrument back into its holder, clasped his hands and lowered his head on the head rest. Before passing into a light sleep, the image of his boss came into his mind. The man was far younger than him but had managed to make so much money. He had many residential houses in Dar-es-Salaam, cars, petrol stations and delivery trucks. He also possessed hotels, guest houses and a six storey building at Kariakoo.

Issa-Mahid looked about thirty-six or younger. When did he start making money successfully? The question boggled Bakari's mind. Issa-Mahid had told Bakari that the secret with him was his discipline: that he went around all the time with a rosary made of pea-sized beads on his hand, and would keep on moving the beads. That brought him luck, perseverance in his work, and the urge to keep searching for more and more money.

Whenever Issa-Mahid talked, he based his rationality on making money. Listening to him, one would be convinced that Mahmood wished that all the money in the city belonged to him. He would not at any moment behave as if he had enough money already. He liked to have people working for him, although many of his workers complained that he did not pay them well. He would always bargain with his workers to offer them as little as possible. His associates complained that Mahmood did not allow anyone owing him money to pass by him. He would insist on being paid to the last shilling. He could also be ruthless to those he saw as wanting to reduce the money he owed. He had his henchmen whom he would send to sort out any competitor or person threatening his quest for making money. His major weakness was with women. He adored beautiful women and would spend lavishly on them. He seemed to have an insatiable appetite for them, such that he did not seem to be getting enough. He wanted to go out with all the beautiful girls he saw in town.

Bakari was now more at ease that Issa-Mahid went out with his sister-in-law. Mwajuma's sister, as one of Issa-Mahid's mistresses, would help to cement the business bond that was forming between them. Bakari longed to possess a car as well. He knew how to drive, after taking lessons with the numerous cars at Amboni in Tanga. One of the drivers, a good friend of his, allowed Bakari to drive his Corolla. Bakari ended up breaking the gearbox, but had managed to acquire the necessary skills to find his way on the roads. Bakari had then used three thousand shillings to get a licence through one of his friends who worked at the revenue office. All that Bakari needed was a bit of practice, as it had been nearly a decade since he last drove a car.

Next to the bridge at the Dar-es-Salaam International Airport were two medium sized jets, parked close to the bridge's entrances. The wide bodied jet, which Bakari arrived with from Nairobi, taxied to the furthest bridge and manoeuvred to its gate. There were passengers already in the airport lounge, some picking their luggage from the revolving belts. The level of humidity in the lounge, coupled with the heat wave from the tarmac, made passengers from Europe swelter with discontent.

A baby carried by an elderly passenger cried and filled the otherwise quiet afternoon outside the airport lounge. Bakari clutched his bag and moved past the metal barriers outside the airport lounge doors. Bakari looked ahead and saw his friend moving towards him, waving his hand. They met halfway about twenty metres from the arrival doors. Omari embraced Bakari and patted him at the back. The smile on Omari's face was exuberant. He asked Bakari how his trip had gone, and immediately extended his hand to reach for the briefcase.

'They did not ask to see inside, at the gate?' Omari asked.

'No, they just allowed me to pass,' Bakari answered, his face showing no expression.

'Issa-Mahid will be very proud of you,' Omari said.

# CHAPTER 9

A remarkable cool wind was finding its way in between pavilions at the Dar-es-Salaam's trade fair along Kilwa road. Between the Nigerian and Kenyan pavilion, a draught blew some dust and discarded paper bags into the air. Bakari used a pamphlet he was holding on his hand to cover his face from the dust. Otherwise, the ambience at the trade fair making the popular 'Saba-Saba' day, was jovial, with whole families taking time to visit the different pavilions at the grounds. Strings supported on tall poles bearing multi-coloured flags hung above the grounds. The flags flattered in different directions responding to the wind. Loudspeakers attached to some of the poles provided different announcements, sometimes playing Swahili and Lingala songs.

Bakari supported himself on one of the poles and removed a wooden speck that had found its way onto his shoes. Unfortunately, the colours around the pole had not dried properly and they had left blue and white stains on his hands. He bent down to wipe the paint on the grass and sniffed his hands. He remembered seeing decorated, flag bearing poles like those long ago when important heads of state used to visit the country. Those days as a student at Pwani region, he and his friends would line up on both sides of the road and gaily wave little flags when the motorcade of the head of state went by. After the motorcade had passed, Bakari and his friends would not immediately return to school, but disperse into the edges of the townships to look for mangoes.

A pack of multi-coloured balloons were released into the air and went soaring above the trade fair grounds. Bakari saw some of the balloons being sold at a nearby pavilion, and he surmised that they were filled with a very light gas that made them airborne. The few well-dressed kids playing ahead of the shop shouted hysterically as they saw the balloons rising. It reminded Bakari of his young children, and he sighed in remorse. He wished he was holding them with both his hands, moving around the grounds like other parents were doing at that moment. He had not heard from his kids and wife for quite a while. This aspect made him feel inadequate both as a man and as a parent.

Bakari stopped at the Woods Industries pavilion, and through the window displays, got lured inside. They were displaying beautiful pine furniture that included dining tables, sofa sets, and beds. Bakari was attended by a young man who assisted him with the prices of the items on display. He instantly fell in love with a six chair dining table, and a double bed complete with an eight inch mattress. He was going to make an order for the two items and instruct that they be delivered to house five hundred fifty five, along Chekereni Road in Sinza.

With the arrival of the furniture, his house would be complete. The bed he used at present would be moved to the spare room. Since moving into the new house, Bakari had already acquired a double door fridge, and a good second hand gas stove. He however used the gas stove only on special occasions, especially when he needed to impress a guest in the house. On normal days the meals would be prepared from a small, Chinese-made paraffin stove. On days he managed to get a cheap consignment of firewood from Kisarawe, he would use the three stone open air stove that was set at the extreme corner of the house. With fuel such an expensive commodity in Dar-es-Salaam, all means had to be found to use the cheapest type of fuel available. Cooking using electricity was reserved for the super rich. With the escalating costs of the Luku provisions cards, the irregular rationing of energy, and high prices of electric cookers, one wonders if there was still anyone cooking using electricity in Sinza.

Bakari had hired a young man to help him with the household chores and care for the house when he made his overseas business trips. He flew to different destinations at least once a month, and had been doing that for fourteen months now. Bakari was waiting for an Italian expatriate working at a petroleum company to leave so that he could buy his Toyota Cressida saloon. The Toyota was still in a good condition and could offer many kilometres of service. Once he acquired the car, it would give him enough freedom to move and meet his other business associates wherever he desired.

In the meantime, Bakari depended on hiring taxis, or persuading his new found friends possessing cars to take him to Ubungo and Mwenge, where he was running a bar and a grocery shop in the respective townships. Running businesses without a reliable means of transport could be burdensome especially when quick decisions had to be made. Sometimes he needed to make frequent trips during the day to check if the shop had enough stock. It was more critical with the bar, as he had to pitch up at Ubungo at night to make sure customers were getting proper service and there were no security problems.

Whenever Bakari was undertaking assignments for Issa-Mahid, he would be driven to all the necessary destinations by Issa-Mahid's drivers. Bakari wouldn't dare use Issa-Mahid's cars when tending to his personal businesses. Issa-Mahid had discouraged Bakari from having other businesses besides working for him. Issa-Mahid wanted to control and monitor all Bakari's moves.

Bakari was also sceptical about asking Omari for assistance using his Ford van. Omari had acquired the van after only three months of the new business. He had helped Bakari to move his acquisitions into the new house at Sinza, when Issa-Mahid eventually allowed him to occupy it. That was the last time Bakari had requested assistance from Omari. He felt uncomfortable over the way Omari pestered him with his personal affairs: wishing to know everything he was doing, where he went and with whom he was spending his spare time. Bakari in turn, was not being given the chance to know anything about the activities of his friend, or his other business ventures.

One day Bakari was having evening tea at a popular tea-room in town with an influential bus operator from Moshi. Omari happened to be passing there and saw them. The following day Bakari had been summoned by Issa-Mahid to his petrol station and given a severe dressing-down, followed by threats. Issa-Mahid had cautioned Bakari to keep away from businessmen from Moshi, citing that they were very crafty and quick to mislead other people. Bakari was annoyed for being reprimanded, but his anger was mainly directed to the man who imparted the news to Issa-Mahid. Bakari did not expect such double-crossing from a man who was supposed to be his friend.

He still handed the briefcase to Omari whenever he arrived from abroad, but lately, that was where their association ended. They would only meet again momentarily, when Omari handed over the proceeds of their business to him. Bakari was increasingly feeling exasperated, and found it unfair that he had to do everything in the business deal through Omari. His audience with Issa-Mahid was only when he was summoned to receive warnings or to be scolded. On one of these admonishment sessions, Bakari had expressed his reservations to Issa-Mahid, but Issa-Mahid had told him that for the business to run according to plan, they had to adhere to the laid-out scheme.

Bakari's face had shown dissatisfaction with Issa-Mahid's verdict, but had quickly cowed into submissiveness when Issa-Mahid popped his eyes out in an intimidating manner. Striking his finger on the desk, he had reminded

Bakari of the oath of allegiance he had taken, and the consequences of violating their agreement. When Bakari was about to step out of the door, Issa-Mahid brought to Bakari's attention that he now slept in a respectable house and ate three times a day because of his generosity. If Bakari kept on grumbling about how the work should be done he could find himself sleeping on verandas and feeding himself from dustbins.

Bakari was back in Sinza. It was in the evening, and he was having his late lunch. With his new found fortune, women were not hard to come by and he now had a steady girlfriend at Ilala. Bakari avoided keeping a woman permanently in his house, as he was convinced that the now fully furnished house had its owner. Bakari was advancing well with the preliminary formalities of bringing back the legitimate owner of the house. The two goats he was ordered to deliver to her uncles' house at Ukonga were long dispatched. One of the goats had been sacrificed immediately upon delivery. Bakari had witnessed the goat being spread on an open fire, and quickly devoured by the hungry folks.

Bakari was also required to deliver three large cocks, to compensate for each child he made with Mwajuma. As a matter of fact, Bakari ended up delivering four cocks, because one of the three he left at the compound of Mwajuma's aunts in Mkulanga was black. According to traditions, as Bakari's purpose was to reconcile with his wife by appeasing her relatives, bringing them a black cock implicated wishing them bad luck. A black cock could only be offered to a medicine-man to make enchantments for someone. The aunts had refused to return the black cock to Bakari upon delivery of a replacement, claiming they were not sure if Bakari would eventually send it to a medicine-man to churn out a powerful spell that would captivate their niece.

On his own initiative, Bakari had also sent three pairs of khangas, inscribed with the right messages to Mwajuma in Mtongani. He had to move all over Dar-es-Salaam to find a green khanga emblazoned: 'I have gone thin thinking of you', and paid twenty thousand shillings for it instead of the usual eight thousand. The red and brown ones with subtle messages 'My heart is aching', and 'I would do anything to be next to you' respectively, were relatively easy to find. He had wrapped the khangas in good colourful foils and delivered them to his trusted emissary. The porter, an aunt of Bakari who at one time lived with him in Tanga, had reported that the presents were received with encouraging enthusiasm, and a shy smile had appeared on the face of the receiver.

Sitting on a lazy chair at the back of the house, Bakari's eyes brightened as the thought of these developments emerged in his mind. His mouth was also celebrating as he ate the lightly spiced rice with roast beef. He had a bottle of an ice cold Serengeti beer next to him on a small stool.

The houseboy came through the back door and informed Bakari that there was a car parked at the front of the house, and the driver wanted to see him. Bakari enquired from the boy the type of car, and the houseboy told him it was a white Isuzu Trooper.

Bakari did not want the guest to come and interrupt him at the back. He had only just begun enjoying his roast meat, and the plate was still full. In addition, there were sacks and boxes of merchandise for his grocery and bar that Bakari did not want his guest to see. Why should Bakari lay everything bare to his associates, whilst they shared very little with him? Lately, his supposed friend had started lying to Bakari about obvious things. Last week he told Bakari that he had sold his restaurant at Kariakoo to an Asian trader months ago. Bakari met the servant-girl working at the restaurant, and she assured him that she was still employed by the same boss, who showed up every evening to collect the day's proceeds.

Bakari rose from the seat, collected three pieces of meat and tossed them into his mouth, then waved at the houseboy.

'Take the plates and put them in the oven,' he said to the boy.

'And the beer, Mzee?'

'Replace the cap firmly and put it in the fridge, next to the freezer; be careful not to spill it!'

Bakari wiped his mouth and approached a tap fixed on the wall. He placed his mouth on the tap and drew some water in his mouth. He rinsed his mouth for a moment, then spat the water on the grass. He then entered the corridor towards the front of the house. There was a door left open, leading to a spare bedroom where he sometimes used to put other commodities. Bakari snarled, and murmured accusations at the houseboy for always forgetting to close the door whenever he cleaned it. Bakari opened the front door and stepped out.

'Salaam Aleikum, did I wake you up?' Omari asked with a smile on his face.

'Salaam, I was wide awake.' Bakari's face was normal and he extended his hand to Omari.

Why should Omari think he was sleeping at that time of the day? the question surfaced in Bakari's mind. His friend had not found him sleeping during the day ever since they knew each other. Even when struck with a bout of malaria, Bakari would be found tucked in a lazy chair in the veranda, but not stretched on a bed. Had Omari lately begun seeing him as someone who was fast asleep and not keeping in touch with what was taking place between Omari and Issa-Mahid? Suspicions were brewing up in Bakari's mind. Ever since he got that glimpse of the full drums of chemicals at Omari's restaurant in Kariakoo, and saw his friend's behaviour following the incident, Bakari's degree of trust over his friend had been diminishing.

'Bakari, I won't be coming in; I just brought you a message from Mahmood.' Omari was talking hesitantly, sometimes avoiding his friend's eyes.

'Nice animal you are having there,' Bakari commented about the sparkling Isuzu waggon with blue and green stripes running on the sides.

'Oh, it is nothing, Bakari; just one of those things in life.'

Omari laughed in a satirical way, and played with the bunch of keys on his hand. He lifted the other hand to touch his balding head, following Bakari's eyes as he surveyed the car, waiting for more praise from him. Bakari just felt the texture of the metallic white paint, and knocked gently at the bonnet of the luxurious four-wheeled drive vehicle.

'By the way, Omari, you left Kariakoo?'

'Ooh yes, I was to tell you that . . . ?'

'But I heard it is four weeks since you moved.' Bakari's voice was low, and a frown appeared on his face.

'Sorry Bakari, I moved to Mikocheni – gosh, surely you have nice stuff in this area.' Omari's face had quickly moved to eye a woman with a big bottom walking on the side of the road. Bakari disregarded Omari's mischief and remembered that Omari had once taken him to the house when he was putting finishing touches to it.

Omari was still looking at the lady disappearing around the corner, shaking his head and murmuring conceited comments. He was hoping Bakari would join him in giving a couple of obtuse comments, as it used to be when they were young or at the time Bakari depended on him for his survival. At that time, Bakari trusted him and would join him in cracking jokes and teasing women passing in front of Omari's restaurant. He had accepted Omari's reasoning that whatever sins he accumulated during the day would be washed out when he went for prayers in the evening.

Bakari was leaning on the station-waggon waiting for Omari to answer his question.

'Now Bakari, let me first tell you the message from Issa-Mahid, as I have to get back to his station right now.'

Bakari looked at the round shoulders of his friend dressed in a new T-shirt. The flannel stretched as it encased the lower part of Omari's abdomen. His chocolate face was shining. The sides of his wide cheeks and lower chin were covered by numerous tiny pimples gained by shaving. His green trousers were fastened a little bit over his big belly, and went down well to a pair of brown leather sandals. His toenails were curved downward, and one or two nails on both feet were missing. Bakari moved his eyes from his friend's well polished feet, back to his chestnut eyes.

'Issa wants you to prepare yourself for an urgent trip tomorrow morning,' Omari said.

'Where to in such a hurry?' Bakari showed signs of disappointment.

'He said you should just pick your passport and bag, and be at the petrol station at six in the morning,' Omari said.

Bakari placed the matchstick he was using to poke his teeth between his lips and patted his shirt pocket. His right hand pulled out a squashed packet of Sportsman, and a match. He withdrew the match from his mouth and placed the cigarette in its position. He crouched down, struck the match on a smooth stone, held his hands around it, then lit the cigarette. Bakari puffed and some of the smoke found its way to his friend's face. Omari made a characteristic snort, twisting his broad nose in a peculiar manner.

'Puff, I can't stand cigarette smoke these days,' Omari complained.

'Oh, since when, Omari?'

'It just somehow chokes me.'

'Oh, sorry for that, then,' Bakari said as he inhaled more smoke.

'Anyway I am on my way, Bakari; don't forget tomorrow morning!'

Bakari did not say anything else; he watched Omari swinging into the leather seats of his station-waggon. The engine started in a blooming purr, before jerking out of the pavement. The dust caused by the wide radial wheels overwhelmed the smoke coming from Bakari's nostrils. He had no chance of expressing his dislike of dust to Omari as the car had already disappeared behind the corner.

Bakari sat again at the back of the house, and reached for the meat on the plate. He placed a large piece in his mouth and chewed. It was already cold and not tasting as nice as before. Bakari reached for the beer glass and put it in his mouth. It was flat, after being kept open for a long time. The taste of the food, coupled with the message Omari brought him, eradicated whatever appetite he had had. He pushed the stool away from him and called the houseboy.

'Take this away,' he said, without looking at him.

'Didn't you like the beef, Mzee?' the young man asked.

'It gets tough when cold.'

Bakari watched the young man slowly collecting the plates, and deduced that there was something he wanted to say.

'Can I drink the rest of the beer, Mzee?' the young man asked in a low voice.

'No!' Bakari said without hesitation.

The young man shrugged his shoulders in a peculiar manner.

'Since when did you learn to drink?' Bakari raised his voice.

'I . . . I thought instead of pouring it away . . .' the boy stammered.

'Have you been drinking my beers lately?' He raised his voice even higher.

'No, Mzee, I swear I have not.' The young man's voice was shaking.

The two eyed each other, and for a moment Bakari gazed at the boy with an uncompromising expression on his face. The young man was wearing tight shorts exposing a pair of smooth thighs. He then remembered the complaints the young man made to him four days earlier, concerning harassments from the broad shouldered butcher living up the street.

'If you drink and continue wearing shorts like that, it will encourage that queer butcher to go after you,' Bakari said.

'You said something, Mzee,' the young man retorted after a while.

'I asked, is the fat butcher still bothering you?' Bakari raised his voice.

'He hasn't touched me again since you talked to him, but he keeps on winking at me, Mzee,' he said in a timid voice.

'I will go and confront him one of these days.'

'Please, Mzee, and I also detest it when he sticks his tongue at me.'

'And you should stop reposing in front of him,' Bakari grunted.

The boy took the stool and moved into the kitchen again. Bakari watched him leave and remained wondering what prompts a man to desire someone of his own gender. He had heard several stories of passionate relationships between men in Dar-es-Salaam, but had not encountered a vivid case. Bakari consequently disputed the arguments that the habit was widespread along the East African coast. He came from a coastal region himself, and did not have any feelings towards another man. He considered himself straight and totally masculine. The young, freaky men he saw dancing the indecent Chakacha dance some time ago, were said to be involved in fostering that immoral act.

As for the queer butcher, Bakari usually saw him shuffling his heavy feet on the dusty roads of Sinza, wearing a worn out white cap and oversized tunics. He was big, with a massive belly, endowed with round eyes and kept his mouth perpetually open. He talked throwing his hands around, and always winced his body in a peculiar way. Bakari had yet to confront him over his houseboy's complaints that he had been pinching his buttocks. Bakari had once witnessed the butcher in a brawl, and had appreciated his punching power. It was safer for Bakari to approach him in a cautious and diplomatic manner.

Bakari glanced at his watch and rubbed a little scratch on the side of the glass. He was thinking of walking to the Deluxe Bar to get some fresh air. The Deluxe had a television set and video recorder, and showed exciting movies in the evening. He had vowed to come with his own television set and video recorder next time he travelled overseas, but was not yet comfortable with the security situation at the house. When he left in the morning to do his business, and the houseboy went to the market, the house remained without anyone. Video recorders were hot property to thieves, and a small opportunity given to them would be used with terrible efficiency. The thieves are capable of jacking up the burglar bars and yanking the electronic devices hidden in any part of the room.

If there was someone else staying in the house when he and the houseboy were out, this could guarantee the safety of his newly acquired property. This awakened in him another sentimental feeling. If his wife was there with the kids, the house would not be left deserted at any time. The kids would play around and liven the house, bringing the warmth required and deter any intruder from taking a chance. The mother of the house would organise the furniture, utensils, and other possessions, bringing the liaison lacking in the house.

The sudden trip overseas Bakari was to undertake, threatened to interrupt the strategy he was trying to win Mwajuma back into his life. In a day or two, Bakari was planning to send to Mtongani a suitcase full of clothes for his three kids. At the weekend, to celebrate Idd-el-Hadji, he had organised a surprise boat trip to Zanzibar with Mwajuma. According to Bakari's plans, and the way he knew Mwajuma, she would not have the heart to turn down such a trip. She would just buy time before accepting the offer, to demonstrate to him all over again that she was hard to get. Bakari was convinced she would eventually succumb and show up at the boat's breakwater bay early on Friday morning. Bakari would not have wasted his time, but put his case to her point blank, and make sure Mwajuma moved to Sinza the following Monday.

He walked down the street, and some dust was blown on his face. Bakari covered his eyes for a while and spat. A motorcycle passed him, going to the other side of the street. The rider wore a helmet, but the passenger he was carrying behind him had his bald head exposed. The little scar patch on the passenger's head reminded Bakari of the man he met yesterday morning on the other side of Sinza township. At first Bakari had failed to recognise the assistant logistic manager as he walked towards him. It was only when five feet remained before approaching him, that Bakari realised who the man was. Bakari gasped in disbelief to see the man he once hated, and who he held responsible for his dismissal from the port, in such a despicable state.

'Kibosho, is it really you?' Bakari had gasped, and immediately the grudges he held against his former assistant manager disappeared. It was obvious that he was in crisis from the way he appeared. The belly that used to hang below his belt was no longer there. His cheeks were drawn in, and he had grey hair all over his head. Worse, he walked unsteadily, knocking his knees. The assistant manager's voice was not the usual authoritative blare he used to intimidate Bakari and his friends.

He had admitted to Bakari without reservations that he had lost his job and was destitute. 'Kibosho, tell me what had happened to you?' Bakari even dared to address him using the derogative name given to him by the workers he used to terrorise at the fumigation section. The pitiful man had recited in brief about the fresh scandal that had rocked the Port and sent, amongst others, the fumigation section into upheaval. The latest scandalous earthquake shook the whole Port management, resulting in firing of personnel, and transfers. As was always the case, the topmost echelon remained unscathed, only shuffled from one department to the other. Those who bore the blunt of the tremor were the likes of Kibosho, who left their desks unceremoniously, bundled into the back of police vans.

Before Bakari parted with Kibosho, the former manager had divulged a secret that left Bakari totally baffled. Concerning the ugly scar on his head, Kibosho had told Bakari it was inflicted by unknown men who assaulted him on the streets a month earlier. Kibosho was not convinced that the motive of the assailants was to mug him, but suspected they could be some former employees at the Port, or henchmen of his new boss. The real shock to Bakari came when Kibosho revealed the name of his new boss. He was staying in Mikocheni, and Kibosho suspected he could have been responsible for him losing his job and spending nine months at the Ukonga prison.

Bakari thought for a while as he took a seat at the Deluxe Bar. 'You should not fully trust another man in this world,' Kibosho had sadly said to Bakari when they parted. Bakari was beginning to get the meaning of this statement as he thought of his business partners. Each day that passed, and following each overseas trip he took, his partners grew richer, but kept him further from knowing the other details of their trade, besides carrying the brown leather bag. The waitress arrived at Bakari's table and greeted him. She was smiling at him as he was generous in offering tips.

'Your usual, isn't it?' she asked him.

Bakari was still immersed in thoughts, sometimes nibbling his fingernails. He then looked at the short woman talking to him.

'No, I will have Kilimanjaro instead,' Bakari replied.

'Ai, you have resigned from Serengeti?' she said while gesturing to him.

'Bring a warm Kilimanjaro, so that I can drink it quickly.'

Bakari watched her moving away, and wondered what type of a man would be attracted to a woman like that. Apart from her lean, flat chest, she stood on dry, slender legs, that supported a small back. What she lacked in beauty was compensated for by her quick service and good nature. That was the reason why Bakari always left her with a tip. They also served nice goat's meat at the Deluxe. When Bakari came craving for some roast goat with hot pimento he would look for that particular waitress, as she would surely come with a plateful of selected savoury roasted chops.

Lately Bakari had been having painful cramps in his joints and tendons. A medical assistant friend of his had warned him against taking lots of goat's meat. The effect of too much indulgence had already shown itself and there was a danger that it could provoke a severe case of gout that could impair his movements. He had taken some medication given to him by the same medical assistant, and was feeling better. The notion that he should quit eating roast goat's meat and reduce the beer he took was hard for Bakari to accept. What would be left for him to enjoy then? Should he drink soda and chew sweets at his age?

They had been telling him the dangers of so many things and he was now getting confused. He was told to abstain from dating women as he could catch an incurable disease. He shouldn't eat fatty foods as he would get a heart attack. They warned him against smoking otherwise he might contract lung cancer. He was waiting to be told not even to come out of his house otherwise the decaying and neglected buildings of Dar-es-Salaam might crumble on his head.

The waitress had placed the beer on the table and opened the cap using an opener made from a cow's horn.

'Why, what is going on with you today?' she asked him.

'I have to leave for somewhere soon,' Bakari said as he downed a whole glass.

'Aha, to someone I know, isn't it?'

'No, not what you are thinking,' Bakari said without even looking at the barmaid.

'If not a woman, what are you thinking of?' She winked at him.

'I am thinking of business deals.'

'Ai, you have changed a lot these days,' she smiled at him.

Bakari took the last glass and lifted it to his mouth. He then belched loudly, took his purse, and offered a five hundred shillings note to the lady. He waved at her not to bother looking for the fifty shillings change. She smiled at him and acknowledged the tip. Only a few clients in that part of the city were generous or cultured enough to leave tips to the waiters. Bakari was thus making a name for himself as a man who was well off, not stingy, and a true gentleman. He stood up and pushed the chair behind him. Bakari made his way to Shekilango Road and waited for a bus.

He watched a new BMW saloon with a low spoiler moving slowly along the road. The spoiler kept on scratching on the big bumps along the rough road. The BMW was not the type of car to be used on Dar-es-Salaam roads. It was made for European roads that were flawless. As the car passed him, Bakari observed that the driver was a young man with a clean-shaven head and an earring in one ear. The other ear was kept busy with a cellular phone. He was driving, at the same time talking loudly on the mobile phone, so that Bakari could hear the contents of his conversation. Bakari suspected that the person on the other end of the line had hearing problems, or the line was so bad that the young man had to shout like that. When the young man finished the last hump on Shekilango Road, he pushed his foot on the accelerator and roared down the road.

An open three-ton truck stopped near Bakari and the conductor shouted out that it was going to Magomeni. Bakari saw that there were plenty of empty seats, but would not clamber on it. He found it rather risky and cumbersome to hold on the hanging rope and hoist himself over the drop-sides to reach the seats. Besides the inconvenience, he considered himself to have outgrown the era of clambering on these transporters, vulgarly known in Dar-es-Salaam as 'Chai-Maharages'. Bakari turned his face and looked away, waiting for a more presentable minibus to come along.

The minibus rattled into some pot-holes as it made its way past the Jangwani grounds. Bakari looked through the window of the Hiace and shook his head. The road was recently repaired, but already had so many pot-holes. No one was doing anything at the city council, Bakari thought to himself. The Toyota minibus took a turn towards Magomeni Mapipa and the conductor hanging at the door banged hard on the side of the bus. The driver stopped in the middle of the road and the passengers got out. Drivers of other vehicles following from behind hooted in distress, some of them shouting abusive words at the driver of the minibus.

The minibus moved on, negotiated another turn, and Bakari signalled to the young man at the door. The young man slapped the bus again. The bus this time left the road, moved to the side, and Bakari got out. Bakari walked down the steps made on the escarpment, till he reached a gravel road.

Suddenly he heard noises from behind him. Bakari turned and saw a group of about twenty young men, women, and children running down the street. He stood on the side of the pavement to let the crowd pass. As they approached he noticed that there was a man wrapped in khangas and forcibly made to run ahead of the crowd. He had seen such multitudes before, and Bakari was convinced it was another of those notorious thieves being given a hiding.

The crowds were singing, jeering, and clapping their hands as they pushed forward the culprit.

'Adulterous, adulterous!' the women's exuberant voices were heard above those of men and children.

The victim was sometimes showered with sand and plant leaves. He even had flowers and bird's feathers stuck in his unruly hair. Bakari realised the throng was not beating a thief, but were in a 'Kindumbwendumbwe' session. The poor devil must have been caught sleeping with someone's wife, and was now being made to pay for his sinful deeds. He was being paraded along the streets, receiving blows, being pelted with stones, spat at by women, and insulted by men. By that time the crowds passed where Bakari was standing, he got the opportunity of observing the victim from close quarters.

His face had been smeared with oil, and several flowers tucked in his hair. He was bare breasted with a khanga wrapped on his waist. He appeared not to be wearing anything else under the khanga. The one who caught him on the act with his wife must have removed his underpants before handing him over to the multitudes to begin the Kindumbwendumbwe session. His face was showing great distress, pain and humiliation. If he were a thief, he would have been a dead man by now. As this was an adulterous affair, the crowds had another agenda for him.

'He is one of us now!' the women were chanting gaily.

'Yes,' someone spoke from the crowd, 'he has already been deflowered by the husband of the woman he was caught with.'

Bakari tried to make meaning of the statement, but no one was prepared to stop and explain to him. The crowd just ran down the street with their victim. He stood aside until all the participants had passed and the dust settled.

Bakari continued walking with his hands in his pockets. It had been a while since he last strolled in the streets of Magomeni. He had always bypassed Magomeni when coming from Ubungo where he had once stayed for a while. Magomeni was considered to be too near to the city centre by bus, and it was regarded uneconomical to stop by when coming from Ubungo, and have to pay the full fare again to the city centre. For those walking on foot, Magomeni was judged to be too far from the city if you had to drop off there then walk all the way to Dar-es-Salaam city centre on foot. It was thus not strange for people from Kimara, Ubungo, and even Manzese to stay for a long time without visiting the township.

Walking along the faded, tarred street, Bakari appreciated that despite the pitiful condition of the streets in Magomeni, at least they were better made and maintained than those of Sinza. The township was popular with the first crop of African politicians conceived during the days of the struggle for independence. It was by then considered a township for the elite and upcoming African young men and women.

The African politicians resided there, because they were denied living in areas reserved for Europeans and Asians. When they left the township after independence and moved to the posh areas previously excluded from them, most forgot to come back and visit those they had left behind. The tarred roads that were built by the colonial authority were left to decay into trenches, some turning to gravel roads again. These thoughts came into Bakari's mind particularly when he stumbled into some of the furrows along the streets, coming close to spraining his ankles.

Bakari eventually reached a little house at the corner of Njombe Street, and made his way past the veranda. He had to go around two streets before discovering that obscure and sewage infested street at the end of Mapipa. Some old scrap cars were abandoned on the side of Njombe Street and made the remaining width of the road passable only by pedestrians. The scraps had been left as fossils, as most of the flat metal parts had been cut off to make charcoal stoves. Two or three soiled ducks and hens splattered in the muddy waters looking for worms to feed on.

He entered the house that was made of clay and cement blocks, and knocked at the second room on the corridor. Bakari knew he would find the man at home. The battered chap had no money, lived in a cramped room, and had no friends. With these predicaments, a man had few places to go. He had long ago sent his wife and kids to Moshi, and remained behind to face life head on. Being unemployed, and depending on sporadic businesses to make money, makes life unbearable in a city like Dar-es-Salaam.

The man opened the door and smiled at Bakari. At least someone had taken the trouble to come and see him. He felt embarrassed, especially when remembering the tumultuous times when they were together at the Port.

'Kibosho,' Bakari called him, 'where is a nice bar around here, where we can sit, have a beer, some meat, and talk business?'

'Thank you for thinking of me, Bakari.' Kibosho's eyes were full of remorse.

'Let's go,' Bakari said.

'Very few people remember even to greet me these days.'

'No sweat. I think we can talk some things of common interest,' Bakari said as he held his arm.

They were about to leave, and Bakari looked at the former manager's weak frame. His hair was thinning, while his body seemed to be declining. It could be a result of the difficult conditions he was going through, but the rash on his arms, sizable pimples on the sides of his mouth, and the dryness of his skin was something anyone would be concerned with. The man was constantly turning to look backwards and sideways, as if haunted by someone.

'Bakari,' he hesitated, blinking his eyes repeatedly.

'You said something, Kibosho?'

'The landlord does not allow me to leave the house.'

'Why?' Bakari seemed surprised.

'He says till I pay the last two months' rent.'

'Don't be silly, how can he do that?'

'That is his order, I cannot go further than the veranda.'

'I can't believe you have been cowed like this, my dear assistant manager.'

'Life is tough for me, Bakari.'

'I know all about this rent thing – how much do you owe him?'

'Seven and a half thousand,' he said in a low voice, looking at Bakari with his sickly eyes.

Bakari remained quiet for a while, then took the little notebook from his shirt pocket. A chain fell out of the notebook, and he bent down to collect it. It was a twenty four carat necklace that had a solid golden heart hanging on it. Bakari lifted the necklace close to his face and examined it with a smile.

It looked sumptuous and an item that could overwhelm whoever would be the recipient. Kibosho was also glancing at the ornament suspended on his friend's broad hands.

'I got it from a street vendor for only five thousand shillings,' he said to Kibosho.

'Five what? The jeweller's price for that necklace could be as high as forty thousand!' Kibosho quickly replied.

'It is from these young boys, they don't even know the value of gold.'

'Who are you going to present it to, Bakari?' Kibosho asked with a smile on his face.

'None of your business.'

The man made a croaking laugh and coughed. His health looked quite controversial.

'Okay Kibosho, take this ten thousand note, call the vagabond landlord here, throw it to him, and tell him to keep the change.'

'I would rather keep the change myself.' Kibosho sounded sombre.

'I say this is my money; I will give you money if you cooperate with me!'

Kibosho grabbed the money and rushed through the corridor to the back of the shabby house. Bakari sympathised with him as he shuffled his feet along the corridor. Despite the animosity the former manager had shown him at the Stores Department, Bakari saw no need to hold grudges on him any more. The man was going through tremendous hardship, and his physique was crumbling. He had served a prison sentence, lost everything in life, and was left as a wretched of the land. Which hunter wastes his bullets on a dying beast? What he saw from Kibosho was a warning of how a man can be when everything has gone wrong with his life. Bakari was determined not to find himself again in a similar situation of having a noisy and disrespectful landlord shouting at him.

When he came back from the forthcoming trip abroad, Bakari planned to confront Issa-Mahid with a proposal to purchase the Sinza house. He reckoned that he had made sufficient money for his boss for him to be prudent enough and keep his promise of letting Bakari keep the house.

A while later, Kibosho reappeared at the veranda. The wrinkles on his chapped face had disappeared and a placard of relief was evident in its place.

'Let's walk to the Mapipa Sunlight Bar, they roast delicious goat's meat,' Kibosho said in a panting voice.

Only a few cars moved on the streets at that time of the day. The two men could walk in the middle of the street, thus avoiding stepping in the numerous channels of dirty and sewage water emanating from the various houses.

'Since when did you know your new boss?' Bakari asked the man seated on the opposite chair at the Mapipa Sunlight.

'Quite a while ago,' Kibosho said as he lowered the beer glass onto the plastic table and licked his lips.

'Did you know that Omari and I were associated?' Bakari made a direct enquiry to his mate, looking at him in the eyes.

The former assistant manager shied his face from Bakari's eyes and licked his lips again. The lips were so dry and chapped he had to keep them daubed with saliva all the time. It appeared as if he was looking for the appropriate words to respond to his previous subordinate. Today, Kibosho was answerable to Bakari and felt embarrassed.

'I mean, Kibosho, did you know of the chemicals deal between me and Omari?' Bakari raised his voice a bit.

'Yes, Bakari,' Kibosho said quietly, and downed the rest of the beer from the glass.

Bakari tapped on the table and heaved. He took his glass but failed to drink from it. He placed it down and looked at Kibosho again. He now noticed that Kibosho had another wide scar on his chest. Bakari wondered where he got that one from; nonetheless, he saw no reason to probe him over his personal life. He might have been attacked by gangsters and survived, so asking him could revoke painful memories. Yet someone who had been working at the Port with Bakari before he left, had alleged that the store's deputy manager was at one time involved in a car hijacking racket using arms of war.

Bakari thought Kibosho could have got the scar from his smuggling activities, but had no way of confirming his suspicions. Bakari was aware that the manager was immensely hated at the Port, and when someone is hated, many allegations about him do appear from many quarters. From the dubious ventures the former manager used to do at the Port, the various allegations about his personal life, and his deceitful look, Bakari was aware that he was not seated with a saint. The man had his weaknesses and shortcomings, like every other man intending to survive in the harsh and difficult terrain of Dar-es-Salaam. Bakari was not concerned with all these; he had another agenda with him.

'Tell me more about what you know, Kibosho,' Bakari said.

'At the time you and Omari were on the chemicals' deal, Omari was also my associate, responsible for distributing a larger consignment which we organised to deliver at his place.'

Bakari called the barmaid and instructed her to bring another bottle of

Safari lager for his companion. Bakari turned to the table and eyed Kibosho again.

'And what happened then?'

'You see, Bakari, every time I went to Omari to collect my part, he would give me less than a third of the cash I expected.'

'What would be his explanations?' Bakari's eyes were now wider with excitement.

'He would tell me his agents stole the money, or lost the consignment.'

A while passed without either of the men saying anything. Bakari's eyes were attracted to an old picture of a Masai warrior leaning on his spear. He supported himself on one leg and folded the other at the knee. They were Africa's most photographed tribe. It made Bakari wonder whether the interest was generated out of their traditional clothing and pierced ears, or was it a fashion for every tourist coming to East Africa to photograph a Masai? They were proud of their culture and that was admirable, but it was another issue to be made into objects of marvel. Bakari was not in agreement with that viewpoint.

Kibosho cleared his throat and called Bakari's name:

'Do you know whom Omari said was his main agent, and responsible for most of the misappropriation?'

'May I take a guess?' Bakari's voice was down with apprehension.

'You are right, Bakari; unfortunately your name always popped out of Omari's mouth.'

The plate of roast goat's meat was already on its way. Kibosho could not wait for the plate to be lowered on the table. His trembling fingers were reaching for a couple of meat chops.

Bakari took his glass and kept it in his hand, his right arm supported on his lap. He was full of thoughts and kept quiet. He turned to look sideways and got a vision of the Seventh Street of Tanga Municipality. Nearly twenty years ago, in a house made of coconut palms, a young man had lain sick with a severe headache. His health was so critical that some local Sheiks had come to read for him some verses from the holy book. Despite the prayers, the young man still gulped and coughed with his tongue sticking out. Earlier on, when he started showing these symptoms, the young man's relatives had summoned a renowned Zigua medicine-man to come and attend to their kinsman. The medicine-man had come with his appropriate pots, sea shells and beads, and performed an elaborate healing session. Upon the traditional doctor's departure, the young man's temperature had soared even higher.

When Bakari finally arrived and took the critical patient to Mkwakwani hospital, the doctors found he had chronic malaria, and he was treated with quinine drops fed directly into the normal drip solution. According to the doctors' assertion, if the young man had remained at home for six more hours, he would not have survived. After three days at the hospital, the patient was on his feet and was allowed to go home.

Bakari had saved Omari's life because he was his friend. That friend lived to betray him and caused misery to him and his family. Bakari sighed loudly and looked at Kibosho. The former assistant manager was busy munching the goat's meat. Bakari sympathised with him; maybe he had not eaten meat for a while.

'It is said that once you help someone, don't hang around expecting to be thanked,' Bakari said.

'To correct you, Bakari, they say don't wake up someone who is asleep; otherwise you will fall asleep yourself,' the sacked manager said.

At that time, Bakari realised Kibosho had already eaten three quarters of the meat on the plate, while he had not touched even a piece.

'Kibosho, I have a job for you, will you cooperate?'

'Anything, Bakari. It is time for the injured to work together, and get compensated for the injustices done to them.'

Kibosho had finished a third bottle of beer, and the night was still young. Bakari had to get up early in the following morning to be at Kariakoo by six. That meant waking up at four in the morning, preparing himself, and catching two buses in order to make it for the appointment. Issa-Mahid, besides being a Swahili, was very strict with time, especially when he had to do the waiting. His numerous mistresses were aware that if he promised to pick them at five, they had to be at the agreed point at five, even if he ended up turning up at six owing to unforeseen circumstances. If he miraculously happened to turn up exactly at five and found she was not there, that would be the end of the relationship.

'Kibosho, before you start your next beer, let me explain to you the details of the job I want you to do.'

'Go ahead, Bakari, I am still sober!'

# CHAPTER 10

Bakari sat at the pavement, took a cigarette and lit it. Ten minutes remained before six, and the morning was nice and moderate. The usual heat at that time of the morning was not there today. Many buses were already moving in the streets, overwhelmed by a fleet of Toyota Hiaces competing for passengers on their way to work. Mahmood's petrol station began work at six in the morning; at that time the attendants were making the necessary preparations, such as checking meters and preparing water buckets.

Bakari peered at the gate of the station, expecting to see any of Mahmood's cars appearing, as the time had already gone to quarter past six. It was not easy to predict which car he would pitch up with, on any day of the week. When Issa-Mahid went home for lunch, he might come back in the afternoon in a different car. Those who observed him were baffled by his style. They didn't see any reason, if he already possessed a new four wheel Toyota Landcruiser, why he should need a Mitsubishi Pajero, Nissan Patrol and a Range Rover? What bothered the observers most was Mahmood's style of work and meeting places.

He had a desk, files and a telephone in every one of his business sites, in addition to the two mobile telephones in his pockets. No one could tell for sure in which office he would be working the following day. It was very common for him to start in the morning, say, at his hotel, and end up the day in the restaurant along Independence Avenue. Only when he fixed an appointment with someone would he be at the designated place. Even then the time of his arrival would be equally baffling. Mahmood could arrive at six in the morning for a meeting scheduled at eight. His critics had acknowledged that he had the instincts of a cat. He would choose his steps, and calculate his moves. He was a man who thinks before he leaps.

Bakari kept on waiting, not caring what other people thought of the man he was expecting to meet. What occupied his mind now were issues pertaining to his own concern. He appreciated that he was in association with a real enemy. When he faced Omari the next time, he would handle him with caution the way he did when attending to live electric wires. The chemicals he had been smuggling from the Port, according to his conviction, were to be sold to enable him and his dear friend Omari raise some extra money for their families. His friend, on the other hand, was using the opportunity to enrich himself and poison the very man who was risking his life and career to help him. Bakari brushed his head in an attempt to rid his mind of those disturbing thoughts at that moment.

As Bakari sat on the hard surface, he tried to work out the reason that prompted Issa-Mahid to summon him to Kariakoo. If the reason was simply to send him to a trip, he could have given the ticket, money for spending, and the sacred bag to Omari as was always the case. Omari was available and came to see him yesterday; why wasn't he included in the meeting today?

On the other side of the road Bakari saw a face he always saw in the local television station walking hurriedly down the road. The man must be hurrying to work, shrivelling his feet on the tarmac. The newsreader was supposed to be a celebrity, and a celebrity should at least be a person in a position to afford the basic things in life such as a car, even if it were a simple one. Bakari quickly remembered that amongst the things the country lacked was a celebrity class. It had no movie stars, artists or sports personnel of local and international standing. The only appreciated and celebrated personalities belonged to the political and ruling clique.

Twenty past six and the boss had not shown up. If Bakari knew Mahmood was going to be that late, he would have retreated to a tearoom along Uhuru Street and had some tea. He had woken up early, journeyed to Kariakoo, and had had no time for breakfast. Bakari kept on looking at the passers-by, knocking his knuckles on the empty barrel next to where he sat.

Memories of his long conversation with Kibosho the previous night surfaced in his mind and caused the smoothness on his brow to crinkle with wrinkles. Some time ago, he had a glimpse of drums full of chemicals at Omari's restaurant. Bakari had totally forgotten about those drums until Kibosho mentioned that Omari was hoarding chemical drums in his storeroom, and had collected other containers which he used to dilute the chemicals before distributing them to his clients. Kibosho had also revealed to Bakari that he and other senior officials at the stores department were purposely purchasing chemicals that were approaching expiry dates so that they might easily dispose of them. As the chemicals were resold in other containers it was not possible for the clients to know the chemicals were out of their useful shelf life.

When Omari felt that he no longer needed his business partners to supply

143

him with the chemicals, he decided to play them against each other. The time the rubbish disposal truck approached the area next to the old containers where Bakari's smuggled drums were hidden, the deputy manager had placed security personnel to intercept the truck when the drums were being loaded. The manager had been tipped off by Omari.

Bakari got these hints as Kibosho downed another bottle of Safari lager. Bakari had always wondered why the scandal had not led to his immediate dismissal from work or even being jailed. 'The way I knew Omari, made me hesitant to fire you. I was not sure what he could do to me. He could have planned that in revenge, you would organise hooligans to beat or even kill me,' Kibosho had confessed.

Bakari was forced to order a plate of cow hoofs and gravy made of offal, to keep Kibosho talking. He had talked and revealed a lot. A hot gravy prepared with plenty of green pepper provoked more thirst, so more beer had to be provided for Kibosho. He ate and drank like that but remained so thin. Bakari wondered what Kibosho's body did with all the food he consumed. Kibosho's thinness could have been provoked by frustrations of losing his job, but it shouldn't have been followed by ugly pimples over his face and neck.

The man's health was not an issue of great concern to Bakari. Kibosho's willingness to cooperate and take part in a master-plan Bakari had designed to avenge the wrongs done to him was all he wanted. It was time Bakari also played the same game his associates were playing on him. The outcome of the plot would also ensure that what had been deprived from him was compensated. Kibosho had grudges with his boss as well, but yielded to him to earn the meagre wages he survived on. No one else had come to Kibosho's rescue after losing his managerial position at the Port.

As part of the wider plot against Omari, Kibosho had even suggested poisoning him. Bakari had hesitated at that idea, suggesting that he did not want his hands soiled by someone's blood. He would just let his criminal associates sort themselves out without his involvement.

A loud siren went in a nearby factory. Bakari looked at his watch and turned to watch uniformed men rushing into the building. Without doubt it did mark the start of production. The factory started work very early in the morning, observed Bakari. If work started at half past six, when did the workers leave their houses, taking into consideration the transport problem? He was biting his fingernails again as he sat thinking of other people's issues. Along the road, two little children in school uniform, each held by a man and a woman, were talking and shrieking loudly. They looked happy, and the couple that was walking down with the kids were young and well dressed. They ought to be a happy family, Bakari presumed.

When the word family crossed his mind, a flash of relief resurfaced in Bakari's heart. His resourceful aunt had brought encouraging news from her last visit to Mtongani. Mwajuma had enquired about the health of her husband, and wanted to know who he was staying with at the new house. The aunt had divulged everything about the house to Mwajuma, and her interest grew. It had taken nearly an hour of narration, without the aunt forgetting to emphasise that there was a gas stove and a double door fridge in the kitchen. The aunt revealed to Mwajuma of Bakari's plans to bring along a television set and video recorder on his next trip overseas. There was also the hint of Bakari acquiring a beautiful car. She assured Mwajuma that her nephew had not brought any other woman in the house, but cautioned her about the dangers of delaying in making decisions. 'Men are so weak and vulnerable, my dear sister-in-law; act now, or you will live to regret it,' the aunt had declared as she left the house in Mtongani.

The aunt had turned up at Bakari's house to give him the news. As it was always the custom in Dar- es-Salaam when someone came to visit with good news, Bakari had sent his houseboy to a nearby bottle store to purchase five beers. She drank three and Bakari had two. The aunt was large and talked loudly and aggressively. Bakari had agreed to her proposition to purchase for her two large cool-boxes she needed for selling frozen juices in the market. The aunt had also suggested that Bakari find her a pair of khangas similar to one of those he took to Mwajuma, except that the messages written on them should be different.

She realised the dangers of wearing a khanga that had the same message as the one Mwajuma was wearing, especially if it happened that they met at her house. Mwajuma could end up misunderstanding the aunt, and get confused about her intentions. The words imprinted on a khanga are supposed to send a message to the reader that is considered much more powerful than the wearer can say with her own mouth. Being a mediator, the aunt had to take an unbiased stance to both parties. If she were to spot a pair of khangas that gave out the same message as that Mwajuma wished to convey, there could be a misinterpretation that could easily end up in a conflict. Swahili women knew this very well and were always taking precautions.

A blue BMW made its way into the petrol station, and jerked to a stop at the side of the main building. The number plates were peculiar: a white plate with the letters written in light blue. Between the letters was an emblem, or coat of arms, that was unfamiliar to Bakari. There was a sticker on the bonnet with the words 'I love Gauteng' clearly visible even from afar. Bakari had heard of the name being of a city or town, but he could not recall in what country it was. What he was aware of was that he had seen quite a few luxurious cars with similar number plates moving in town.

From loose talk he picked up in town, he understood that the cars came from what was popularly termed as 'down South'. He overheard some people suggesting that the cars were cheaper to get than those from Japan or the Middle-East, and Bakari was not surprised as he had even seen young men, those wearing earrings on one ear, driving Mercedes Benzes bearing funny number plates. The Benzes were almost brand new, looking extraordinarily elegant, except for damaged door locks or broken windows, usually replaced with polyethylene sheets.

The windows of the luxurious saloon car that had just pulled in were heavily tinted, so that it was impossible to determine who was the driver, or how many people were in the car. From the way the BMW drove into the petrol station, it was not difficult to surmise who had just arrived. As soon as Mahmood came out of the car, he began shouting at a petrol attendant, asking why the drums of oil littered the entrance of the office. With his hands on his waist, Mahmood called the foreman, and in a high voice inquired something from him, the meaning of which Bakari could not interpret. Maybe Bakari's attention was distracted by the long, straight hair of Mahmood's passenger as she came out of the car. She had lazily pushed the door back and it partially shut itself with a gentle click.

Bakari glanced at his watch: it was ten to eight. His back was stiff, as a result of the long period he had spent sitting on the elevated wall. His host had arrived, but was still surveying the compound, occasionally shaking his head. It appeared that Mahmood was a man who liked perfection and got easily agitated to see things not done according to his standards. Mahmood walked to the other side of the building, and Bakari could hear him shouting from there. Finally, Mahmood realized Bakari's existence, and waved at him to follow him into the office. He left the young woman dressed in black tights pacing up and down on the pavement with her handbag slung over her shoulder.

Bakari reached the innermost office of Mahmood. It was not new to him, as he had taken his oath in it. Only on this occasion did Bakari realise how weird it actually looked. It could only be accessed after going through two doors. The office had a single window, and a split unit air-conditioner refreshing it. There was a big, old safe on the wall that seemed to have been built and reinforced with hard steel. There were pictures hanging on the wall, and from the way they hung, it looked as if they were moved from time to time, or concealing something on the wall.

Mahmood took a white phone on the edge of the table and pressed on the digits. He then lifted up the receiver and held it close to his ear. Mahmood waited for a while without saying anything, then replaced the receiver. He then pressed an air-phone on the wall and spoke to the doorman, who always stood outside the door, dressed in military boots, cap and uniform and clutching a big baton on his hand. Mahmood asked him to take the girl he came with to the guest lounge and make her comfortable. The guard was also ordered to tell the tea lady to provide the girl with soft drinks and snacks.

Mahmood appeared to be thinking of something, then suddenly turned to Bakari who had all the time been sitting quietly on the chair in front of Mahmood's desk. His face appeared stunned, as if Bakari had just sprung up from the floor and suddenly appeared in front of him. His lips moved a bit but no words came out of his mouth. He just held his hands together, and brushed his freshly shaven chin. Mahmood then widened his eyes and leaned forward on the desk, facing Bakari.

Bakari also stared at the thin moustache of his boss. He felt annoyed that Mahmood had used another ten minutes since he walked into his office without even acknowledging his presence in the room. Mahmood could be having lots of things preoccupying his mind, but at least he should have greeted Bakari, and found out how he had woken up that morning. Bakari was suspicious that Omari might have lied to him about the meeting time. It appeared as if Mahmood did not necessarily want him that early. Even eight o'clock would have been acceptable. A flash of anger crossed Bakari's face when he perceived Omari's mischief. He however consoled himself, knowing that he would soon find a way of putting a stop to his friend's roguery.

'Bakari, something is very serious here!' Mahmood said, interrupting his tormenting thoughts.

Glittering and finely polished gold rings decorated Mahmood's fingers on both hands. He always wore open-necked shirts that exposed a thick golden chain. Another chain hang on his left wrist, and moved to and fro when he gestured with his hairy hands.

'Mzee, first let me say "Shikamoo" as we did not even get a chance to greet each other this morning,' Bakari said in a voice that was softer than usual.

'I am telling you, someone is trying to play a monkey trick on the business,' Issa-Mahid virtually snapped back at Bakari.

147

'What tricks, Mzee?'

'Guys, remember what we pledged to each other!' Issa-Mahid said with his thin moustache moving up and down, 'one of us will soon be turned into food for the hyenas in the forest.'

'But, what has happened, Mzee?' Bakari's voice was tainted with uncertainty.

'Wait, I am the one who is doing the talking!' Issa-Mahid snapped again.

Bakari was very much aware that Issa-Mahid could be a very dangerous man if annoyed. He had heard of Issa-Mahid's ruthlessness when dealing with his adversaries. As a renowned mafia boss, he would not hesitate to shed the blood of any of his associates, or workers whom he suspected to be double crossing him. He had his hit-men carrying pistols, and he would assign them to different tasks when there was a necessity. The former owner of the hotel Mahmood acquired, was found in the valleys of Msimbazi with a bullet lodged in his head, and the police could not find the murderers.

Mahmood initially ran the Kariakoo petrol station as a junior partner with his distant uncle, who perished in a freak accident along the Mikumi road on his way to Iringa. The death had aroused a lot of speculation, as Mahmood had been seen in Morogoro the same night the accident happened. Mahmood had denied the allegations, saying that he had not left Dar-es-Salaam that whole week.

His most spectacular stunt was a gun battle between him and another gang-leader in Kunduchi. Residents of that area were kept awake at three in the morning as the two men exchanged fire near the beach. When Issa-Mahid realised that the opposite side could not fire any more, he quickly rushed to a nearby police station and reported that a gang of people had fired at him and tried to hijack his car. Issa-Mahid said he fired back and put his foot on the accelerator. The bandits had kept on firing at his car but he managed to outrun them. To add more weight to his story, Issa-Mahid had fired one shot at his own car, at the fender on top of the front wheel, to appear as if the shot came from the bandits.

The police had gone to comb the area Issa-Mahid had indicated to them and found a body with two bullet holes in the chest. The police also found a pistol still on the wrist of the bandit with a light-brown complexion. Issa-Mahid was only called to make a statement, before they took the curly-haired and bearded body of the deceased to the mortuary. The authorities had accepted Issa-Mahid's story, and the matter ended there. Being a prudent man, Issa-Mahid had offered a modest cheque to the authorities in appreciation of their understanding and kindness to him.

It was only recently that someone narrated these stories to Bakari, so he gawped at Issa-Mahid with awe.

'Someone is tampering with the powder!' Mahmood croaked, pushing his head forward.

Bakari felt a slight chill forming on his back. As there were only three people in the syndicate, Bakari could suspect only one person. Whenever he arrived from overseas trips the bag was collected from him at the airport. Even when he was sent to deliver a consignment, the bag would be brought to the airport and offered into his hands only when he was about to check in. Bakari had no access to its false compartments. The furthest he had extended his fingers was to sample the different spices that were always packed in the open compartments. The mixture of spices and strong deodorants were used to make the sniffer dogs sneeze when they attended to his bag.

'Mzee, you know yourself that I don't even know what the powder looks like.' Bakari's voice was unsteady.

'I swear to Satan himself, that I am going to find out who among us is responsible, and when I discover him . . . let me not finish.'

Mahmood suddenly stood up, jerked back his chair, and moved to a cupboard where he took the bag Bakari had got accustomed to. He turned it upside down and tapped it.

'You are leaving for Europe this evening.' Mahmood's eyes were aimed at Bakari's face.

Bakari just sighed, a sign of succumbing to his master's wishes.

'I am going to stuff the bag with hot pimento powder and clove granules. These are your samples to advertise to the clients, and you are the export agent. Mind you, the ornaments are already packed in the secret chambers, so be careful.'

'Mzee . . .' Bakari said in a low voice.

'Now listen, from Amsterdam you are to catch a flight to Rio de Janeiro, in Brazil. There, my connections will pack you with first grade stuff: the Colombian extract. Remember not to leave the spices behind in Amsterdam!'

'Mzee, I was saying maybe this time you will increase my spending allowance.'

'What, more money? No way, when I travel I use even less money.' Mahmood had frowned.

'Sometimes I only pay for accommodation and nothing is left for food.' Bakari was behaving like a child asking for more food from his mother.

'Listen, I do travel the same routes you use, and I know the expenses. Now I don't want to hear any more of your complaints – am I clear?'

Bakari had his mouth full. Mahmood was indeed travelling the same routes, to establish contacts with suppliers and buyers. More importantly, he travelled to collect and make payment to his agents. Mahmood also travelled with a briefcase, but one full of money and not spices. His bag contained invoices, cheque books and receipts, but no secret compartments. He was a perfect international businessman, jetting from capital to capital to seal business deals. Mahmood's invoices revealed that he was a curios and wood products exporter. He also imported cooking oil, sugar, and pastry for his distribution stores.

Bakari reached for the bag from Issa-Mahid, although the boss did not release the handle immediately. He seemed as if he wanted to impart more advice to Bakari before letting go his precious possession. Mahmood Issa-Mahid had recited the message to Bakari, in a clear and well pronounced assertion. Bakari finally took hold of the bag and felt that it was heavier than usual. Mahmood's free hand then reached for his golden rosary and jerked it over his wrist to fall on his fingers. His thin, sienna lips moved as he recited the rosary.

Bakari watched Issa-Mahid's face, especially his shining forehead as he prayed. Below his neck, he wore a collarless shirt that was strapped neatly on his neck. On the side of the shirt pocket was a golden pen with a logo at the top. His stomach filled the shirt to a considerable extent, although Mahmood could not be said to be a fat person. The leather belt on his waist was shiny, and the pair of trousers he wore must have been cut from very expensive material. With the thin moustache on top of his upper lip, Mahmood looked distinguished, like a seasoned diplomat from the Horn of African region.

He always appeared firm and confident whenever he spoke to his subordinates, and all those he believed owned less money than him. Today as he worked on the rosary, his face showed signs of anxiety. Perhaps Mahmood was working too hard, and was becoming dissipated. Bakari had noticed a slight quiver on Mahmood's hands when he handed the bag to him. On his forehead, that always shone radiantly as a result of the make-up he used, were short lines running across it from the sides of his face, diving down along his nose.

Bakari's wide left wrist was clutched on the handle of the briefcase, although he had rested it on the floor. He was not sure what would be Mahmood's reaction if he were to let go the handle. He felt like asking Mahmood something at that time, but did not have the courage. Some sun's rays were penetrating through the curved window on the side of the office, shining onto Bakari's face. He did not feel the effect of the heat though, owing to the air-conditioner that was hissing in the room. Bakari also felt like smoking, but that would only be possible if he were outside, away from the vicinity. He did not want Mahmood to bark at him for allegedly attempting to set the petrol station on fire.

'When you arrive back, the bag will be collected from you by Omari as usual. He will be waiting for you at the car park, not the passenger section as he usually does,' Mahmood said.

Bakari could not surmise the reason that made Mahmood change the rules of the game on this occasion. He was however convinced that Mahmood now distrusted Omari. The thought that he and Omari were now being viewed in the same light, brought a strange sense of relief to Bakari. The act of being summoned into Mahmood's secretive operational room was a landmark to Bakari. He could not determine outright if it was a sign of increased trust in him or if Mahmood just used the occasion to express his reservations on the ways the business was being handled. What Bakari did not forget was that Mahmood was unpredictable, reacted capriciously, and was capable of going to any lengths to protect what he thought belonged to him.

Bakari was to wait in another small office until the time Mahmood's driver took him to the airport. It had to be a time when Mahmood was free as well, as he had to follow them behind with his car and make sure they were heading to where they were supposed to go. Issa-Mahid would simply remain in his heavily tinted car in the parking lot, and watch from there that everything was going according to plan. It is also from there that he could jet his BMW sports car into safety in case of an unforseen occurrence.

Before Bakari left Issa-Mahid's office, he remembered another issue he had long wished to discuss with him. In a rather timid voice, Bakari mentioned something about the house in Sinza.

'No, no way!' Issa-Mahid responded as he shuffled through a pile of files. 'You still have to work hard for it.'

'Pardon, Mzee . . .'

'I said you have to work extra hard before I give you a chance to buy the house!' Issa-Mahid raised his voice.

Issa-Mahid then ushered Bakari to the other office as he had important telephone calls to make.

When Bakari was out of the room Issa-Mahid moved to close the door. Before the latch clicked, he opened it again.

'Even if I make a decision on the house, I won't accept instalments. It should be the full amount in cash.' Issa-Mahid then latched the door.

Bakari sat alone in the small room and thought. He looked around the dark blue room. There was a small, heavily grilled window just below the roof. The window was small and allowed little light to pass through it. There was a chair and small table with an attached bench on the side of it. Bakari stood up, moved around the small room and pushed a little door on the side of one of the walls. There was a small squat toilet pan, a tin of water on the side and a cistern on top. Bakari was curious to know the purpose of that small room in the complex that made part of the petrol station.

He still paced the weird room and reached the only door that gave access out of the room. The door was thick, made of hard wood and reinforced with metal bars. To his astonishment, he discovered that the door was not openable from inside. Bakari gasped in disbelief when he realised he was virtually being held in solitary confinement. An air of annoyance crossed his mind. Simply because Issa-Mahid gave him the bag, he had to lock him up as well. Was it made like that to deny him communication with the outside world?

He slowly approached the loose chair in the room. He stood beside it and stared at its fading burgundy material. It reminded him of a similar chair belonging to an old paramount chief of the Wasambara tribe he had seen at a house in Korogwe. Bakari recalled seeing the old man seated on the chair with a black whisk resting on his shoulder. He looked frail and desolated. He was the last of the Great Shambalai dynasty that ruled the mountains of Lushoto, and lived to see his power disintegrating after independence.

Bakari's reminiscence of the ailing chief, who later wasted away a forgotten man, cautioned him to the unfairness that might occur to someone's life. If Mahmood kept the dungeon for keeping his captives or his disobedient workers, what mistake had Bakari done to find himself there? There were noises outside; Bakari paused to listen. He brought his concentration back into the room when he discovered that the noise was made by a deflating tyre from the repair section. He touched the couch, and discovered that the seat of the chair was detached from the backrest. Bakari shoved it a bit, and saw that it unfolded. So the sofa could be turned into a bed as well. Bakari appreciated that it was indeed a versatile room, and guessed that Mahmood used the room for many discreet activities.

After folding back the chair Bakari sat and pulled the bag close to him. He detached the flap and opened the briefcase. The divisions in the bag were the same as he always knew them, and he felt the padded area between the material that made the divisions. He was aware that the numerous trips he made with the odd bag had made lots of money for his boss and his associates. One of them could even afford a one-storey house in Mikocheni, and a brand new four-wheeled vehicle. He bore the risks and got paid, but only an amount that precluded him from even making a deposit for a simple house. His savings would only allow him to purchase second-hand furniture and a few domestic appliances in the house. A portion of these savings in the first place came from his own personal businesses.

A wind of anger blew over Bakari's face as more thoughts of this act of unfairness merged in his wits. He tapped the bag repeatedly and blew a faint whistle from his wide lips. An old song of Ahmed Kipande was being simulated through the whistle. Bakari could not recall the title of the song, but it expressed the artist's suffering, as he kept on singing of a heartache. Kipande's heart ached because of love, and praised the woman in his song, confessing that he had no replacement for her in his heart. Bakari loved the song, and although it was an imitation of a Lingala number played by a Congolese music group, Kipande's Swahili version was undoubtedly better composed.

Even the chords from Tanzania's most famous musician could not soothe the exasperation gripping Bakari's heart as he paced the little room in which he was being held incommunicado. The rising temperatures in the room augmented the indignation he harboured against those who were using him as a human shock-absorber to enrich themselves. As he paced the small room again, sweat beads developed on his broad face; at the same time a strange idea he had not thought of, was unfolding on the horizon.

Bakari moved to the sofa where he had left the bag, raised and examined it. His crinkled face relaxed, and he took a deep breath. He had seen a similar bag the last time he flew to Amsterdam. A cunning smile was developing on his face as the witty plan kept on surging in his mind. Bakari quickly saw at his disposal two weapons he could use to fight back. An identical bag to the one he was holding and his new-found comrade, Kibosho, were all he needed to begin the campaign.

He stretched himself on the sofa and clenched his teeth as he thought. Bakari would strike at his enemies with such an impact that they wouldn't bother him again. He would purchase the identical bag in Amsterdam and get some spices, deodorants and bread flour to stuff in it. They waged war against him, abusing his integrity, and messed up with his life. As a payback to his associates, that is the bag they would receive when he got back home. They gained most and he gathered the crumbs under the table. This time he would unload the secret chambers of the authentic bag and keep the loot. Bakari even bit his lips as details of how he would deal with his partners played back in his mind.

Suddenly the door jerked open, Bakari stumbled from the chair and stood up. In an inexplicable panic, he used his foot to kick the bag away from his feet. Mahmood shot his query eyes at him, and for a moment, refrained from saying a word. Mahmood gazed at the man he found in that confined room, surveying him from head to toe. Perhaps Bakari had not slackened his face sufficiently to disguise the vile image that had been plastered on it. In turn, Mahmood's instincts were putting him on a cautionary guard. He again stared at Bakari with a frightening glare, then moved close to him as if to attack him. But he stopped a metre from Bakari, and spoke in a low, yet vibrating voice:

'You are leaving now for the airport.'

# CHAPTER 11

The dimly lit streets were narrow but well paved, sufficient to separate the tall block of flats that were arranged in a row. It was the noisiest suburb in greater Amsterdam, accommodating mainly Surinamese, Asian and African immigrants. Cars rushed through the narrow streets, sometimes jerking, stretching and hooting unnecessarily. The atmosphere was in contrast to the affluent areas of the city where the middle and upper class Dutch families lived. Groups of youths, mostly from broken or single parent homes, roamed the streets in gangs, listening to obscene music and exchanging narcotics. When the sun sets in that neighbourhood, it is safer to be indoors, rather than to brush with the coloured prostitutes prowling the streets, or knife-wielding young men, representing the lost generation of the immigrant population.

Bakari was in the corridor of the seventeenth floor, in a maze of flats contained in that complex. He was seated in the bastion of Issa-Mahid's associates waiting for further instructions after delivering the expected consignment to them. He was not going to take with him the payment for the six packets of Tanzanites, red rubies, and other precious stones he delivered, as that was not part of his brief. From there Bakari would carry another load to a given destination. All that depended on those who hired and paid him for his services. In his jacket he always kept his passport and ticket in a secured zipped pocket, just in case of any eventuality. He was in a zone which he wouldn't know when to vacate in a hurry, or to change flats at short notice. The suburbs were also a haven of police immoderation, as frenzied midnight raids were not uncommon.

It was spring in Europe, the temperatures were low, but still a person could remain outside, provided he was equipped with a padded jacket. Trees growing by the road adjoining the flats had blossomed, and the colours of their flowers paralleled the different colours of jackets and sweaters worn by the children of the tenants playing below them. There was a railway station a short distance away from the flat where Bakari was putting up, and

155

the movement of the passenger waggons on the lines, coupled with the humming noise of the electric engine, could be felt at the balcony.

Bakari had used the telephone of his associates to make a call to Mapipa Sunlight Bar in Dar-es-Salaam. He had asked the barman there, who had become his friend, to send someone across the road to a tenant of what was known as Mzee Tangawizi's house. Bakari was to phone again in an hour's time and at that time Kibosho would be at the Sunlight Bar waiting for the call. As he waited for Bakari's phone call he would be entitled to a bottle of Safari Lager on credit, courtesy of Bakari. Bakari would come and settle the bill on arrival from overseas.

Mahmood Issa-Mahid had shown his determination in monitoring the movement of his bag all the way to the airport. He escorted his driver who took Bakari to the airport to make sure he did not stop or speak to anyone along the way. What Issa-Mahid had forgotten was the advancement in communication technology. While Issa-Mahid sat in his Mitsubishi Pajero entertaining his teenage girlfriend in the humidity of Dar-es-Salaam, Bakari from Amsterdam was speaking with Kibosho at Magomeni. They were conversing in Kiswahili, and Bakari had informed his associates at the flat that his wife was sick and he wanted to know her condition. The associates did not suspect anything. Issa-Mahid, enjoying the company of the seventeen-year-old schoolgirl outside an ice-cream parlour, would not suspect that there was a plot being hatched.

The noise at the immigrant flats continued well into the night. Some of the residents could speak English, though a majority spoke a mixture of Dutch and other languages. Bakari could not understand the pidgin slang. The next morning as he sat with one of his associates and another friend in a small restaurant, Bakari could not join in the conversation. He spent his time ogling a couple of dark complexioned women with long hair, laughing sheepishly at the counter. The girls were tattooed on their arms and thighs and looked unpleasant.

Bakari's other thought was to find some time to go and buy a huge plastic bag in the flea markets.

'Why do you need it?' the associate asked Bakari, talking in broken English.

'To put my shopping in.'

'But all the stores here wrap what they sell in bags.'

'I need a strong one that I can re-use for other things back home.'

'At your home, you have no plastics?'

'We have, but not big and strong.'

'Or, will you use it to make a roof of your hut?' the chap with fluffy hair laughed.

'My house is made of tinned roof.' Bakari did not see anything funny to provoke the chap into laughter.

'But I saw on TV you Africans living in huts with plastic sheets as roof – some written UNHCR.'

Bakari had no answer as he had no knowledge of the impact of Western television station's depiction of the African continent in Europe. The chap he was talking to was looking more African than European, but as he had been born in Europe, his concept of Africa was of a land of misery, conflicts and refugees. It was unfair to blame him for that misconception. The major world news corporations had successfully implanted in him the notion of the Africa they wanted him to have.

A brief silence endured as Bakari waited for his friend's answer, concerning the time he would take him to the flea market. Bakari indeed needed the bag to put inside what he intended to purchase at the duty free shop at the airport. It was so vital that no one should see him making the purchase at the airport, as he was aware that it would appear cumbersome and suspicious to be carrying two identical briefcases through airport controls.

Piercing noises could be heard inside the airport terminal bridge, as the passengers moved inside it. The bridge terminated at the door of a huge Jumbo jet. Bakari had spent a considerable length of time surveying the different shops that composed the extensive duty free market. He had salivated at the many different consumer items on display, and wished he had enough money to purchase them. He saw cars that were cheaper in comparison to the price back home. All that was required to do if he had the money, was to place an order for one and have it delivered to Dar-es-Salaam. Bakari realised that the value of each consignment he carried in the bag to Europe could purchase even five cars, yet the money was not designed to be shared with him. He breathed heavily and shook his head.

A moment later a smile formed on his lips. He convinced himself the era of not affording anything in his life was now coming to an end. With the master-plan he was devising, even a four-wheeled luxurious vehicle would no longer be a dream to him. He had managed to converse with Kibosho for fifteen minutes and was convinced that Kibosho had taken note of all the details. Luckily Kibosho was still waiting for the call at the bar when Bakari finally managed to get through, although there was a delay of two hours from the time he was supposed to call back the Mapipa Sunlight. The delay was due to telephone lines to Dar-es-Salaam being hard to get. The instruction to the bar's supervisor that he should keep Kibosho waiting with an incentive of some beers had paid off. When Bakari eventually finished talking to him, Kibosho had emptied his fourth bottle of Safari lager, and had signed the bill to be settled by Bakari when he arrived back.

Bakari boarded the plane, and was assigned to row fourteen, seat number two hundred and fifty-eight. From there onward it was not easy to know what was going on in the outside world, except for the little village that comprised the passengers of the massive plane. It made little sense to look outside as everything was blue. There was a black man seated abreast to Bakari, wearing wide-rimmed spectacles. As they were the only individuals having the same complexion in that section of the plane, the man leaned towards Bakari:

'Hi, I am Dexter from Trinidad,' the man said and grinned.

'I am Bakari from Dar-es-Salaam,' he cleared his throat.

For a moment Bakari analysed his companion's grin, that extended from the sides of his face without exposing his teeth. Such grins were not common with the Swahili people he knew. When the Swahili laughed or even smiled they would open their mouths and expose most of their teeth. It therefore was a predicament for toothless people, as they were restricted from showing that important act of emotion. It was still a long way for the Swahili to perfect the shrewd art of grinning.

'I bet that is in Africa, right?' The man tilted his head.

'Yes, Tanzania, East Africa.' Bakari raised his voice a bit.

'That is interesting. I hear a lot about the continent, but I have little idea of the different states.'

'Pardon,' Bakari had difficulties in understanding the man's accent.

'I mean, what main features, or what outstanding aspects characterise your country in Africa?' The man spoke gesturing with his arms.

Bakari thought for a while, trying to digest his fellow passenger's words. He nervously cleared his throat again:

'Many animals: lions, elephants, in Serengeti; big mountain Kilimanjaro.'

'Oh that is interesting; now tell me are you on holidays or business?' He moved his mouth in a funny way, and adjusted the rim of his spectacles.

Bakari looked down and wished the gentleman would stop talking to him. His English was limited, and he only used it when it was necessary to get through during his travels, and communicating with his associates. He was not groomed to withstand an interview such as the one he was going through.

'I am visiting friends in Brazil,' Bakari just mumbled the words without even looking at the man.

Bakari then quickly bent and reached for a newspaper at the back of the chair ahead of him. He unfolded it and lowered his face on the page. The man said something else, but Bakari was not concentrating. Peace had returned to him and he lowered his head on the head rest. As he relaxed, his vision travelled miles over the ocean, and landed at the East African coast of Dar-es-Salaam. The statements Issa-Mahid had uttered to him made his head agitate with confusion. Bakari really feared Issa-Mahid could do something bad to him unless he acted quickly. Bakari felt haunted and suspected that Omari had twisted events around so that all the blame and suspicious could be placed with him.

Otherwise, Bakari feared that Issa-Mahid could be using sinister tricks of playing around with his associates, thus bringing them into clashes in order to detract them from colluding against him. Issa-Mahid would be the one to benefit if all those working for him distrusted one another. Divide and rule is not a new strategy. It has been there ever since human beings began organising themselves, being preferred by the wicked ones, and those who ruled with authoritarian practice. Whenever Issa-Mahid talked, he used threats to put his message across.

Before leaving his petrol station, Issa-Mahid told Bakari that he became aware through Omari that Bakari was involving himself in businesses with other people. Issa-Mahid had reminded Bakari of his earlier instructions to him not to engage in any other endeavour besides the business he was doing at present. He had thus given Bakari two days on his return from this trip to wind up all his other activities and report to him all the side businesses he had been doing and the people involved. Issa-Mahid insisted that he wanted to know from Bakari the source and amount of money he had invested in these ventures.

Bakari heaved his head even further on the head rest and bit his lower lip. He distrusted both men and was not sure of their real intention. He reached for the earphones on his lap, placed them over his head, and switched on the buttons on the panel.

The music was classical, with vocals in a language he could not understand. For the rest of the flight, Bakari used the ten hours in the air with different activities. He took some time watching the movies, listening to music and thinking. The plane eventually touched down in Rio de Janeiro. The warm and humid air at Rio was not new to him, as it was similar to the weather he was used to in Dar-es-Salaam. Some of the faces in the city were like his, although most of the people were of mixed races.

159

Bakari searched for a telephone booth and made phone calls to the numbers provided to him by Issa-Mahid. Bakari waited at the Peixe-do-Sal café for the contacts to come and fetch him. His contacts came after a while and took him in a car. The two men and a woman in the car were taking him to the unknown. Most of the time they talked amongst themselves in Portuguese. Bakari was left out of the conversation; only once did they talk to him, informing him of Issa-Mahid's visit to Rio, two weeks earlier. Issa-Mahid had come to put everything in order before he sent his messenger, Bakari.

Issa-Mahid had indicated to Bakari prior to his departure from Dar-es-Salaam that this operation was a big one, and was supposed to be very profitable. The consignment he had sent Bakari to collect was of high quality and was in high demand with tourists visiting East Africa. Issa-Mahid had instructed Bakari to be extra careful, otherwise millions of shillings would be at stake. Although Issa-Mahid had said this to Bakari in a stern voice, he had refrained from making the usual threatening gesture of moving his finger across his throat. He had done that too frequently to his associates and workers, but they still dared to defraud him and go against his commands. Perhaps he needed to prove to them that he was really capable of carrying out his threats, for them to take him seriously.

In a meek voice Bakari had assured his boss that he would indeed be careful and do exactly as he was instructed. Issa-Mahid had nodded his head as he saw him out of the door, to the car waiting outside the petrol station. Issa-Mahid had closed the passenger door for Bakari, and instructed his driver to drive Bakari straight to the airport. A while later, Issa-Mahid started his car and trailed behind them. All the time Issa-Mahid was talking to him, Bakari had his head bent and avoided eye contact with his master. He was portraying an image of a faithful and meek subordinate.

The low opinion his boss and associates harboured against him was what he needed to perfect his treacherous master-plan. He had long realised that they considered him incapable of doing anything that needed a lot of thinking. That could have been the reason they selected him to be a messenger to fly with the bag from one capital to the other, without knowing how the arrangements were made, or deals struck.

Bakari gnashed his teeth when these thoughts came to his mind, but he quickly convinced himself that his time for revenge was around the corner. He had approached a travel agent in Amsterdam and made changes in his flight schedule. His original flight was from Rio de Janeiro, Cape Town, Johannesburg then to Dar-es-Salaam. Bakari scheduled a flight that left earlier for Luanda, Angola, then arrived in Nairobi on Tuesday evening. He would spend a night in Nairobi, then catch a flight on Wednesday that arrived in Dar-es-Salaam almost at the same time as the flight from Johannesburg.

Bakari's contacts in Rio, after fixing him with his valuable package, took him to the airport transit hotel. There he was supposed to spend the night before catching his flight to Cape Town at six the following morning. They bade him farewell, got into their cars and left.

The sun was not beaming in the sky, but the temperatures were still high. Bakari was feeling strange in his stomach, and attributed the nauseous feeling to the bizarre fish he ate with his hosts at one of their houses. He found Latin American seafoods to have an unusual taste, and had vowed not to eat it again. Bakari moved into his lodging and waited for about half an hour, sufficient time for his contacts to have gone far, or to be convinced that he had really settled in his room, that is, if they waited to monitor his movements.

Bakari peered through the window of the second floor building, and realised that there were three other wings making the rest house of that airport complex. There were flights of stairs at the edge of each wing, winding from the fourth floor to the ground. From his window he could not see the runways, except for the air-control tower, adeptly teetering above the rooftops of other structures. He kept gazing on all sides, and when he was convinced everything was quiet, he quickly changed his clothes and put on a wide brimmed hat and artificial spectacles. He then opened the big plastic shopping bag he had come with from Amsterdam and took out a brown leather briefcase. Bakari worked on the briefcase: trampled on it, and dragged it along the floor to make it look used. He took several cushioned polyethylene bags from his suitcase and stuffed them into it. Bakari exchanged the briefcase with the usual one packed with precious effects, and sealed the flowery bag.

He then quickly moved out of the room and went past the reception into the airport lounge. The bill for the room was already paid in advance by his associates. Only five minutes were left to check in for the flight to Luanda. Bakari checked in his multicolored shopping bag, and proceeded to the immigration control.

They were already calling for passengers to board the airbus parked on the tarmac. Before boarding the Luanda-bound flight, the security officials routinely asked Bakari to review his hand luggage. Confidently, Bakari gave it to them, and the officials shuffled the bags of perfumes, soaps and toiletries that were inside.

'Having a lot of presents with you, eh?' the officer commented.

'We have shortages of these basics in our country.' Bakari was solemn.

'It's a pity, you guys ought to improve your economies.'

161

'Maybe if you people come and counsel us.'

The officers at the desk grinned at him.

'We wish you a nice flight, sir,' they said to him.

The plane taxied to the end of the tarmac, then stood motionless for a few moments, waiting for instructions to take off. The plane rumbled along the runway, then its nose lifted up. Bakari swallowed, sniffed and recited a short prayer. He was not a very committed religious person, but there are occasions when one usually retreats to one's faith.

At eleven in the morning, a man in a straw hat disembarked from a Kenyan Airways jet and headed to the arrival lounge. He adjusted his glasses so that his eyes could peep at the top floor of the building at the Dar-es-Salaam airport complex. Bakari did not recognise any face amongst the few people who stood up there. A few more paces and he would be at the arrival lounge, safe from anyone who would have otherwise recognised him. He wore a red jacket. Anyone knowing Bakari wouldn't expect him to wear red, as it was the colour of Simba Sports Club, the soccer team he disliked. Being an avowed follower of the Young Africans Sports Club, his colours would have been green or yellow, or a combination of the two.

Bakari went through the passport control section. The humidity inside the airport lounge was overwhelming. He wondered why the authorities did not instal air-conditioners in such an important infrastructure. The airport building was supposed to give the first impression of the country to the visitors. A visitor having disembarked from a comfortable air-conditioned plane would be disappointed to be subjected to the gruelling heat inside the lounge. The visitor would immediately begin to suspect he had landed in a country simmering with hardship and desperation.

Wiping his brow with a handkerchief, Bakari waited at the rotating belt for his checked in luggage. Many types of suitcases and boxes moved with the belt. There was a life-size teddy bear wrapped in clear plastic sheets moving there as well. Bakari was surprised, wondering why anyone should bring such a huge doll. He could not envision a child playing with a bear of that size. He saw a woman dressed in tight fitting trousers lifting the bear from the belt. Bakari imagined what the huge teddy bear could be stuffed with in its artificial body. The answer was not easily available to Bakari. He himself was waiting for a replica of the briefcase he carried on his hand, stuffed with prohibited and sedative material.

Eventually Bakari saw the plastic shopping bag, as intact as he had first checked it in Brazil. He got hold of the bag and pulled it off the belt. He placed the bag on a trolley he found near the revolving belt, and pushed it towards the customs desk. There were about thirty other passengers standing alongside the belt waiting to collect their luggage. No one would have taken special note of a man in a hat and spectacles, yanking a very normal shopping bag from the belt. Less interest would be shown to an average person pushing a trolley across the airport lounge, especially when there were over twenty other men and women doing a similar thing. Even when Bakari left the trolley a few metres from the customs desk, and the trolley was taken over by another man (a worker of the airport), no one cared.

Bakari approached the customs man and lowered his handbag ahead of him. Bakari had waited for fifteen minutes in the queue to present his handbag for checking by the customs officer. As he flipped open the briefcase's flap, there was a thunderous noise of a huge plane as it touched down on the runaway. The huge sound disappeared beyond the building, leaving the lounge's windowpanes vibrating from the tremor the jet caused. Bakari watched as the customs man went through his bags, and interrupted his concentration by enquiring from him what airline had just landed. The officer confirmed to Bakari that it was the Alliance Airlines' Jumbo from Johannesburg. A smile escaped from Bakari's lips and he sniffed. He accepted his briefcase from the customs officer, and was satisfied that things were going according to his plans.

Bakari lowered his hat so that the brim touched his spectacles. The edges of his eyes were surveying all sides of the building, not to be surprised by anyone sent by Issa-Mahid to spy over the airport lounge. Issa-Mahid could have posted a man to check on all movements at the airport as he was expecting Bakari to be landing at any time. The spy could have arrived earlier, and manage to see through Bakari's disguise. Bakari would have to find words of explanation of how he managed to arrive ahead of his scheduled flight. As he was thinking, he could hear the whistling sound of the jet taxiing at the runway, closer to the lounge.

The worse danger remained the possibility of being spotted by Omari. Issa-Mahid told Bakari that Omari would come to collect the bag as usual. As Omari was now rich and had many contacts, Bakari feared that by mere chance, Omari could have come a bit earlier to the airport and been given permission to walk inside the airport lounge by the officers at the door. With money everything was possible; rules and regulations could be bent to allow the rich to have their way wherever they wanted to go. This always happened, especially in poor and underdeveloped countries, where most of the laws are enacted to bind only the common man in the street. If Omari were to get in the lounge he would have easily recognised Bakari even behind his disguise.

Bakari did not leave the building at that time. Instead, he asked the customs officers to allow him to proceed to the baggage reclamation office. Bakari was directed by one of the officers and moved to a cramped office filled with pungent sweat odour. The officer in the room looked tired and demoralised by the excessive heat and damp ambience in his untidy room.

'When was the last flight from Kampala?' Bakari asked.

'Oh, on Monday, one plane came late in the afternoon,' the man replied without looking at Bakari.

'Was there any television set that came unaccompanied?'

'You mean unclaimed?' the officer spoke in a hoarse voice, a foul smell coming from his mouth.

'Yes . . . yes, a seventy inch screen.'

The officer twisted his mouth, and shook his head. His thick fingers were tapping on the table :

'Mmhn, I don't recall seeing such a big set.'

'Maybe you should check amongst the goods received.'

The officer moved from his chair, took a bunch of keys from his drawer, and approached a door on one side of the little office. The store had boxes and parcels dumped all over the place without arrangement. There was a big box at the bottom of long polythene wrapped aluminium spikes. The officer asked Bakari to help him clear some of the boxes along the way so that they could get access to the big box. At this time Bakari could hear the creaking sound of the rotating belt, coming from the airport lounge. He knew that the passengers from Alliance Airlines were already into the lounge, and would soon be proceeding to the customs desk.

'Mmh, this is not a television,' the short man in uniform grunted.

'So it is not here as yet.' Bakari appeared to be pensive.

'Were you expecting a set?' the man asked Bakari.

'No, I flew from Kampala with the television set, but on arrival at the airport it was nowhere to be found.'

'Maybe it was left behind in Kampala. Usually when planes are full, some of the luggage, especially that not accompanying the passengers, is left behind.'

The officer proceeded to check in his registry book, flipping the pages of the worn out book. He regularly wetted his finger on his tongue as he continued turning the pages. At the same time Bakari saw through the glass window that the first batch of passengers from the Jumbo jet were already at the customs desk. He kept on looking at the officer paging his book, at the same time peeping through the window of the reclamation office till he saw three of the new passengers from Johannesburg going out of the door. Bakari was now convinced he had bought enough time, and could leave the airport building as well.

'Never mind, officer, let me leave and I will check with you again when the next flight from Kampala comes.' Bakari was preparing to go.

'Maybe check on Monday . . . by the way, what is your name?'

Bakari was already out of the office and walking towards the door. He emerged out of Dar-es-Salaam arrival lounge, behind two European gentlemen from Johannesburg. Bakari had removed his straw hat, spectacles and red jacket, and had placed them in the suitcase containing his clothes whilst still in the reclamation office. By the time Bakari left the exit door, his flowery shopping bag had long been wheeled out of the airport lounge by the people he made arrangements with.

Bakari stopped by the side of the road and disregarded the scores of taxi-drivers offering to take him to town. He glanced over the parking area expecting to see the bald head and protruding stomach of his friend. Bakari's eyes were not rewarded with any sign of those features. He crossed the road and went over the low fence protecting a line of withering flowers that had not been watered for weeks owing to lack of water. In a country that had abundant rivers crossing it, the precious liquid was a luxury limited only to a few households in affluent areas.

He glanced from one end to the other, expecting to see a sleek Isuzu Trooper parked somewhere. Bakari saw a pick-up carrying about six women draped in khangas moving to park in an open slot. Amongst them was one covered from head to toe, leaving only a set of beautiful, captivating eyes. She seemed to be the centre of attraction, and Bakari could tell that she was being taken to be married, most probably to a rich man in Zanzibar. Otherwise, if she was to marry in the mainland, the accompanying party wouldn't incur the expenses of going by plane.

The sight of a carousing wedding gala sent Bakari's imagination some thirty-five years back to Kisarawe. He recalled as a young boy venturing with his friends into the 'Mdundiko' dance. When a new bride finally emerged from seclusion and was handed over to a man chosen by her parents, her sisters, brothers and relatives would clutch their drums, tins, traditional percussion, whistles and anything else that could make noise and hit the streets. Little kids would be excited by these processions, and join them, singing along. The children would follow the processions without realising the distance they had strayed from home.

When the Mdundiko procession finally disbanded, the children would be left stranded and crying. It had happened to Bakari a number of times, being left stranded far from home. Fortunately, his famous surname in Kisarawe had always helped him to be identified and promptly returned to his parents' home. His mother had always rebuked him for straying from home: 'Be careful, my son, there are people up there who are looking for children like you.' His mother was referring to cases of children being abducted and sacrificed for ritual purposes.

A flash of headlights attracted Bakari's attention, and he moved towards the direction of the car that signalled him. It was a white Suzuki Vitara, but Bakari could not determine the identity of the person in the car. He was nevertheless convinced that it could be Omari, as he now had lots of money and could afford changing cars. The fact that the car had tinted windows similar to the Isuzu Omari owned, removed doubts from Bakari that he would find Omari seated behind the driver's wheel.

Bakari approached the driver's door, and the door opened gently. He peered inside, and was greeted by the muzzle of a revolver. Behind the greyish barrel was a short-haired man in sunglasses. Apart from the shock that greeted him, Bakari's eyes managed to get a glimpse of his boss's terrified face as he sat between the two burly and serious looking gentlemen also in dark shades. The men in shades all had automatic pistols in their hands.

'Give me the briefcase and climb in the car fast!' was the cold instruction from the short man who was aiming the revolver at Bakari.

# CHAPTER 12

Celebrations held annually to celebrate the harvesting of new crops, usually run during the first week of August. When the harvest has been good, and there is a generous supply of food, many households in the coastal regions, will consume only that food which they have grown themselves. At this time they will not go to the market and buy maize flour ground from unselected maize corn. Last season's beans and groundnuts remain unsold in the markets, prompting the vendors to lower prices. When Bakari paid a visit to Mwajuma's grandparents in Rufiji during the harvest season, he was treated to a delicious meal of fried cassava, dowsed in fresh honey. He also consumed a number of calabashes of coconut beer.

That same evening in Rufiji, Bakari heard of the availability of free refined beer at a wedding celebration. A pint or two of Safari lager to complement the coconut beer he had consumed earlier, was what Bakari wished to accomplish for that day. Bakari had forgotten a vow he had made earlier in his youth, not to mix traditional and modern beers. The last time he had had such a concoction in Tanga resulted in him tottering from the bottle store he was drinking, surviving being run down by a bus, and vomiting down the street. Along the way, Bakari had molested a couple of women and had their husbands charging at his flat the following day, threatening to have him castrated. Neighbours and fans of Coastal United, the team he was playing for, had to come to his rescue, thus saving him from the hostile men.

That evening at Rufiji, a tipsy Bakari had discovered the place hosting the function, thanks to a heavy Lingala beat coming from the house. After a couple of beers, he had left the function feeling on top of the world. He came to a bend and found a mango tree with ripe fruits. Bakari was not prepared to let go anything that looked delicious pass by him. He took a stone and threw it up the tree. The stone went astray, and instead of bringing down a ripe mango, it brought down a hive of wild wasps. The cone shaped object fell directly on Bakari's shoulder, and from it emerged four huge wasps that wasted no time in injecting their stings into his body.

The pain, and the horror that gripped Bakari at that moment, sent him reeling down the footpath, screaming close to insanity. He jumped up several times and fell on the ground. He hit shrubs and tree trunks, and the venomous essence from the wasps made him vomit the blend of coconut and barley beers he had consumed. He then passed out.

When Bakari woke up later at a local Rufiji medical centre, he had the same confused feelings as he was having today at the Keko Detention Centre. It was not Bakari's first time in a detention centre, but it was his first experience waking up bruised by the blows he had received from fellow detainees. Detectives who brought him and Issa-Mahid to the cell did not abuse them physically, but simply interrogated them. The two spent long hours answering questions of allegedly being involved in drug trafficking. Both men denied vehemently even knowing the look of illicit drugs, let alone trading in them.

The briefcase Bakari came with was taken by the detectives and thoroughly searched. The detectives were not to give up easily; they went to the extent of tearing it to pieces, thinking there might be something hidden in the thin leather walls. Someone seemed to have tipped off the detectives about the impending arrival of Bakari with a nice cache, and they had staged a surprise for him. Where Mahmood came from to be caught up in the detectives' net, was still an issue that baffled Bakari, at the time they sat together on the bench facing their interrogators. After eight hours of interrogation they were then remanded in custody.

Bakari and Mahmood appeared fresh and well groomed, and had attracted the attention of hardened inmates. Inmates who have spent months in remand cells without appearing in court have an indecent habit of sexually abusing new arrivals on the very first night they get locked in the cells. The criminals were anti-social elements in society, having no one to bail them, or buy their freedom from detention, so they had nothing to lose from their disgusting actions.

Bakari was, however, not to submit with his hands down. He put up a resistance which resulted in the hangover he was now experiencing. He was thrown on the floor and flung to the wall, but refused to allow anyone to cling on his back. He had also delivered devastating blows to his adversaries, but on balance he received more than he delivered. Mahmood was only good in issuing verbal threats, but had no physical strength to fight off the desire of the hardened criminals. He depended on knives and the pistol he carried most of the time. He was thus not that lucky and became a victim. Bakari himself, reeling from the punches to his body, could not help

Mahmood from being abused.

The following morning, Bakari was still coming to terms with the turn of events from the time he left the airport lounge. He was expecting to find Omari at the edge of the airport lounge waiting to collect the briefcase. Bakari was convinced that it was an opportunity Omari would not have wished to miss. Omari would probably have relished taking the briefcase and delivering it to Issa-Mahid, thus allaying any suspicions from him that he had been tampering with the briefcase on previous deliveries. That would have been in line with Bakari's plans, as Omari would have handed over to Issa-Mahid a briefcase without the loot. Issa-Mahid would therefore have had no doubt who was his traitor.

That did not happen, and now Bakari found himself in detention with his boss. What was Issa-Mahid doing at the parking lot, and where did the detectives come from? Bakari could not come up with the answer. He was relieved that out of the briefcase, the detectives would not find any evidence to incriminate him.

Bakari was seated on the cell floor, watching Issa-Mahid leaning by the wall on the opposite side of the cell. There were six other inmates, all seated, not uttering a word. During the day they were calm. Their violence commenced only at night after lights off. Bakari could not catch Issa-Mahid's eyes, as he stood looking down. If Issa-Mahid had managed to collect the briefcase from him, Bakari's plans would have been jeopardised, and he would have been in grave trouble. It appeared to Bakari that Issa-Mahid had come with a disguised car to spy on him and Omari to see what transpired at the airport from the time Bakari arrived till he handed over the briefcase to Omari. Perhaps Issa-Mahid would have then followed Omari to see where he ended up.

Issa-Mahid's plans must have gone terribly wrong somewhere. Whoever foiled his strategy must have had prior knowledge of his intention to be at the airport area at that time, and first hand information on which car he would use.

What transpired was out of the scope of Issa-Mahid's imagination. He could only take a wild guess at those who could be responsible for his incarceration. His major predicament at that moment was to find himself locked up in a dirty cell with his subordinate, having been molested by the wretched of society.

There were a few mosquitoes still hovering in the cell at daybreak, vying to sting the already throbbing bodies cramped in that cell. Bakari slapped his hands and squashed a giant mosquito that left a sizable dot of blood on his palm. He proceeded to rub his hand on the floor to remove the stain. At the same time the door of the cell clanged and was flung open.

A prison warder walked in and called Issa-Mahid and Bakari to follow him. Issa-Mahid quickly heaved himself from the wall and dashed to the door.

'Not so fast,' the burly warder growled at him, holding Issa-Mahid by the chest.

It appeared strange to Bakari to see a man of Issa-Mahid's stature, supposed to be respected by everybody because of his wealth, being spoken down to in such a manner. Bakari felt a funny sensation of relief to see Issa-Mahid being on the receiving end for a change. The two men were pushed down the corridor, with the warder following behind. They eventually reached the same office they had been bundled into the night before.

When the two men were left alone, Issa-Mahid uttered his first words:

'Bulls,' he crowed.

Bakari did not know how to respond to that curse. There was an intriguing question he wanted to ask Issa-Mahid, but refrained, in order to allow Issa-Mahid to express himself first.

'I am really going to kill someone when I get out of here.'

Bakari looked at him again and cleared his throat.

'What happened to us to find ourselves here?'

'Do you ask me, or should I ask you?' Issa-Mahid's voice was highly pitched with anger.

'But I had only arrived from overseas!' Bakari showed surprise.

For a while Issa-Mahid remained quiet. His face was showing signs of forming a rash, especially around his chin. He had not shaved. The smoothness was not in place, and it became obvious that to look as elegant as he usually did, Issa-Mahid needed considerable time to prepare his face before leaving his house in the morning. The face he wore that morning in the prison office also revealed that he was much older than he normally looked.

Mahmood Issa-Mahid spoke Kiswahili fluently, with a characteristic coastal accent. Some of his employees maintained that Mahmood was born out of the country and came as a young man from Mombasa. They say that after working for some other businessmen from the Horn of Africa, and deceitfully making money from them, he had used a sizable portion of the money to buy himself a passport and citizenship. He got married and divorced a couple of times and would use some of his former in-laws as a proof of relatives if anyone dared to challenge the rightfulness of his citizenship.

The more money he made, the fewer of those in authority cared to know to which country he paid allegiance.

Mahmood was still twitching his fingers and biting his lower lip in apprehension before turning to Bakari again:

'Have you been opening your big mouth lately?' Issa-Mahid was virtually snarling at Bakari.

'How could I do something to victimise myself as well?' This time Bakari's voice was also raised and jerky.

'Someone is playing a cat and mouse game here!'

'Where was Omari, I was expecting him?'

Issa-Mahid stared at Bakari and shook his head. They both sat silently waiting for the authorities to come and tell them the purpose of the meeting.

In the midst of the confusion and humiliation, a sound idea was coming to Bakari's mind. His plans had not misfired altogether. At that moment, Bakari presumed that Kibosho would have managed to get the plastic bag from the airport worker who had assisted Bakari to smuggle it out of the arrival lounge. Bakari assumed that Kibosho had taken the original briefcase full of invaluable material, removed all the hidden packets from the secret compartments and placed them under the sewage manhole at his Sinza house. Bakari had also instructed Kibosho to go and put the polyethylene bags of bread flour contained in the open compartments of the briefcase in the secret roof aperture at Omari's house in Mikocheni. Kibosho was then directed to plant the briefcase a bit further inside the hole in Omari's roof.

The original plot could still be carried out with some adjustments. Bakari wished he could reach Kibosho and quickly inform him not to leave the polyethylene bags and the briefcase in his boss's roof to avoid further risks. Instead he should carry the loot to the designated manhole and dispose of the briefcase immediately. This was very important, as a discovery by Issa-Mahid of an extra briefcase would indicate that Bakari had been up to dirty tricks, and he would pay with his life.

Bakari was continuously tapping his foot on the floor as he thought. Issa-Mahid meanwhile was getting irritated by the vibrations his mate was making, causing the bench to rattle. He turned and stared at Bakari.

'Why is your body shaking, are you casting away demons?' Issa-Mahid rebuked him.

Bakari relaxed his foot and took a glance at Mahmood. The respect and fear he used to harbour against him was gradually fading. He was aware that Mahmood still eyed him suspiciously. Somehow, Mahmood seemed to be reading his mind. There were signs of insurgence on Bakari's face. It was

171

easy for a man like Mahmood, a master of deception himself, to detect when one of his associates showed an unsteady character. Bakari did not care much any more. Every time Bakari saw him, Mahmood appeared elegant and noble; today, he sat on a bench with a foul stench coming from his armpits. Mahmood pretended to be too much of a macho man, but his status had been reduced after being sexually abused by other men in jail.

A detective walked in the room and stood in front of the two culprits.

'We are going to release you for now, but the investigations against you will continue.' The officer paused and looked alternately at the two men.

A clear sign of relief escaped from Mahmood's lips. He was about to say something, but the officer interrupted him.

'We take your fingerprints and photographs; in addition we will retain the car and the briefcase.'

'But the briefcase . . .' Issa-Mahid was alarmed.

'Shut up!' the officer yelled at him, 'I did not ask you to speak – otherwise I will leave you to rot in the cell.'

Bakari looked at Issa-Mahid cowering in a way he had not seen him do before. Bakari was vehemently relieved that the briefcase would not be coming out. It was up to him to seize the opportunity and proceed with his vengeful plans. A complete picture of how he would proceed from there with the plot was materialising in front of his eyes. Bakari was simply waiting for permission to leave the Keko Prison.

The mid-morning sun was shining intensely as the metal gate of Keko Detention Centre creaked open. On the gravel road outside the old stone complex, rusty tins, coconut shells and other types of garbage littered it. The bumpy road descended towards some government buildings, used for storing old and unused belongings. Bakari and Issa-Mahid walked along the street. Issa-Mahid asked Bakari if he knew of a place they could sit and make a phone call. Issa-Mahid felt embarrassed looking so dirty and walking on foot.

'We can move towards those buildings, there is a restaurant,' Bakari answered.

'Are you sure we won't meet respectable people there to tease me . . . us?'

'It is mainly frequented by workers of the factories here, not senior staff or managers.'

They got to the restaurant and went in. There was no telephone, as would be expected from a restaurant serving the rank and file. Issa-Mahid cursed the waiter for that, proving that his boastful manners were hard to eradicate even at that time of distress. Issa-Mahid even inquired if there was anyone with a cellular phone nearby. His own cellular phone remained in the Suzuki waggon, impounded by the police until they finished their investigations.

'Let's send someone to take a taxi; we can go to Sinza first, then you can call your driver from there,' Bakari suggested.

A waiter from the hotel went to the main road, leaving the two gentlemen in the restaurant. Issa-Mahid was so hungry that he could not resist Bakari's proposal that they take some tea with a couple of buns and chapattis. It had been a while since Issa-Mahid ate in such a low class environment, but hunger had no respect for anyone. He could hardly talk, as he tore the chapatti with his agile fingers, and sipped the tea noisily.

Before Issa-Mahid rose to riches, at the time he arrived with his father from Mombasa, he spent his early teenage years herding cattle in Singida. He stayed only with his father, who was a night watchman at a district provisional store. They were so destitute that his father had to steal from the same place he was supposed to guard, for him and his son to manage. Today, Issa-Mahid was feeling queasy eating from an old plastic plate. He gobbled the food and sipped the tea noisily, yet cursed and condemned everything: the walls of the restaurant, the scratchy music playing, and the untidy tables.

'Why should I be eating shit here, is what I can't understand,' Issa-Mahid said through a mouthful.

Bakari was busy stuffing a huge chunk of chapatti in his mouth, and lifted his cup to his mouth. He then looked at Issa-Mahid and thought it could be the appropriate time to speak his mind:

'Mzee, our associate's houseboy has been telling me that he saw his boss holding a peculiar brown briefcase and removed some powdered stuff from it.'

'Come again, Bakari, you are talking in parables.' Mahmood stopped the cup halfway to his mouth.

'I say, I thought I should mention to you that Omari's houseboy saw him removing what appeared like white powder from a briefcase to a cavity in his master-bathroom's roof.'

'How could that be, the briefcase is with the police?'

'The houseboy said it was a month ago.'

'Why didn't you tell me before?'

'How could I? Was I supposed to say anything against Omari to you?' Bakari frowned and braved Issa-Mahid's eyes.

Issa-Mahid had finished the three chapattis on his plate when the waiter walked into the restaurant again and informed him that the taxi was waiting for them outside the restaurant. Bakari paid the restaurant's bills as he was the one with money in his pocket. Issa-Mahid had taken out all his notes and coins the night before, in an attempt to bribe the detectives when they pounced on him at the airport parking stand. The officers had taken the money, but refused to set him free. Issa-Mahid had vowed to get even with the officers when he got a chance.

That chance would be hard to come by unless Issa-Mahid wished to stir up more troubles with the authorities. His arrest had come as a surprise to him. Issa-Mahid was convinced that with the money he had spent, most of the decision makers in the security forces were on his side, and disinclined to interfere with his business. The only explanation could be the existence of dissidents within the forces who were excluded from the gifts he normally made available to them. For Issa-Mahid to continue operating with impunity, he had to unearth this dissident segment and pay his dues to them so that they might not interfere again with his affairs. If the present matter was however going to be shelved, he would prefer to let it wither away and be forgotten.

As Issa-Mahid sat at the back seat of the speeding taxi, he became surprised to be released from detention so quickly. He was convinced that the detectives must have discovered the hidden packets of narcotics in the briefcase, and had solid evidence against him and his companion. For them to be released, Issa-Mahid suspected the detectives must have kept the haul for themselves, and released the two culprits so as to down-play the whole case.

The officers are going to make a lot of money for themselves, Issa-Mahid thought. He knew it would be reckless to go back to the police and claim his briefcase. For his own safety, he thought it was not even sensible to attempt claiming back the Suzuki. What he had to do now, was to find the traitor who set him up, and fix him before he created more troubles for him and his businesses. Contortions had formed on Issa-Mahid's brow as he thought. His jaws were moving up and down in thought.

He was not even aware that Bakari was talking to him.

Mahmood kept quiet and disregarded Bakari's attempt to draw his attention to two women who were fighting on the side of the road. His contempt for Bakari augmented at that moment as he looked at his thick lips parting in amusement at that trivial encounter. He was concentrating on issues that could bring a solution to the mayhem that had occurred in the business and Bakari was busy distracting his attention to two mad women. Mahmood was also thinking of what to do with Bakari as well after he had settled his score with his betrayer.

The taxi took a turn out of the Shekilango road and joined a bumpy street going through a corrugated metal fence that reflected the sound of the exhaust of the taxi. Eventually it stopped in front of a low wall painted in green. Bakari was the first to get out of the taxi. Moments later, a dispirited Issa-Mahid slowly shoved the creaking back door of the taxi and stood up. He gently locked the door and moved towards the house without even saying a word.

Bakari collected his change from the driver and joined Issa-Mahid at the veranda. Bakari knocked the door and after a while the houseboy appeared. The young man gaped in amazement at the physical state of his boss and his guest, but was afraid to make any comment. He simply ushered the two gentlemen in the house.

'Can I offer you a beer, Boss?' Bakari spoke to the man seated at the sofa.

Up to now Issa-Mahid had not spoken a word to Bakari; he appeared to be immersed in deep thoughts.

'What type do you have?' Issa-Mahid spoke in a low voice.

'I think, Kilimanjaro or Serengeti; let me check with the boy.' Bakari was moving through the corridor.

'Never mind,' Issa-Mahid waved him down, 'I only take the imported Heinekens or Amstels.'

'I will get myself a bottle then,' Bakari said as he moved to the kitchen.

He needed an excuse for a quick word with his houseboy. The young man had retreated to the yard, washing a shirt under the tap. He had not noticed that Bakari was coming behind.

'Hey,' Bakari shouted at him, 'I told you not to let the water run like that.'

The boy closed the tap and stood up, looking at his boss. Bakari waved at the houseboy and walked with him to the edge of the yard. Bakari noticed that the grass around the house had only been partially mown, and the dried grass had not yet been raked. Bakari felt annoyed as it was more than a week since he instructed the houseboy to do the work. Under normal circumstances, he would have raised his voice and rebuked the young man in the strongest terms. It seemed, nonetheless, that the boy was becoming immune to being shouted at by his boss.

The more Bakari shouted at him the less effective he became in his job. Two weeks earlier Bakari had got so upset when the houseboy allowed a nice piece of steak to burn to charcoal in the stove that he had lost control of himself, slapped the boy on the neck, and threatened to fire him on the spot. After seeing tears rolling on his timid face, Bakari felt pity and changed his verdict. He became remorseful and even apologised to the young man for slapping him so hard. Bakari had offered him liniment to apply to his neck, where fingermarks resulting from the blow were appearing.

Bakari was not in a fighting mood as he pulled the young man to the yard. He looked on all sides to make sure that Issa-Mahid was not following him, then whispered to the rather timid young man:

'Has Kibosho been here as yet?'

'No, I have not seen him,' the houseboy whispered back.

Bakari turned and headed back into the kitchen. He thought of going to inspect the manhole at the edge of the yard, but desisted. He opened the fridge and took out a beer. Bakari then moved to the living room. He found Issa-Mahid seated and surveying a vase placed on top of a table.

'Were you expecting someone to come?' he asked without looking at Bakari.

'No, why?' Bakari's heart skipped a beat, and stood with his beer in his hand.

'I saw you surveying the whole yard.' Issa-Mahid now turned and eyed him.

'I . . . I was finding out from the boy where can we get imported Amstel beer near here,' Bakari said, avoiding Issa-Mahid's face.

'Typical of a Swahili, he either thinks of his beer or women; nothing else.'

'But Mzee . . .'

'Cut it out, Bakari,' Issa-Mahid interrupted him with a raised voice. 'You are aware where we are coming from, but you seemed to be relaxed already. I expect you to join me and plan what are we to do next.'

Bakari felt uneasy. It appeared Issa-Mahid was suspecting him of something he could not figure out precisely. Bakari wished Mahmood would leave his house so that he could move swiftly to ascertain other aspects of his plan. The non-appearance of Kibosho seemed to put Bakari's plans in disarray.

'I will get you my new shirt and a pair of clean trousers then,' Bakari suggested to Issa-Mahid.

'Of course, I cannot arrive at home with these clothes. I also want to ask you a favour.'

Issa-Mahid stood up and moved close to Bakari. From that closeness, Bakari experienced a foul smell from his boss's uncleaned mouth. Mahmood's eyes were however shining and fixed on him as he always had done prior to the occurrence of the current problem. The stare eroded the confidence that had been building up in Bakari, and at that moment, he placed the bottle of beer on the table and clutched his arms behind his back.

Although Issa-Mahid had surged towards Bakari and was only a few inches from him, he did not utter a word, and Bakari found himself the first to speak:

'Boss, someone must have plotted to put us in this mess,' Bakari said, braving Issa-Mahid's eyes.

'What makes you so sure?' Issa-Mahid had lowered his voice.

'We were three associates in this business; only the two of us got into trouble,' Bakari said.

Issa-Mahid looked at him without showing any expression on his face. He just moved an extra step towards Bakari, and he was very close to his face. Bakari could now feel the characteristic garlic smell mingled in the foul mouth odour.

'I want you to keep your mouth shut, and don't tell anyone what has happened to me . . . or us, am I clear?'

'Not a whisper from me, Boss,' Bakari was feeling relieved that Issa-Mahid had not made a threat.

'Good, then leave other things to me. Someone's body will be made into a meal for the hyenas very soon.'

Bakari bit his lower lip and nearly allowed a smile to escape from his mouth. That would not have been a wise gesture; he wasn't sure in the first place whose body Mahmood was referring to. The time was therefore immature and too early for him to celebrate.

Issa-Mahid moved to the room to take a shower and change into new clothes. In the meantime Bakari, as instructed by his boss, went to a neighbour to make a phone call to Issa-Mahid's office. A driver was to come immediately to Sinza with the Nissan Patrol. The story that everyone would be told was that Issa-Mahid and Bakari had gone to Mahenge to buy precious stones, and on the way, towards the steep Uluguru mountains, heavy rains had caused the Suzuki to skid out of the road and overturn. Issa-Mahid and Bakari had managed to jump out, but the Suzuki went hurtling down the cliff.

Bakari assured his boss that was the story he would tell to anyone interested to know of Issa-Mahid's absence for two days.

Issa-Mahid had indeed gone to Mahenge several times to seek precious stones, but had not taken Bakari on any of his visits. He had gone with Omari on a number of occasions, and was depending on Omari's expertise in defrauding the diggers. They would leave Dar-es-Salaam with fake stones of different shapes and colours, concealed in pockets. Omari was good at the game, and could easily hide a stone in his broad fingers without arousing suspicions. He would usually take a stone from a seller, and pretend to be examining it. Omari would rub it on his hands, check it against the sun, attempt to grind the stone with his teeth, and drop it on the sand, claiming to see how it repelled the sand. During this examination process, Omari would switch the stone with a fake one of similar structure from his pockets. He would then offer the stone to the seller and claim it was not valuable at all.

Issa-Mahid had stopped taking Omari with him, after it happened that on several occasions when he reached Europe and tried to sell his stones, he found out that some of them were cut from coloured bottles. The prejudices Issa-Mahid suffered from such embarrassments offset the gains he got from depending on Omari's tricks in swindling the poor diggers. Mahmood had preferred to make the trips alone, or accompanied by his girlfriends to keep him company along the road.

When Issa-Mahid appeared again in the living room looking cleaner and smarter, Bakari thought it was the appropriate moment to ask for a return favour.

'Now Boss, what about my request for the house?' Bakari pronounced the words with the deserved eloquence.

At that time a rich humming sound of a powerful diesel engine could be heard outside the front door. Bakari paused for a while, watching Issa-Mahid as he adjusted his collar.

'Look here, if we solve the mystery of this hiccup, and you behave properly, I will think about it.' Issa-Mahid was at the door, and moved to the car.

'But, Mzee, I have taken all the trouble for you, agreed to uphold your integrity, and . . .'

'Oh, come on, mate, there is nothing I hate more in my life than having someone trying to hold me to ransom!' Issa-Mahid charged at Bakari.

'I did not mean that, Mzee . . .'

'Then hold your guns, till I reorganise myself first!'

Bakari went to see his boss out. Issa-Mahid quickly ushered his driver out of the driver's seat and took control of the steering wheel. He started the vehicle and revved the accelerator.

'Stay at home all the time, so that when I need you, I can get hold of you immediately,' Issa-Mahid shouted before jerking the car out of the pavement into the rough road.

When the Nissan disappeared around the corner, Bakari rushed inside the house and quickly inquired from his servant if there had been any other message for him or a visit from any other person.

'Oh, I nearly forgot, Mzee, your aunt came and was looking for you,' the houseboy said.

'Which aunt?' Bakari said without concentrating.

His thoughts at that time were with the whereabouts of Kibosho. Anxiety was building up in Bakari, as he was aware that if Kibosho were to falter at any point in the execution of the plan, the whole plot could misfire with serious repercussions.

'Your aunt, the fat one with a light-brown complexion,' the houseboy emphasised.

'Oh, I see, when was she here?'

'Well, she said she had good news for you from Mtongani.' The boy's voice was stammering.

'Mtongani?' Bakari rose his voice in excitement, 'what else did she say?'

The boy had nothing else to explain, and with mixed feelings Bakari paced the living room with his thumb in between his lips. Good news coming from his wife and children in Mtongani was of great interest to him. The choice now was critical, and it was becoming difficult for Bakari to apportion his priorities. After a while of thought, he made up his mind to rush to Magomeni, check on Kibosho, collect his stuff, then hire a taxi to rush him straight to Mtongani.

There was a Hiace minibus along the Shekilango road with the destination Manzese. From Manzese there would be many buses going to Magomeni. A person rarely spent five minutes at a bus stand. It was exactly at one in the afternoon, and the radio on the dashboard of the microbus was transmitting the news from Radio 3. The national chairman of the CRCRC opposition party was at loggerheads with the general secretary and some other senior members of the party. They were fighting over the misprint of their logo and abbreviations on the thousands of blouses ordered from outside the country. The top officials feared that the mistake would realise less revenue from sales of the blouses, and there would be less money to go between them.

The officials threw verbal abuse at each other, as they regarded the incident an issue of national importance. One faction among the warring parties wanted their followers to march into the streets condemning the party's chairman for collaborating with the printing company to cause such an upset. The other faction disagreed and wanted the party to change its logo and the abbreviation of the party's name so as to coincide with the error appearing on the blouses. They claimed that this was the best alternative to avoid losing all the money used for ordering the blouses.

Bakari, seated behind the driver, requested him to play a musical cassette instead of continuing with the news broadcast. Twelve minutes had elapsed from the commencement of the broadcast and the reader was still on the same political issue. Bakari's request was turned down by some keen supporters who were heading towards their bases in Manzese.

Bakari alighted from the minibus and walked for about ten metres to take the connecting bus to Magomeni. He sat more comfortably in the twenty-six seater bus that was playing a loud Ndombolo song from the Congo. A woman wearing a tight shift-dress clambered into the bus. Bakari ogled her and she turned her face away from him. Bakari's eyes followed her until she reached the back seat where she sat. After a while Bakari regained his composure and wondered why he was distracting his concentration from the more important issues he had planned for the day.

It was two thirty when he reached the shabby house in Magomeni. Bakari entered the house and met one of Kibosho's neighbours in the corridor. The man greeted Bakari and quickly pointed at the door of Kibosho's room.

'What happened?' Bakari quickly asked the chap.

'Broken down,' the short man answered.

'Who did it?' Bakari asked, as a ray of horror ripped across his body.

The chap ushered Bakari out of the house and back into the street. At that time plenty of perspiration was forming on Bakari's brow.

'They broke down his door and splattered everything in the room,' the short man said with a scratchy voice.

'Who . . . who did, and why?' Bakari stammered so much and he was finding it hard to maintain an upright posture.

'Let's move up the road and I will tell you what I saw that night. It is not safe to stay here; the police were here in the morning,' the man said to Bakari.

# CHAPTER 13

Hooters of different buses and the movements of informal vendors at the Magomeni bus station were driving demons in Bakari's head as he tried frantically to get a taxi. It was seven-thirty in the evening, and so dark already, that it had become impossible to see clearly whether a car coming from the front was a taxi or a normal passenger car. Most of the taxis in the city did not carry a display on top, so it was not easy to distinguish them. Eventually one passed by, and Bakari had to shout at the top of his voice for it to stop.

He sat at the back and ordered the taxi to speed him to Mikocheni, using the Drive-In road. The other alternative, through the Morocco road, was too congested at that time of the night. The taxi was old, and the best it could do was nothing more than sixty kilometres per hour. There was heavy traffic as well along the Bagamoyo road with numerous commuter buses stopping now and then to drop off passengers. Bakari was becoming so impatient that several times he had to slap hard on his thigh in frustration.

The taxi paused in transit in a long queue after the Salander bridge. A traffic police officer was directing movement of the traffic, and had stopped cars coming from the Bagamoyo road, to give a chance to cars coming from the Kinondoni road. The officer was busy waving at the cars to pass, urging them to move faster. Bakari sat stiff in the taxi, knowing that the situation was out of his driver's control. He unwound the door window all the way down, and could feel the scent of sea water moving up the Msimbazi creek. The water had a pungent smell, and he felt it more seated in the car than he normally felt when walking along the road. Maybe it was psychological, but his nostrils were giving him that message.

Eventually, the taxi surged forward and continued towards the Namanga shopping complex. There were fewer cars on the road, as most of them had taken the road towards Oyster Bay. Bakari pulled his thin beard and sighed heavily. Things were moving in circles, bringing total confusion to him. He could easily guess the identity of the man driving an Isuzu Trooper, responsible for ransacking Kibosho's room in Magomeni. According to

Kibosho's neighbour, the man came in the middle of the night with a group of thugs. With a single kick he had forced Kibosho's door down, and let in his men. The motive for the assault on Kibosho's room remained a mystery to Bakari.

He knew that there could be many possibilities that prompted Omari to do such an act. Bakari feared to think of some of these options. The possibility of him striking it rich following the Brazilian trip was becoming increasingly remote. Kibosho took the original briefcase packed with rich narcotics worth millions of shillings and was supposed to send the consignment to Bakari's house. Bakari hoped that Kibosho had not opened his wide mouth and made careless remarks that jeopardised the whole scheme.

Bakari cursed Kibosho for being so irresponsible. When Bakari briefed him of the scheme, Kibosho assured Bakari that he understood it perfectly well. Where could he have gone wrong then? Could it be that Kibosho was being trailed by Omari's spies and they intercepted him immediately after taking the bag from the airport? Bakari regretted his decision to work with Kibosho. Only now did Bakari recall that Kibosho was a crook and responsible for having him fired at the Port.

After he got sacked from the Port as well, Kibosho worked as a servant at Omari's house, sometimes helping with other businesses belonging to Omari. The former deputy manager had stooped that low in order to avoid possible starvation. Kibosho told Bakari that he took part in putting the finishing touches to Omari's house in Mikocheni, and knew it in detail. Kibosho claimed that although he worked hard for Omari, he was paid a meagre wage and always got insulted. Kibosho was thus bitter with Omari. The bitterness was augmented after discovering that Omari was responsible for brewing the scandal that had resulted in him losing his post as assistant manager, and a six-month spell at the Ukonga prison.

When Bakari and Kibosho conversed at the Mapipa Sunlight Bar, Kibosho had expressed his desire for revenge. Bakari took his word and trusted him. He gave Kibosho the chance to retaliate and also make some money. With his shirt hanging on his skeletal body, and hands shaking as he held his glass of beer, Kibosho had agreed to cooperate. Bakari's frequent travels overseas and the numerous presents he brought had won him friends at the customs. The officers had helped him smuggle in his television set, video recorder and a music system.

On Bakari's arrival from Brazil, one of the officers had been assigned to take the plastic shopping bag through the back of the arrival lounge, as far as the ticket offices. From there Kibosho was to take the bag, jump into a taxi, and speed to Sinza to offload the drugs into the manhole. Kibosho was to choose a time he was sure Omari was not at home, and take the shopping bag with him to Mikocheni. A chill passed over Bakari's spine, when he envisioned Kibosho being Omari's agent. Perhaps Kibosho had informed Omari of the whole scheme, and Omari had encouraged him to go ahead, then double-crossed him as well towards the end. But if this was the case, and if Omari tipped the police to come to the airport to surprise Bakari and Issa-Mahid, Omari would have known that Bakari was not carrying the right briefcase.

Seated in the taxi, Bakari recalled the intention he had to purchase his own car from the departing expatriate. Bakari had not organised enough money to pay for it. He had initially hoped to accumulate enough funds from his side activities, but he had fallen short of his target. Constant interruptions and threats from his boss not to engage in his own business, meant he had to hide himself when doing them. A business that is being run whilst the owner is in obscurity, fearing to present his face to the clients, hardly succeeds.

Before his current plan went astray, Bakari had even planned to acquire a four-wheeled vehicle, in addition to the saloon he expected from the expatriate. He would have two cars, and had envisioned that when Mwajuma returned to him he would teach her to drive and leave the saloon with her. These dreams were quickly dissipating from his mind as he sat at the back of a tottering taxi, going to the unknown. Bakari needed to stop his racing and perturbed mind, and ask himself what he planned to do at Mikocheni. The desire to reach the destination, though, was overwhelming him.

The taxi carrying Bakari reached the junction at Morocco road and stopped at the traffic lights.

'Just go past them, there is no car on the other side,' Bakari said to the taxi driver with a trembling voice.

'No, I don't want trouble,' the driver spoke with a sullen face.

'Trouble with whom?' Bakari's voice went up.

'The traffic police – what do you think?' The driver also raised his voice.

'With five hundred shillings they will let you go!'

'Who will give them the five hundred?'

'You of course, it is part of your overheads.'

'Just leave me to do my driving the way I know.'

Bakari cursed him, but at the same time the lights turned to green and the car behind the taxi hooted. The driver jerked the car and it stalled. Bakari cursed again and slapped hard on his thigh. The driver tried to restart the car, his face showing exasperation. On the third attempt it started again, but the lights were turning from amber to red. A flurry of horns and insults could be heard from the cars behind the white taxi. Bakari had raised his hands to his head, unable to do anything else but to wait.

He still had a faint ray of hope lingering in his mind. In it, Bakari hoped Kibosho had remembered to off-load at least a packet or two of the narcotics from the secret compartment and had placed them in Omari's hiding place. If Bakari reached there in time and manage to locate the hiding place, he would have at least a packet that could fetch hundreds of thousands of shillings in the streets. If he was lucky he might find other packets from previous trips that Omari had taken from the briefcase and replaced with packets of bread flour before handing the briefcase to Issa-Mahid. Omari might also have some gem-stones and money in cash stashed in the same hiding place, to which Bakari could help himself.

In forming these thoughts Bakari did not get the feeling that he was a potential burglar on a mission to unlawfully break into someone's house. He felt justified to go and collect what belonged to him and not Omari. If he was going to steal, he would be stealing from a big thief, and according to his conviction, it was justifiable. Bakari sighed loudly again, causing the driver to look at him in amazement.

This was the same man he had bailed out of a long prison term in Tanga, two decades earlier. Omari had gone without food and nearly starved, and Bakari had given him money. When Omari was gasping with high fever at the Bumbuli Hospital, Bakari had forced some hot porridge in his mouth and had had to duck when Omari vomited it out at him.

Perhaps Omari had not forgotten all these good deeds Bakari had done to him. Maybe Omari was preparing a feast for his friend in anticipation of his visit. All the dubious things Omari had done to Bakari could have been aimed at eventually bringing the best out of Bakari as a way of thanking him for being such a good friend in Tanga those many years ago. Possibly Bakari failed to recognise it this way, distrusted Omari, and found himself where he was at present: full of anxiety. Bakari was passing into a light phase of hallucination as the taxi surged on.

The taxi eventually took a turn to Mafichoni road. After it had moved for half a kilometre, Bakari ordered the driver to stop and he got out. He would finish the rest of the distance on foot. He gave two thousand shillings to the driver, but the man protested, demanding another thousand. Bakari did not want a row with the sulky driver at that time, and tossed two five hundred shilling notes through the window, and jeered at him.

'The only thing you will gain in your life is to collect money on the floor!' Bakari sneered again.

The driver did not respond, he just looked at Bakari and bent down to pick up his money.

The light on the street was provided by the bulbs from gates and spotlights from the big houses along the road. Few cars moved along the street, and only one or two people could be seen along the whole stretch of the road.

After walking for a while, Bakari saw Omari's house from a little distance, and realised it was dark, except for a fluorescent tube near the entrance. Bakari had been there before, but had not been accorded the opportunity of being shown around it. The host had allowed him to come and sit on the veranda and consume a bottle of beer. It was a one-storeyed mansion with a newly painted front entrance. Bakari could only get a glance at the living room where Omari entertained guests he considered conformed to his newly attained status. Omari's relatives from rural areas, and low level business associates like Bakari were entertained on the plastic chairs in the patio. Omari had a Persian carpet in the main living room, and in order to avoid it being trampled upon, had to restrict the number of people in the living room.

As Bakari approached the house, he noticed that the small door on the main gate was left ajar. That signified that someone was in the house. There was no car on the driveway, and Bakari made his way in, walking on the grass. He expected to find the security officer from the guards' unit standing at the gate, to ask him if Kibosho had been there, and find out the whereabouts of his boss. Bakari would then go around the wall encircling Omari's house, look for a suitable place, and climb on it. He would use a stone to crush the pieces of broken bottle sticking above the wall and jump inside. Knowing that the guard would only be at the main gate, Bakari would approach a small window on the side of the house and make his way into the house. Kibosho had given him a brief plan of the house when they were drinking together prior to his departure to Amsterdam.

With the absence of a guard at the main gate, Bakari shuffled his feet further on the grass towards the house. Panic seized him, as he drew closer to the veranda. How could the place be so deserted, when he knew Omari always took necessary precautions? Bakari stopped and tried to listen if there was any noise in the compound, or vicinity. He was convinced at that moment that it was highly unlikely to find Kibosho at the house.

With his heart beating, Bakari recalled the story of Kibosho's neighbour in Magomeni. The neighbour confessed that when Omari came to look for his servant, he was in a high state of anger. Other tenants of the house were

185

gripped with apprehension when they heard noises and insults being hurled at two in the morning. The tenants had gathered and watched helplessly as Omari and two of his lieutenants broke down the door, cautioning the neighbours not to stop them. They had asked where Kibosho was, calling him a big thief, and threatened to burn down the whole house if the tenants did not inform them where the culprit was hiding.

The landlord, a man in his seventies, had come out and pleaded with Omari, explaining that no one had seen the culprit for two days. It was at this point that someone suggested that Kibosho might have gone to Moshi. Omari had proceeded to search Kibosho's room, turning upside down the few possessions that were in the room. What had Kibosho taken from Omari to make him search for his servant so desperately? Perhaps even at that time Omari could be searching for his servant somewhere in the wilderness.

Bakari was convinced that Kibosho could still be somewhere in Dar-es-Salaam, maybe drinking his life away at an obscure bar. Bakari was becoming bewildered by these thoughts as he continued moving stealthily along the grass in Omari's compound. He then reached the servants' quarters at the back of the compound where Kibosho used to spend some nights when he had to work late for Omari. Bakari knocked at the door but there was no reply. Bakari tried the door, and it was ajar. It was dark and Bakari was scared to put the lights on. He moved in the dark room and called the name Kibosho. He felt haunted and decided to leave the room. When Bakari held the door again, he noticed that the latch was hanging loose. He concentrated his eyes on it and realised it had been broken. Someone must have broken down this door as well.

Bakari became fully convinced that there was something weird going on in that compound. What could have incited Omari to move all over the place breaking down doors? That is, if he were responsible for breaking down the servants' door as well. From their days in Tanga, Bakari knew Omari as a very intemperate person. Omari used to pick up fights over trivial things that a reasonable person would simply disregard. He would argue with his friends about soccer, and when a friend despised his team, Omari could get upset and throw a punch at him. Bakari had always avoided arguing with him over the Young Africans and Simba Sports soccer teams. They favoured different sides and there was always a potential danger of conflict whenever the two teams played.

Time was passing and no solution emerged in Bakari's tormented mind. He was standing at the servants' quarters, undecided what to do next. He must have been standing for ten minutes waiting to see if an illusionary image of Kibosho would appear from somewhere. As he thought, Bakari remembered about the message from his aunt coming from Mtongani. Mwajuma was prepared to come to Sinza with the children. Bakari was supposed to have left a while ago for Mtongani to collect her, if it were not for this emergency. The time could be around eight in the evening. If he had to leave Mikocheni, he would arrive at Mtongani at ten at the earliest. People at Mtongani would be surprised to see him coming at that time, but he would not lose the opportunity to pick up Mwajuma.

For her to come to Sinza, be comfortable and at peace, Bakari needed money. A woman becomes a good and happy wife if there is money in the house. He had experienced problems with her before when he had no money, and was not prepared to allow the situation to recur. Bakari had come to Mikocheni hoping to recover what he reckoned belonged to him.

The teacher who taught him during the last year of primary school always emphasised fighting for one's rights. The teacher was a political refugee from a country in Southern Africa which Bakari could not recall outright. The bearded man had a scar on his cheek that he proudly showed to his pupils, telling them he sustained it in a shoot-out with the colonial police during a demonstration. The teacher had promised Bakari and his other pupils that when his country finally got independence, he would invite them for a visit. Bakari remembered seeing the teacher for a few more years after finishing standard seven, but had not heard of him since.

All of Southern Africa was now free from colonial domination, so the teacher must have gone back home, to occupy a senior position. As had been the case with many other Southern African exiles who made emotional promises to their Tanzanian friends, he too must have promptly forgotten about his friends when he departed. Bakari sighed at these thoughts and stepped out of the servants' quarters. He moved on the paved footpath to the kitchen area of the main house.

Apprehension seized him when he thought of moving into the main house. It appeared as if there was no one in the main house. How could everyone leave such a luxurious house unattended all the way from the gate? Bakari realised he could not achieve anything standing outside the kitchen biting his nails. He looked in all directions and approached the kitchen door. If he was caught there, there would be no excuse, but he would be considered as a burglar, and could find himself in a police station.

Bakari tried the kitchen door, and the latch remained on his hand. He quickly dropped it on the floor as if it were burning his hand. There must be something very weird about the house that evening. He quickly left the kitchen area and retreated back onto the grass. From there he listened to hear if there were any other movements. The place was as still as if he were alone in the whole area. Bakari moved around the building until he came close to the gate. There were no signs of movement anywhere in the vicinity. He turned around and moved back towards the kitchen. Bakari tried a window: the burglar bars were all over the place. Bakari thought of going to check the front door, but the light from the gate shone there and it was risky to approach it without being detected.

From afar, Bakari noticed that the front door was half-way open. Someone could be inside, he thought. He found it strange and scary that the house was left in this way, and was now convinced there might be a trap set up.

Bakari decided to abandon the search and move out of the compound. He quickly crossed the grass, reached the gate and jumped out. He rushed up the street, but after a hundred metres he stopped. Bakari was becoming undecided. How could he leave the house without knowing where Kibosho was and the fate of the bag? It was extremely important at least to know what had transpired with Omari from the time he left for overseas. If the bag had fallen into the wrong hands, or if Kibosho had revealed the plot to Omari, then Bakari's life would be in great danger. It was better to confront Omari, find out what he knew, and try to sort out issues with him before they reached Issa-Mahid.

If Omari had caught Kibosho with the bag in his house, he wouldn't have gone looking for him at Magomeni and broken down his door. Omari would have sorted him out there and then, and Kibosho's body would have long been fed to the fish in the Indian Ocean. Equally logically, if Kibosho had recounted the whole plot to his boss, Kibosho wouldn't need to be a fugitive; instead he would be seated comfortably at Omari's servant quarters sharing at most some crumbs from the loot.

Bakari turned and headed back to the gate. This time he came thumping his feet on the ground and even knocked at the gate. He knew that there was no one there, but he did that anyway. He then walked on the paved footpath, shouting 'Hodi' for everyone to hear that he was coming. He reached the middle of the compound and called on the guard at the top of his voice, but each time he would hear the echo of his voice on the fence wall. Bakari moved to the half-open front door and knocked at it. He shoved it, shouting 'Hodi' time and time again. When he realised there was no reply, Bakari pushed the door and walked into the lounge.

Bakari called out asking if there was anyone in the house, pretending he came for a visit. It was quiet, save for a flip of curtain caused by a slight wind. Bakari braved the switch on the wall, and switched it on. It only lit a dim wall light. Bakari called the name Omari again and waited to hear if there was any response. There was a big photograph of Omari with his arm around a pretty woman with a light complexioned face, and long hair. Bakari recognised her as the mixed race woman Omari had taken as his new wife, after he became rich and moved to Mikocheni. Bakari was not expecting the woman to be in the house. Kibosho had told him two weeks earlier that Omari had flown her to Dubai for a medical check-up. The woman was expecting their first child.

The staircase wound up to the first floor. Bakari put his foot on the first step, holding on to the banister. He called his friend's name again, apprehension seizing him. Bakari decided to move upstairs. There had not been any response to his calling, but the house appeared to be in order. There were no signs of any commotion or burglary, yet the kitchen door seemed to have been broken. Doors broken, yet the house seemed to be in perfect order. What could have been the motive of whoever decided to gain access to the house? Bakari turned and looked behind him as he reached the top of the stairs.

He tried to open a door, and it was open; he peered inside and from the size of the room it appeared to be the children's room. Omari had not brought any of the numerous children he sired from different women to live with him at Mikocheni. The present wife was sophisticated and adorned with Western culture, and would not tolerate having children of other women. She did not believe in extended families and had ordered Omari to restrict the number of his relatives cramming into Mikocheni. According to information Bakari got from Kibosho, the new wife had even insisted that Omari's mother slept at the servant house when the sick old lady came from the village to visit her son.

Bakari called Omari's name loudly before trying another room. This time he found the door locked. Bakari went for another door at the corner and gently twisted the round steel knob. The knob turned fully and the door snapped open. With a slight chill forming on his back and a trembling voice, Bakari called Omari's name. The room was dead quiet. Bakari felt sweat beads developing on his brow as he took the first steps into the large carpeted room.

Bakari hesitated; he was not sure if he heard a slight noise from somewhere. He now sweated profusely, his hands shaking so much that he had to rub his hands to dry the sweat. At one point he thought of abandoning everything, dashing out of the house and running as fast as possible out of that haunted manor.

189

But as he had gone this far, there was no point in turning back. The secret hiding hole for Omari's loot should be somewhere near where he stood. A few more brave moments might enable him to get hold of the prized bag with its valuable contents. If Kibosho had forgotten or failed to find the secret compartment in the briefcase, it would be even better. The whole consignment had a street value of millions of shillings. Such an amount of money would enable him to build a house, buy himself a brand new car, and even take Mwajuma and the children for a shopping trip to the Emirates. The stakes were high, so the risks were justifiable.

# CHAPTER 14

Bakari held the door of the master bathroom and unlocked it. He was greeted by the sweet scent of a mixture of perfume and toilet soaps. It was quite dark in the toilet to figure out the position of the false ceiling hole. Being a smoker had its advantages; a smoker carries a matchbox most of the time. A flicker from his match would produce enough light to find his way in the room, without causing too much light to attract someone from outside.

There was an ironing table on the other side of the toilet, and that is what Bakari needed. He extinguished the match, took the ironing table, and cautiously climbed onto it. He stretched himself till his hands reached the roof made of thin wooden strips. He had his palms on the ceiling, pushing up at intervals. His hands were also feeling for a latch or button that might need to be pressed for the door to open. Bakari struck another match and surveyed the roof. It all looked even; or perhaps the dim light given by the match could not allow his eyes to notice fine demarcation lines on the ceiling.

What his eyes managed to catch were neat shelves packed with a range of different sized bottles. These were the arsenal of cosmetics and accessories belonging to the lady of the house. It was a clear manifestation of the expenses Omari had to incur to maintain his new spouse. It was also apparent that in order for the fair woman to stay with him, the man had to be on continuous search for lots of money. Quick money in droves does not come easily, especially if one wants to be on the safe side of the law. But if one has a wife who regularly demands to be flown to Johannesburg for shopping, and who wants to host lavish parties for the rich and famous, money has to be found even from the wrong side of the law.

Bakari continued with his search on the ceiling. He stepped from the ironing board, moved it into a new position and climbed onto it again. All along, the timber strips defied his hands and the wood remained tightly in place. Bakari felt as if the ironing board was wobbling; he quickly moved from it and stepped on the ceramic basin. The basin appeared more secure, and from there Bakari felt the roof again. He then stepped from the basin, onto the top of the cistern. The distance to the roof was now extended, and Bakari had to stretch his hands even higher to reach the ceiling.

Bakari came close to toppling over when his hands suddenly lifted a plank on the ceiling. For a moment he tried to balance himself, but the top cover of the cistern moved. Bakari held onto the shower riser pipe that saved him from falling to the ground.

With a weary smile on his face, Bakari felt the sides of the hole he had discovered. His exploring fingers went from side to side, hoping to grasp something that would widen his smile. He had forgotten a bitter lesson he had learned while working for the fumigation centre at the Port. He had once wandered into an open store with little visibility. The store was always kept locked, and on that occasion the storekeeper had forgotten to turn the key before leaving. Bakari thought he could find a weighing scale or a strapping machine that he could smuggle out and sell for a couple of shillings.

It happened during the days Bakari was going through severe financial problems. He moved in the damp store, his hands feeling every area of the room. He felt something and tried to lift it, but the item was too heavy for his hands. His hands reached a shelf on one corner of the room, and felt something. Incidentally, Bakari's fingers triggered a mouse trap that snapped on the back of his hand. The guards were not very far from the store, so Bakari had refrained from screaming despite the sharp pain that surged up his arm. He had swallowed, bearing the awful pain; he lowered his injured hand from the shelf and doddered out of the store. The mouse trap was still clinging on his hand as he rushed out of the door and into the toilet.

This evening, Bakari's fingers were not to meet a painful surprise. On the side of that secret hole, he felt something like a bundle of paper slips. He pulled down the first bundle, balanced himself on the cistern, and held it in the palm of his hand. A grown up man like him did not require the assistance of light to recognise a bundle of shillings. Without even thinking, he sniffed the bundle and his nose gave him the confirmation he needed. For those who were more experienced in dealing with money, they could tell the denomination of the notes from the variety of pungent smells they carried. Bakari was not that perfect, but was sure that Omari would not waste his time stuffing a hundred or two hundred shilling bundles in such a valuable and restricted area.

Bakari stuffed the bundle in his pocket and lifted the hand back to the hole. He heaved himself further up, and felt more bundles. Breathing heavily, he stuffed more and more bundles in his pockets, pants and shirt. His senses were shut off from everything else that was happening around him. His feet were wobbling and body streaming with sweat as his hands worked. He wished he had come with a big bag to collect everything that he felt in the hole. If he had known that things were going to be this easy: to find the house wide open and placed at his disposal, he would have hired a van to come and clear it up.

Then there was a loud bang. Bakari came tumbling down and crashed on the floor. Then everything became quiet.

The neighbourhood of Mikocheni housed people of high income and of high standing in the society. Nearly every building was surrounded by a high wall, sometimes with warnings at the gates of fierce dogs, or surveillance by security systems. Few people knew exactly what happened with their neighbours, and in some cases, neighbours did not know one another. When they needed to communicate, they would use a phone or leave a note at the gate.

Such a way of life was detestable in the Swahili areas. In Kiwalani, people living in a radius of one kilometre knew each other by name and tribe. Housewives within the ten house cells would even be aware who was cooking chicken on a particular evening. If a housewife entertained a lover, news would move from house to house, and eventually reached the ears of the husband. For this reason, educated Swahilis and those who could afford it, would flee from these cramped residential areas, and take refuge in the secluded suburbs.

The secluded, posh areas had their disadvantages as well. Each household was on its own. If thieves managed to force their way past the security guards, or silence the dogs, then there was little chance of escape for the dwellers of the house. They ended up entrapped behind their own high walls.

The single loud bang of gunfire coming from a house in Mikocheni would have been heard by several neighbours. None of them bothered to come out of their houses to find out what had happened. They took it as an issue that didn't concern them. It was not their habit to get involved in other people's affairs. Some would even deny the loud bang was the sound of gunfire, assuring their spouses that a car might have backfired.

One or two of the neighbours already knew Omari by now. Omari had invited them to the cocktail parties he used to host. These neighbours were aware of the existence next to them of an exceptionally sophisticated lady with long hair. The lady would not open the door of the car unless her husband or the driver did it for her. A blunt shot coming from that house should have aroused interest from these neighbours.

Meanwhile in the besieged house, Bakari found himself sprawled on the floor, with pieces of ceramic surrounding him. The range of bottles of perfumes and cosmetics also came crashing down with him, as he tried frantically to hold onto the shelves. The bank-notes Bakari had stuffed in his shirt and trousers did not help cushion him during the fall. He felt pain on his elbows, and suspected he had sprained his ankle. Bakari stumbled to his feet and attempted to come to terms with the reality of the moment.

His memory had came back to him and he remembered hearing a deafening blast coming from downstairs. If Bakari could recall well, prior to tumbling to the floor, he had heard a groaning noise accompanied by a dull thud, as if a heavy sack was thrown on the floor. Complete silence had returned to the house as Bakari made his way out of the toilet. He shuffled amidst the debris of ceramics and broken bottles, and nearly slipped on some liquid stuff spilled on the floor.

As Bakari tried to reach the door of the toilet he heard some fresh noise from downstairs. Great fear seized him and he quickly struggled out of the toilet to the master bedroom. He stumbled on the bed as it was dark in the room, and moved to a corner. Bakari heard footsteps coming upwards. As a young man in Tanga, Bakari's other interest, apart from chasing women and drinking, was to watch horror movies. When Dracula movies were shown at the Scala Cinema, Bakari would not miss a session. He fancied dragging his girlfriend along and cherished comforting her when she got scared of the acts on the screen.

One scene that always occurred in a Dracula movie, was the part where Dracula prowls to his victim, most likely at night, the action taking place in a dimmed room. The directors of the movies would create the scenes to be sensational. They would lay out the music to enhance the action. A distant beat of a drum would follow the villain as he walked up the stairs. The intensity of the beat would increase on each extra step he took towards his victim. The directors would present grating and frightening music, whose speed and volume would increase as Dracula prepared his fangs to pierce his victim's neck.

The footsteps coming towards Bakari were getting louder, and he could hear a breathing sound accompanying them. There was no music or beat of drums to enhance the intensity of the peril that was approaching. If there had been the sound of gunfire in the house, it was obvious that the person approaching the master-bedroom at that time possessed a gun. If he had used the gun on someone already the chances were there that he would use it on Bakari.

If the person pursuing Bakari was already on top of the stairs, then there was little chance for Bakari to escape. Panic seized Bakari and he poked his tongue out to lick the drain of sweat flowing down his face. His head was heavy, with no solution coming to it. He wondered whether he should just put on the lights, go down on his knees and wait for whoever was coming into the room, to quickly recognise him and maybe forgive him for all he had done. The footsteps were now approaching the door of the master-bedroom.

Bakari took two steps back from the door, his body shaking so much that froth came out of his mouth. Only one reality came into his lame mind at that moment. He had joined the shadowy world and got involved in a narcotics ring; later he had betrayed his associates. He wished he had continued running the small tea-room in Temeke, living a poor but normal life. He would not have made enough money selling fat buns and coffee, but at least he would have made fewer and less perilous enemies. Bakari wanted lots of money and had planned to deviate a whole consignment of narcotics to make money for himself and his new-found associate, Kibosho. It seemed he had picked on the wrong mate. Kibosho had disrupted all their plans, and put his life in danger.

Bakari knew the rewards of such treachery, and how painful it could be. He was aware that he wasn't a guest, but a burglar in Omari's house. The pockets of his trousers were bulging with something that did not belong to him. He regretted having returned to the house after leaving initially. He would have been better off if he knew of the proverb that a house left open without attendance was more dangerous than a cordoned castle with a platoon of guards standing at the gate. Common sense should have dictated to Bakari that Omari would not have left the doors wide open for him to walk into his house unhindered, and help himself on very valuable possessions.

With the functioning of his mind completely under the control of the power that generated fear, Bakari quickly clambered to the top of the dressing table. Bakari's hands wandered around the dressing table, attempting to grab anything he could reach. His ears were still trained on the door, and he heard the door handle being slowly turned. Bakari quickened the pace with which his hands searched the dressing table and its surroundings. His hands eventually felt something on the edge of the table and tried to lift it. It was heavy with a rough surface, but with all his might he hoisted it over his head.

The door was flung open and a bulging figure crashed into the room. There were tense moments of quietness and despair. The figure moved in the room, and after a few moments the lights in the room went on. Bakari's eyes were impaired by the sudden flash of light, but in a split second Bakari saw a bald head below him. In the person's hand was a black automatic weapon.

There was another loud crash in the house, but this time it was made amidst the clatter of hundreds of cast iron pieces spattering over the floor of the master-bedroom. On top of these pieces tumbled two bodies of middle-aged adults, one on top of the other. One of the bodies began letting out a pool of fresh blood from a huge hole in the skull. The other body was still mobile, and slowly it organised itself to its knees. This body, filled with so much pain and stress, belonged to Bakari. He lifted himself from the floor and tried to come to terms with what had happened in those past seconds.

Bakari was born with a strong body, and developed it well during the time he played soccer. One thing that troubled him, though, was to carry heavy things on his head or in his arms. Even at the time he worked at the stores department of the Port, he avoided hoisting boxes over his head, and complained to his supervisor that his arms were not as strong as they appeared. The cast iron vase he had picked from the floor, filled with coral stones to support the artificial flowers in it, could have weighed nearly forty kilograms. Bakari did not comprehend the source of the energy that enabled him to swing the item over his head, and bring it crashing down on his friend's head with such intensity.

Bakari was on his feet, and at that moment, fear had completely left him. He bent down to pick the gun from the lifeless body on the floor. The dead man was still clutching tightly onto the gun, demonstrating the resolve he had to protect his house and property at all costs. Bakari's subconscious mind convinced him that there were other people still haunting him in that besieged house. He took the pistol in his hand and staggered out of the room. Bakari tripped at the door, and the gun dropped from his hand. He quickly went for it and clutched it securely again, his index finger pressing lightly on the trigger.

Bakari could hardly maintain himself upright, as his ankle was badly swollen. There was also a sharp pain from the left side of his ribs, where he got hurt following the fall from the dressing table.

Bakari tottered from the master-bedroom and went down the stairs. When he reached the base of the stairs, he remembered the money. In his pocket, only one bundle remained; the rest had fallen off when he rolled on the floor. Feeling dizzy, Bakari struggled painfully back to the top of the stairs. He ground his teeth with pain and shoved open the door of the master-bedroom. Bakari opened the door to the toilet and brushed his hand on the wall, feeling for the switch till he succeeded in finding it. On the floor were bundles of ten thousand shilling notes, mingled with broken porcelain debris.

Bakari picked up the bundles and dropped them on the floor again. A weary smile escaped from his lips, and he coughed. The pain on the side of his ribs was exacerbated. He moved back into the master-bedroom. He skipped over the body lying on a pool of blood, and did not even feel queasy seeing the body of his business associate. Bakari had killed him using his own hands, by smashing his head. At that time, Bakari was not occupying his mind with what he had done. He was more concerned with the desire to garner as much as possible from the house of a man he bitterly hated.

Bakari removed some curios from a tall stool that was at the far end of the master-bedroom, and threw them on top of the bed. He then towed the stool with a screeching noise on the tiled floor. He did not have sufficient energy left to lift the stool. Bakari pulled it until he reached the toilet and positioned it below the hole in the ceiling. With the florescent light in the room, Bakari appreciated the way the hole had been craftily set, and how well concealed it became when properly shut. He did not foresee Omari being that creative, but he was aware that with all the property he owned in the house, Omari had been far ahead of him in life.

Bakari clambered on the stool and groaned with the resulting pain on his left ankle. He put the left foot on the side plank and balanced his knee on top of the stool. He heaved his body up, making sure he did not place too much weight on one edge of the stool to avoid tumbling over. The height of the stool allowed him to reach the ceiling easily, and he could extend his arm deep inside the hole. His weary, yet eager hands pulled the remaining bundles and packets of white powder from the roof. His searching hands managed to feel a small, but heavy, cloth bag. He pulled it to his chest. Bakari quickly fumbled with the bag and poured on his trembling hand, stones that glittered with the light of the fluorescent tube. His heartbeat increased, as he stuffed the precious stones in his pocket.

When no more energy remained in his hands, and he could not feel any other thing, Bakari slowly lowered his legs from the stool and sat on it. He waited for a few moments to regain a bit of energy, then dragged himself to the floor. He left the toilet again and limped into the bedroom. Bakari searched the room for a container to carry his loot. All the wardrobes were locked and he had no energy to force them open. He then reached for a sheet from the bed and dragged it along the floor. On the way it got soaked with some of the blood spewed on the floor. Bakari did not notice the dark red stains on the sheet, but proceeded to pack it with the bundles of notes and the packets of white powder.

Bakari worked for a while, having to pause from time to time to regain some strength. Half of his body was numb at that time, and he began coughing. The fall he had experienced when he delivered the fatal blow on the deceased, was more serious than he realised. His ribs had hit the edge of the wooden bed. Bakari disregarded his suffering and proceeded to tie the four ends of the bedsheet into a huge bundle. He dragged it from the toilet. The bundle came along, mopping up pieces of ceramic and bottles of perfume. Bakari paused at the door and removed the pieces of glass clinging to the bedsheet, fearing they would rip open his valuable bundle. He eventually moved the bundle to the master-bedroom.

After managing to dodge the body and pool of blood on the floor, Bakari sat on top of the bundle and breathed heavily. He cleared some of the froth from his mouth and sneezed. His chest pained him intensely as he sneezed again. He stood up and felt dazzled, but stubbornly dragged the bundle out of the master-bedroom door. Bakari saw the pistol on the floor; he went for it and tucked it into his trousers. He groaned as his wounded ankle twisted when shuffling along the carpet. Bakari's relentless efforts enabled him to pull the bundle to the top of the stairs.

He positioned the package on the top step and rolled it down the stairs. Bakari limped down to follow his new possessions. At the bottom of the stairs Bakari remembered that he had left the master-bedroom without searching the drawers, or the pockets of his deceased friend. He might be hiding other valuable items somewhere in the room, especially on hidden corners or below the mattress. As Bakari decided to turn and head back to the master-bedroom, he saw a body lying at the other end of the living room.

As he had seen in movies on many occasions, when an actor, the hero of the movie, sees a precarious situation, the first action is to flip out his pistol. Bakari did the same thing and drew the gun from the front of his trousers. He cautiously approached the body on the floor, his finger tightening on the trigger. Having forgotten temporarily his sufferings he advanced to the body and turned it around. Bakari was already dazzled by the incidents that had occurred upstairs, but he could not avoid gasping in horror on seeing the open, yet lifeless eyes of his boss. He quickly drew back and went to stand at the side of the long sofa. He recalled hearing a single shot around the house earlier on. Bakari examined the body and found a small hole on his chest, with blood that had soaked his shirt.

Issa-Mahid was wearing a pair of gloves on his limp hands. Bakari deduced that Issa-Mahid might have come to Omari's house with a clear purpose. He appeared to be a professional assassin by the way he had prepared himself. Bakari wondered what might have gone wrong for the hunter to become a victim himself. It was clear that Omari must have killed Issa-Mahid and was coming upstairs to finish off whoever was making the noise from there. How the two deceased managed to locate each other in the darkness, remained a mystery to Bakari.

At that moment Bakari noticed that there was another pistol at the edge of the wall. Bakari went for it and lifted it up. The gun was bigger and heavier: a masterpiece of a weapon. It should belong to the assailant, and on closer examination Bakari confirmed his suspicious when he found that it was engraved MIM below the safety catch. The gun must have fallen from Issa-Mahid when he tumbled to the ground. He wondered how long the two men had been hunting one another, as it was now apparent that both knew of the presence of the other around the compound and had guns on their hands. Bakari suspected that Issa-Mahid had walked into Omari's compound, somehow immobilised the guard and gone around breaking latches, looking for Omari. All that time, Omari must have been avoiding his assailant, and waiting to get a shot at him.

Bakari had forgotten about himself and used his time pondering over his boss's body. Bakari did not like him much, but the sight of the man lying in a pool of blood made Bakari sad. If he had to choose between the two devils, Bakari would prefer Issa-Mahid to Omari. Bakari would have preferred Issa-Mahid to shoot Omari, rather than him having to break Omari's head with a cast iron vase. Bakari wanted to steal lots of money from Issa-Mahid, but was not after his blood. He would have liked Issa-Mahid to live and send him on other missions, which Bakari could have used to swindle him.

After a while Bakari left the body of his boss and limped back to the base of the stairs. He clutched the bundle and dragged it towards the main door. Then he remembered Issa-Mahid's diamond clustered Rolex watch, and the gold rings he wore. In his pockets he should have some car keys, although there was no car packed on the driveway. From the tag of the keys he would know which type of car Issa-Mahid was driving and he would go around the area looking for it. Bakari also remembered Omari's Isuzu Trooper, which should be in the garage. He thought of making a quick dash upstairs to search for the keys, but he did not have much strength in his limbs. All these opportunities were coming to him at a bad time when he was so badly injured. Feelings of exasperation resulting from Bakari's plans having gone badly wrong were making him hysterical.

Suddenly the front door flung open and three uniformed men jumped into the living room.

'Police – freeze!' said one of the men.

The officer crouched down aiming a Kalashnikov rifle at Bakari.

Bakari was astounded; he did not realise what had transpired in that room. Without thinking, and quite unintentionally, he drew the pistol that was under his belt and hoisted it up.

There were three consecutive bangs coming from two of the policemen at the door. One of the bullets found its target at Bakari's thigh. The other two ripped through his right hand, sending the pistol flying up into the air before falling and bouncing on the tiled floor. The gun fell before Bakari's body slumped to the ground, on top of the bundle he was dragging.

Bakari was still alive, but seriously injured. He groaned a bit before finally losing consciousness. The way things looked, he would need to spend a great deal of time in hospital, and possibly have his shattered right foot amputated. He would then stand trial facing a number of serious charges, including resisting arrest and trying to shoot at the police. Under normal judicial laws that could earn him a life term in jail, with the possibility of parole after twenty-five years. That was not an encouraging development for a man who was in his mid-forties.

The following morning news had not spread in town or in the newspapers concerning the incident at a secluded house in Mikocheni. It was nine in the morning when a Toyota double-cabin van pulled at a fairly good house at Sinza township. From the white van emerged a woman dressed in a green skirt and yellow blouse. She was at her best with make-up and the local Swahili extract 'Ina' painted over her well manicured hands. She wore those colours specifically to arouse more excitement from the man she expected to meet in the house. From the other doors of the car emerged three nicely dressed kids, holding different toys on their hands. They cheered happily and played around. Their mother called them and told them to go quickly to the house and meet with dad.

'Who amongst you wants to be the first to embrace daddy?' she asked the kids.

'Me!' was the unanimous response from the three healthy looking children.

Mwajuma knocked at the door, and the houseboy emerged from it.

'Is Baba in the house?' Mwajuma asked.

'No, since he left yesterday he hasn't come back,' the boy answered in a normal voice.

Mwajuma looked pensive, but she quickly consoled herself and ushered the kids into the house. She had heard that her husband's new job entailed a lot of travelling.

'Children, come in,' Mwajuma said, and instructed the houseboy to help the driver of the van with the luggage.

'Where is daddy?' the youngest child asked her mother.

'Baba will be home soon, dear,' Mwajuma told the child.

Seven hundred kilometres away in Moshi, at the Mawenzi hospital's ward for AIDS patients, a skeletal structure lay on a bed, breathing in spasms. There was a bottle of drip above the man, and the blanket covered only as far as the stomach, exposing his elaborate rib cage. His face was all dotted with ugly open sores. There was little more the doctors could do about that patient. On the board behind his bed was an old clipboard with the name Kidaha Boniface Shoo, more popularly known by his friends by the abbreviation KIBOSHO.